Miss Blaine's Prefect and the Golden Samovar

Miss Blaine's Prefect and the Golden Samovar

Olga Wojtas

FELONY & MAYHEM PRESS • NEW YORK

All the characters and events portrayed in this work are fictitious.

MISS BLAINE'S PREFECT AND THE GOLDEN SAMOVAR

A Felony & Mayhem mystery

PRINTING HISTORY

First UK edition (Saraband): 2018
Felony & Mayhem edition (First US edition): 2018

Copyright © 2018 by Olga Wojtas

ISBN: 978-1-63194-186-3 (hardcover)
978-1-63194-170-2 (paperback)

Manufactured in the United States of America

Library of Congress Cataloging-in-Publication Data

Names: Wojtas, Olga, author.
Title: Miss Blaine's prefect and the golden samovar / Olga Wojtas.
Description: First U.S. edition. I New York : Felony & Mayhem Press, 2018.
Identifiers: LCCN 2018025061I ISBN 9781631941863 hardcover I ISBN
    9781631941702 (trade pbk.) I ISBN 9781631941719 (ebook)
Subjects: I GSAFD: Mystery fiction.
Classification: LCC PR6123.O37 M57 2018 I DDC 823/.92--dc23
LC record available at https://lccn.loc.gov/2018025061

Olga Wojtas was born and raised in Edinburgh, and attended the school that inspired Muriel Sparks's *The Prime of Miss Jean Brodie*. She became a journalist, writing short stories on the side, and her life changed when she won a New Writers Award from the Scottish Book Trust. Obliged—as per the award—to live in a recycled shipping container, she embarked on a novel to keep warm.

The icon above says you're holding a copy of a book in the Felony & Mayhem "Historical" category, which ranges from the ancient world up through the 1940s. If you enjoy this book, you may well like other "Historical" titles from Felony & Mayhem Press.

For more about these books, and other Felony & Mayhem titles, or to place an order, please visit our website at:

www.FelonyAndMayhem.com

Other "Historical" titles from

FELONY&MAYHEM

ANNAMARIA ALFIERI
City of Silver
Strange Gods
The Idol of Mombasa
The Blasphemers

FIDELIS MORGAN
Unnatural Fire
The Rival Queens

KATE ROSS
Cut to the Quick
A Broken Vessel
Whom the Gods Love
The Devil in Music

CATHERINE SHAW
The Library Paradox
The Riddle of the River

LC TYLER
A Cruel Necessity
A Masterpiece of Corruption

LAURA WILSON
The Lover
The Innocent Spy
An Empty Death
The Wrong Man
A Willing Victim
The Riot

Miss Blaine's Prefect and the Golden Samovar

CHAPTER

1

"Who shall I say is calling?"

Madame Potapova's major-domo didn't even look at me, or at the letter of introduction I was waving, as he asked the question. He was too busy glaring at the doorman for letting me in, and at the footman for escorting me across the reception hall.

I announced myself in the Russian style of name and patronymic, and decided to play the exoticism card. "Shona Fergusovna from Edinburgh, the capital city of Scotland. My father Fergus was president of the local heritage association in Morningside, Edinburgh's most celebrated arrondissement. I arrived here yesterday and have come to pay my respects to Madame."

Not a flicker. "I do not know whether Madame is accepting any more visitors this afternoon."

"Well, why don't you ask her?" I suggested. Madame Potapova was elderly, widowed and threw the best parties in Imperial Russia. I was on a mission which demanded that I wangle an invite to the party she would host that very evening.

But before the major-domo could reply, there was a piercing shriek from the top of the marble staircase and an elderly lady plummeted towards us in a flurry of black silk and taffeta.

I dashed over to try to cushion her fall, but I never got the chance. In the wake of the shriek came the scrape of metal on marble and the snap of bone. The gold chain on the lady's lorgnette had caught on one of the banister's artistic protuberances. The gold was obviously of excellent quality, since rather than the chain breaking, it was her neck that broke. She sprawled halfway down the staircase, her head lolling at a 90-degree angle.

"Is that Madame Potapova?" I asked the major-domo.

He nodded, piously crossing himself in the presence of death.

"I suppose that'll be tonight's party cancelled then?"

"Unfortunately so, but since your excellency was not invited, your excellency will not be greatly inconvenienced."

He snapped his fingers to summon a footman. "Her excellency is leaving."

I always try to see the best in people, but I couldn't warm to this bloke. I was very glad I hadn't mentioned what I thought I had seen. Just as Madame Potapova plunged to her doom, it was as though someone had moved on the upper landing, then disappeared into the shadows. I couldn't be sure; time travel seemed to have left me with a bit of visual disturbance.

If I had said anything, I wouldn't have put it past the major-domo to start yelling that Madame Potapova hadn't fallen, she had been pushed. Then some innocent chambermaid or footman who just happened to be in the vicinity would have been executed for murder. I deal in facts, not fancies. And it's a sad fact that a lot of elderly people don't exercise enough to retain good balance.

The footman escorted me across the reception hall and the doorman opened the door.

"Thanks," I said. "I'm sorry you're out of a job."

The doorman's brow creased. "Your excellency?"

"Now that your employer's passed away," I reminded him. He still looked baffled.

"Excuse me, your excellency," said the footman. "I couldn't help overhearing your conversation with the major-domo. I believe your excellency is Scottish."

"Impossible!" gasped the doorman.

I fixed him with the stare I used as a prefect when some gobby second year tried talking back. "Do you have some objection?"

"By no means, your excellency," he faltered. "But your excellency speaks our language so perfectly that I can't believe your excellency is not Russian."

I smiled. "Yes, I'm from Scotland, where I had the finest education in the world." I turned to the footman. "How about you? Any problem with my being Scottish?"

"What I meant, your excellency," he gabbled, "is that perhaps you are not conversant with our circumstances. We are serfs. Whoever inherits Madame's estate will inherit us as well."

"Then I hope she's left you to someone nice."

"It is widely known that Madame has never made a will. We will therefore be given to Our Little Father, the Emperor and Autocrat of all the Russias, of Moscow, Kiev, Vladimir, Novgorod, Tsar of Kazan, Tsar of Astrakhan, Tsar of Poland, Tsar of Siberia, Tsar of Tauric Chersonesos, Tsar of Georgia, Lord of Pskov, Grand Duke of Smolensk, Lithuania, Volhynia—"

"Yes," I said, "I know who you mean. So how do you feel about that?"

The footman and doorman closed their eyes in collective ecstasy.

"It is the greatest honour imaginable for a serf," breathed the footman, "to be allowed to serve Our Little Father, the Emperor and Autocrat of all the Russias, of Moscow, Kiev, Vladimir, Novgorod, Tsar of Kazan, Tsar of Astrakhan, Tsar of Poland—"

I slipped past them through the door as they contemplated their good fortune. It was nice to hear that my language skills had passed muster.

I hadn't appreciated the significance of the parcel of books when it arrived in the library, marked for my personal attention. The accompanying unsigned note said: "Read and inwardly digest," so whenever I had a slack moment, I did. I got through the books on Russian history, geography, architecture, politics, culture and infrastructure in no time, and then moved on to the complete works of Tolstoy in the original. I found they weren't entirely in Russian. A good chunk of the dialogue was in French, spoken by pretentious aristocrats. My French is so fluent that I scarcely consider it a foreign language, but it was fun getting back in touch with my inner Slavonicist.

I was in my flat in Morningside, deciding that it really was time I repainted the kitchen, when the twinges began. At first, it seemed like a touch of indigestion. Then I thought I might be coming down with flu. Then I was convinced that my appendix had burst. I doubled over, gasping, my eyes screwed up as I tried to ride the pain. And when I opened them again, I was lying on a polished wooden floor, looking at a bulbous metal object with a tap sticking out of it. It says a lot for my state of confusion that it was a full minute before I recognised it as a Russian samovar.

I had been told that I would experience "slight discomfort" when time travelling, and I was pretty shocked that I hadn't been told the truth: it was excruciating. Surely I hadn't come over as a wimp who would refuse a mission just because it involved severe abdominal pain?

It was starting to ease off slightly, and I began to assess my surroundings, drawing on my recent reading. I was in an anteroom of a nineteenth-century Russian mansion. The samovar was brass, embossed, stately yet serviceable, and would provide a lovely cup of tea. It stood beside a high-legged settee whose upholstery was old and faded. A large rectangular mirror hung on the wall, its gilt frame dingy, its glass mottled with age. There was the faint sound of dance music next door, the high-pitched chatter of society ladies, the clink of wine glasses.

The sound suddenly got louder—the door was opening. I didn't want to be seen before I knew more about where I was, so I dived under the settee. It might be four decades since I left school, but I have to say I still had the speed and proficiency that saw me crowned class swimming champion.

My view was restricted to floor level. A man had come in. A young man, from the stride. Squeaky shoes. New shoes. Buffed black leather, intricate silver buckles. They paused, as though the newcomer, like me, was assessing his surroundings.

As I peered out from under the sofa, I could see his distorted reflection in the curve of the samovar. He was just a vague shape, but I suddenly had the most extraordinary optical illusion. I thought I saw his head spinning round and round.

I can tell you I was more than a little alarmed. The twinges had been bad enough, but nobody had mentioned visual disturbance. I blinked a few times, then opened my eyes wide and everything was back to normal.

A voice came from the doorway, female, middle-aged, imperious. "My dear Sasha! For shame! What are you doing hiding in here with all the ladies desperate for your company?"

"Countess, you know you are the only lady whose company I seek. Forgive me—I felt quite overwhelmed by the grandeur of this evening, and came in here to compose myself."

The young man's voice was light and attractive, the sort that you could listen to for hours on the radio. I wondered whether he had a face for radio as well.

High heels tapped across the floor towards me. The settee sagged, pinning me to the polished parquetry. I couldn't help admiring the quality of the floor, each wooden mosaic piece meticulously interlocked with its neighbours into graceful patterns. Thankfully, this was a well-kept house, with no sneeze-inducing dustballs. In front of my nose, chubby ankles bulged over high-heeled satin shoes.

"Dear child! You think this is an evening of grandeur? Why, we are all laughing at Lidia Ivanovna for its embarrassing simplicity—the poor creature hasn't the first idea of how to entertain. Secure me an invitation to Madame Potapova's, and then you shall see a proper party."

The settee sagged again as the buckled shoes settled alongside the high heels, but I was less squashed this time.

"If you're certain…" the young man murmured. "Perhaps I'm not ready."

"You are ready, Sasha, and you will not fail me." The tone was threatening rather than encouraging, and then it softened. "I assure you that even now they are discussing who your family might be, and creating the most glittering biographies for you. 'I hear he is the first cousin of the old prince…' 'He is obviously related to the blue-eyed baroness; the family resemblance is unmistakable…'"

There was a pause.

"I shall not fail you," said the young man.

The countess let out a deep sigh of contentment and the settee sagged still further. "To think that tomorrow evening I shall be a guest at Madame Potapova's! Yes, that will be success indeed. Now, enough of this hiding away—you are here to be seen. Escort me to the ballroom."

"I am yours to command." The buckled shoes turned 180 degrees to face the high heels and braced themselves. The high heels moved a fraction of a millimetre, and I deduced that the young man was attempting to haul the countess to her fat little feet. Eventually he succeeded and both pairs of shoes proceeded to the ballroom.

Once the door had closed behind them, I wriggled out from under the settee and tried to make sense of what I'd heard. It was like a reverse *My Fair Lady*. Without the songs.

I dusted myself down, and discovered I was wearing a floor-length lilac evening gown, with long white kid gloves that stretched up over my elbows. Just one other thing to check. I lifted the hem of my gown. Excellent. I was still wearing my trusty Doc Martens. The countess might think she had the edge on me in terms of fashion with her high heels, but she was storing up all sorts of problems for herself in terms of bunions, plantar fasciitis and sciatica.

I pushed open the door and emerged into a ballroom of exquisite proportions. It was easy to recognise the refined style of the great Russian architect Andrei Voronikhin. But despite the room being perfect for purpose, and the music enticing, nobody was dancing. Guests were sitting around in morose little groups. Not even phalanxes of footmen bearing vast quantities of food and drink seemed to cheer them up.

It was time to test out my new skill. My heart was racing, whether from excitement or nerves I wasn't sure.

I thought back to the instructions I had been given: "You must learn to be unobtrusive."

"How do I do that?" I asked.

"What is our greatest attribute? Our mind. You must concentrate and practise."

So I concentrated and practised until the day came that I cracked it, and people started bumping into me in the Morningside Waitrose. Nobody would ever be rude enough to bump into you deliberately in the Morningside Waitrose, so I knew people just didn't see me.

I moved further into the ballroom, blending discreetly into the background as I crossed the magnificent parquet floor. It was made of intertwined leaf shapes in different colours, giving the impression of an autumn woodland. I crept up behind a semi-circle of young women who had turned world-weariness into an art form. They managed to wilt while simultaneously sitting bolt upright. I filed the technique away for future use.

"Who could have imagined it would be so dreadfully dreary?" said one, fanning herself.

"Who could have imagined anything else?" said another. "Lidia Ivanovna simply has no idea what a party is."

"No, I imagine this is the most exciting night of her life. Oh, ladies, that dress!"

They all sniggered.

"That alone was worth coming for," said the first. "Do you think it belonged to her mother?"

"Her mother? You mean her grandmother."

"Well, now we have seen the antique dress, we can be sure there will be nothing of further interest. The champagne is surprisingly tolerable, though. I shall have another glass. And then I shall prise my husband away from the card table and get him to take me to dinner somewhere expensive."

"Let's all have some more champagne, then we'll come with you and the evening won't have been completely wasted."

I drifted past them towards the next group, feeling quite sympathetic towards this Lidia Ivanovna. As far as I could see, the problem wasn't the party, it was the guests.

My fingers and toes started tingling. It wasn't unpleasant, nothing like the time-travelling twinges, just noticeable enough to get my attention. This must be the signal that I was nearing my target, like an internal metal detector indicating a hoard of Viking treasure. It took me a while to establish which direction to go in, but eventually the increase in tingling led me to a slim young woman standing alone in a corner. She was absolutely stunning, with the perfect contours of a classical statue. Her skin was flawless. Unlike the young wives, she wasn't plastered in make-up, and her long, fair hair hung loose rather than crimped into elaborate swirls. She looked in her mid-twenties, and the simple style of her dress showed she was still unmarried.

She was also a bag of nerves, her arms clasped protectively over her chest, her face tight with apprehension.

I walked up to her, my hand outstretched. "Good evening," I said. "Allow me to introduce myself. Shona Fergusovna."

She jumped at being addressed, then smiled tentatively as she took my hand.

"How kind of you to come," she said. "Forgive me for not recognising you. This is the first time I have been out in society, and I'm afraid all of my guests are unknown to me."

So the person I had been sent to help in nineteenth-century Russia was our hostess, Lidia Ivanovna.

"Lovely party," I said.

"Thank you—this is the first party I've ever hosted—indeed, the first party I've ever attended. I had nobody to ask for advice. I'm not sure…" Her voice tailed off as she looked round at the yawning, gossiping guests, and her face tightened with anxiety.

"You know what?" I said. "Nothing gets a party going like a wee jig. Leave it to me."

I crossed over to the orchestra. It was the standard nineteenth-century set of violin, double bass, bassoon, clarinet, trumpet, percussion and accordion, and it couldn't have been a better mix for my purposes.

"Hello, lads," I said, briskly idiomatic, and explained what we were going to do. Then I clapped my hands to get everyone's attention.

"Honoured guests!" I called loudly in French, determined to make an impression for Lidia's sake.

Everyone turned towards me.

"Lidia Ivanovna, your gracious hostess, has spared no expense to make this a memorable evening for you. She's brought me all the way from Edinburgh to teach you some Scottish country dancing. As I'm sure you know, Scottish country dancing is now all the rage at the most fashionable soirées."

There was an uncertain pause and then everyone nodded vigorously, pretending they had known this all along.

"In me, Lidia Ivanovna gives you the crème de la crème," I went on. "I am Shona Fergusovna McMonagle, former captain of the gold medal–winning team from the Marcia Blaine School for Girls. We were specially commended at the Royal Scottish Country Dance Society's spring fling for footwork, flexibility and fervour."

There was an excited murmuring.

"We'll start with a Dashing White Sergeant," I told them. "Kindly get into sets of six, two lines facing one another, boy-girl-boy and girl-boy-girl."

When I choose to, I have the voice of authority. It comes from having been class prefect. Obediently, the guests rose and took their places in the ballroom. I struck up on the accordion I had borrowed from the band. The school gave me a good training in classical music—the recording of me playing Sibelius's violin concerto at the annual prize-giving still raises considerable sums for the fund-raising appeal—but I like to think I'm equally adept at traditional music, particularly on the mouth organ.

As I played, the other musicians gamely following my lead, I called out clear, simple instructions for dancing the reel. "Forward, back, forward! Grab an arm! Twizzle! Hoppity-hop!"

But despite the precision of my directions, it was a catastrophe. The dancers careered into one another, crashing into tables and chairs, smashing glasses, knocking over footmen. Then came an ominous commotion at the far end of the ballroom, and a shriek of "Saints in heaven! Save him!"

Something had gone terribly wrong. I realised there could easily be a panic. If the guests stampeded, there would be horrific injuries. Clearly the only responsible thing to do was to keep playing, Titanic-style, in order to distract everyone. I gestured to the other musicians to play louder while I called the steps with even more authority. The dancers responded to my cool leadership, grabbing, twizzling and hopping.

Peering across the room to the cause of the drama, I saw that a tiny elderly gentleman had become lodged in a portly lady's cleavage and was suffocating. Two immaculately dressed officers rushed up to him, grabbed him by the shoulders and legs and eventually managed to wrench him free. Wheezing, he was helped to a seat where he slowly regained his colour, while the portly lady set about patting everything back into place. And as she made her way to another seat, I caught sight of fat little feet in satin shoes.

So this was the redoubtable countess. I had no doubt where the blame lay: the tiny gentleman would have been completely incapable of steering such a bulky vessel.

Now that the crisis was over, I stopped the band, and the dancers juddered to a halt.

"You see what happens when you don't pay attention?" I said. "Somebody—" (I looked meaningfully in the direction of the countess) "—obviously went forward when they should have gone back. Or possibly vice versa. There could have been a fatality had it not been for the intervention of the military, and that wouldn't have been a very nice end to the evening, would it?"

There was an embarrassed muttering and shuffling of feet.

"You have a choice," I went on. "You can all sit down and listen to the music. But if you want to dance, you're going to have to obey my instructions to the letter. Do I make myself abundantly clear?"

"Please, Shona Fergusovna, please let us keep dancing!" burst out a guest.

"Please, Shona Fergusovna!" cried another. "This is so much fun! We promise to do exactly as you say."

Their faces were so eager that I couldn't help relenting.

"All right. I'll give you one more chance. Strip the Willow. Sets of four couples, boys facing girls."

The dancers went in more or less the right directions, clearly making an effort to behave. So I seamlessly led the band into Hamilton House followed by a strathspey. The atmosphere in the ballroom was transformed from its earlier apathy. The dancers smiled and laughed as they hurtled round the room, and there was an enthusiastic hubbub among the observers sitting at the side, who nodded and clapped along in time to the music.

After a particularly vigorous eightsome reel, I announced a refreshment break and gave credit where credit was due.

"Very well done," I said. "I wish the RSCDS could see you. You'd all be up for dancing achievement awards, elementary level."

Everybody beamed. I could see people beginning to move towards me, no doubt to compliment me on my language and performance skills. But after a round of hand-shaking with the band, I slipped past the guests, fading into the background.

"Just a tea for me," I told a passing footman as I escaped back into the anteroom and sank into the large indentation on the settee.

The footman retrieved the pot from the top of the samovar and poured strong black tea into a glass in a silver filigree holder, adding hot water from the samovar's tap. I prefer my tea with milk, but I knew better than to show myself up as an ignorant foreigner. I was determined to make a success of my mission, which meant I had to fit in.

I retrieved a cube of sugar from the little dish the footman had left beside me and, holding it between my teeth in the tradi-

tional way, took a sip of tea. I was able to identify it as Russian
Caravan, its smoky flavour evoking the camp fires during its
long journey across the steppes. I still didn't know exactly what
my mission was, but I was more than happy to do whatever
was necessary to help our shy, uncertain, stunningly beautiful
hostess.

She was an enigma. Why weren't her parents hosting the
party? Why was this the first party she had ever been to? Why
wasn't she married yet? I sucked the pungent tea through the
sugar lump and told myself to be patient. I had only just arrived.

When I returned to the ballroom, Lidia Ivanovna ran up to
me and clasped my hand.

"Shona Fergusovna, I will never be able to thank you
enough! I was so afraid this evening would be a disaster but you
have saved it for me!"

"Not a problem," I said. "Delighted to help." Not only
delighted but also destined and duty-bound. "That was a lovely
cup of tea, so now I'm good to go."

Lidia tried to smile, but her eyes were clouded. Something
seemed to have upset her.

"Of course, it is time for you to leave," she said. "You must
have many more important social engagements than this. How
kind of you to have come at all."

It was easy to Russify what I would say in English, but I had
to remember that this wasn't the twenty-first century.

"No, 'good to go' is just an expression," I explained. "I mean
I'm going to get them dancing again."

The orchestra members, anxious to learn more tunes,
greeted me warmly.

"Honoured guests!" I called. "You've done so well that I
think you're ready to try one of our more complicated dances, the
Gay Gordons. This is for couples, so grab the person you most
want to dance with."

The guests all raced to partner up. Lidia Ivanovna, entirely
unaware of how beautiful she looked, stood hesitantly at the edge
of the dance floor as couples rushed past her.

From the opposite side of the room came a young man. He was absolutely stunning, the most gorgeous man I had ever seen. Blond hair flopping sexily over his forehead. Chiselled cheekbones. Temptingly sensuous lips. And he was wearing new shoes, buffed black with intricate silver buckles. He certainly didn't have a face for radio: he would have been welcome on any television sofa in the world.

It was clear that he had eyes for nobody but Lidia, and was walking straight towards her, as though the other guests were nothing more than troublesome flies. As I watched, it was like one of those films where everything goes blurred and out of focus except the main characters. All I could see was this one couple, two unbelievably beautiful people preparing to dance with one another. It would be the highlight of the evening. I was already imagining calling the instructions for the Gay Gordons: *Forwards, forwards backwards, backwards forwards, backwards backwards. Gents skip! Ladies rotate!* while the perfect couple danced in perfect harmony.

But before I even had time to pick up the accordion, I saw the hefty lady with the dangerous cleavage totter towards Sasha and intercept him. And just as the countess hauled Sasha into line, Lidia was similarly captured by the tiny elderly gentleman who had nearly expired in the countess's bosom.

This was all wrong. They had to have a chance to ditch their partners. I got through the Gay Gordons as quickly as possible and, just as Lidia and the tiny gentleman came to a standstill beside me, I quickly announced a ladies' excuse-me.

"Excuse me," said Lidia to the tiny gentleman. "I enjoyed our dance very much, but I must take care of my other guests."

She moved to the side of the room where some elderly ladies were sitting, and signalled to a footman to bring them more champagne. Meanwhile, Sasha had been grabbed from the countess by an eager widow, who was then seen off in her turn by a stocky termagant. He looked longingly towards Lidia every time he was spun past her, but she was deep in conversation with the old dears, as far as their ear trumpets allowed.

In vain, I taught the guests Strip the Willow, Wind on Loch Fyne and The Bees of Maggieknockater. Lidia didn't come near the dance floor again, her attention solely on the guests who were too old or infirm to whirl round the ballroom. Sasha had been commandeered once again by the countess, who, when she wasn't dancing with him, insisted that he fetch more champagne, arrange her shawl round her shoulders, find her a footstool, fetch more champagne, take her shawl off her shoulders, and fetch more champagne. He did all this without the slightest complaint.

It was as though everything was conspiring to keep the two beautiful young people apart. Finally, the party started to break up and the guests headed for the cloakroom to retrieve their cloaks.

I turned to the orchestra. "Great gig, guys," I said. "With a bit more practice, you could almost sound like a Scottish country dance band. That would be a nice wee earner for you."

The leader of the orchestra bowed. "A generous suggestion, your excellency, but this was our final performance. We are all about to enlist in the army."

I was quite surprised—nothing I had read suggested that the Imperial Russian Army had a band. But I could see that it might work very well. "If you got the cannons synchronised, you could do a brilliant version of the *1812 Overture*," I said.

"The what?" asked the leader.

It was an awkward moment. I realised I had no idea what year it was. And it would be totally unprofessional just to ask— what sort of numpty doesn't know the date? I couldn't appear unprofessional on my very first mission. So I decided to solve it myself. I would easily be able to work it out from clues. After all, when I'm doing a jigsaw, I always keep the edge pieces aside until the end. And here was my very first clue: Tchaikovsky wrote the *1812 Overture* in 1880, so it must be earlier than that.

"Well," I said heartily, "have a lovely time in the military band. I'm sure there will be lots of rousing martial music for you to play."

The leader shook his head. "We will never play again, your excellency. To be allowed to accompany you this evening has been the pinnacle of our musical careers. We can be musicians no longer, for, without you, our music will have no meaning. During the interval, we decided that our only option was to enlist, because it guarantees us certain death."

The others all nodded enthusiastically. "Mikhail, whose accordion you played, is already making arrangements to have it buried with him," said the percussionist.

"Really?" I said. "Mikhail, are you married?"

"Of course, your excellency," said Mikhail. "We all are. With many children."

"Then isn't it a bit excessive having your accordion buried with you? How about letting your widow and dependents sell it to raise some cash?"

Mikhail lifted the instrument high over his head. "Now that you have played it, your excellency, I will allow nobody to profane it by playing it again," he said. "Rather, I will hurl it to the ground and dance the kazachok on it."

"Oh, please don't do that," I said, worried in case he scratched the fabulous parquet floor. I could see their minds were made up, so all I could do was thank them again for their help, and express the hope that their certain deaths would be swift and painless.

They appreciated the sentiment, bowed to me, and departed.

The ballroom was practically empty, so it was time for me to go as well. I had no idea where I was going, but I had been told that accommodation would be provided.

Lidia Ivanovna was at the grand entrance, bidding farewell to her guests as they prepared to leave in their drozhkies.

"Dear Shona Fergusovna!" she cried when she saw me. "I shall never be able to repay your kindness—I thank you with all my heart."

"Absolutely no thanks necessary. It was a great pleasure," I assured her. "Well done for throwing such a great party and I look forward to seeing you again soon."

As I got to the foot of the steps, an elegant four-wheeled drozhky drew up and the coachman dismounted to help me into the carriage. He was shaggy-haired and heavily bearded, and wore a long shabby coat.

"Home, your excellency?" he asked.

"Home," I agreed, feeling quite excited about finding out where home would be. The coachman set the horse off at a brisk trot and after a few minutes, we overtook a carriage containing the tubby countess and a cadaverous gentleman who gave me a haughty stare.

"Who's that in the carriage with the countess?" I asked the coachman.

"The count," he said and then elaborated, "her husband."

Perhaps coachmen, like taxi drivers, knew everything. "The countess spent a lot of time with a young man, blond, early twenties, slim, unbelievably good-looking," I said. "What's his relationship to her?"

The coachman's reply was blighted by a bout of coughing.

"Did you say protégé?" I asked.

"If your excellency will forgive me."

"Of course—you can't help a cough. So what do you know about him?"

"I have no personal knowledge of the young man," said the coachman. "His name is Sasha and he is new in town. I hear he is the first cousin of the old prince. And he is believed to bear a close family resemblance to the blue-eyed baroness."

"That's very interesting," I said.

And I meant it. First, it confirmed that coachmen know everything. And second, it revealed that the gorgeous young man was being passed off under a false identity. Other people might be hoodwinked, but I was on a mission, and nobody was going to hoodwink me.

We pulled up outside a two-storey house built in a restrained neo-classical style, its white façade enlivened with turquoise and gold decorations. I recognised it instantly as the work of Charles Cameron, Catherine the Great's favourite architect. A really nice touch to give me a house designed by a fellow Scot.

Candles glowed softly through all the windows.

The coachman clambered off his box and waited to help me down from the cushions. This was completely unnecessary, since I still retain all the flexibility I displayed in the school gymnastics team, plus I had the added benefit of the DMs. But I felt it would be ungracious to point this out, and accepted his assistance.

His vast bushy black beard and long straggly hair hid most of his face, and there wasn't enough light to let me see him properly. But there was something endearing about him, like Bambi.

"Thank you," I said. "May I ask your name?"

"Old Vatrushkin, your excellency."

"That was a very pleasant drive, Mr Vatrushkin," I said.

Despite the camouflage of the beard, I could see his face crumple. "*Old* Vatrushkin," he whispered, distress in his voice.

"Right," I said. "Hope to meet you again some time."

His tone changed from distress to bewilderment. "I'm your driver, your excellency. You will see me tomorrow. What time will you require me?"

I had no idea I was going to get a regular driver—another thoughtful touch.

"That's great," I said. "I'll have a walk round to get my bearings in the morning, so I won't need you until the afternoon. Sleep well, and thanks for bringing me home."

"Your excellency." He bowed, clambered up to his seat, clicked his tongue at the horse and drove away.

I walked up to the elegant front door, wondering how many more staff I was going to have. A major-domo, a housekeeper, a cook, a lady's maid, a brace of footmen? I didn't much relish the idea. I wanted to concentrate on my mission, whatever it might be, and I didn't want to be distracted by HR issues.

I looked for a doorbell but couldn't see one. It was really frustrating that none of my reading had told me when doorbells had been introduced to Russia: it would have helped me discover what year it was. I started to knock on the door, and at my touch it swung open.

I stepped into the hallway and closed the door behind me on the outside world, turning the iron key I found in the lock. I leaned back against the door and massaged my face with my fingertips. My jaw was aching after an evening speaking Russian and French.

So this was my new home. I was greatly relieved to see the interior was as douce and sober as the exterior. I would have loathed the architectural excesses of one of Bartolomeo Rastrelli's rococo palaces. Here, the gilding on the walls and ceiling was discreet, the carved woodwork minimal, and there was absolutely no sign of any vulgar neo-classical statues.

"Hello!" I called. There was no answer. Presumably the staff were lined up to greet me in the reception rooms. I took the white marble stairs two at a time. At the top was a small anteroom, and I pushed open its double doors into the salon. No one was there, but the room itself glowed in welcome. The sparkle of the candlelit chandeliers was reflected in the polished mirrors. The sofas and chairs had white-painted frames and were upholstered in a warm peach satin. At the far end of the room was a pianoforte, its lid already open. I couldn't resist. I sat down, and my fingers automatically sought out the notes. I don't think there's any music in the world that's more stirring than our school song.

> "To our great founder, whose great name
> We praise for ever, Marcia Blaine,
> We owe whate'er we have of fame,
> Cremor, Cremor Cremoris," I sang.

Cremor Cremoris. The crème de la crème. Our motto.

As I sat in my new Russian home, I thought back to the pouring wet Edinburgh day that had changed my life. The library was full of people who had come in to take shelter. I became aware of a woman, not one of the regulars, standing dripping in front of my desk, not bothering to take down the hood of her raincoat.

"Good morning," she said before I had time to ask how I could help her. Her accent was local, her tone authoritative. "Do you have a copy of *The Prime of Miss Jean Brodie*? I can't find it on the shelves."

There was a time when I wasn't sure what hackles were. But the mere mention of That Book makes mine rise like cholesterol levels after you've been eating saturated fat.

I fought to keep my tone level. "If it's not on the shelves, then it will be out on loan."

"Yes, I imagine it's very popular."

My fingers tightened round the edge of the desk. "For those who like that sort of thing, that is the sort of thing they like."

"Could you order it from another branch?"

I could, but I wouldn't. I would play no part in disseminating That Book. "I'm afraid I can't. My computer's playing up."

"Have you tried switching it off and switching it on again?"

All the old biddies are technomeisters these days. "I mean, the system's down. It won't get fixed for ages. Council cuts."

"Tell me," there was a new edge to her voice, "is there some problem with this book?"

Where to begin? "Just up the road is the Marcia Blaine School for Girls, which I attended. That Book purports to be about my school, but never has a school been so traduced under the veil of fiction. It is nothing but a distortion, a travesty, a betrayal. That Book mocks the school's dedication to academic and sporting excellence, and exposes us to public ridicule."

That was what I wanted to say, but didn't. Libraries have changed over the years, but shouting at borrowers is still discouraged. I also didn't say, "Whenever people find out what school I went to, they snigger and say, 'So you're a Brodie girl, the crème de la crème.' I am not a Brodie girl, but every single Blainer is the crème de la crème by virtue of having had the finest education in the world."

"Perhaps," she said, "someone else can help me."

I couldn't have that, one of my officious colleagues discovering that That Book was missing, and reordering it yet again. I would log this wretched woman's details and rely on the council cuts to lose them almost immediately.

"May I have your library card?"

"I don't have one."

"Let me sort that out for you." I was reaching for the mouse when I remembered I had told her the system was down, and reached for a notepad. "May I take your email address?"

"I don't have one."

"Your postal address?"

"My address is…fluid."

Sometimes I think Morningside Library is nothing more than an annexe of the psychiatric hospital round the corner.

"Do you have a name?" I asked in my most cheerful-in-the-face-of-adversity voice.

The prospective borrower pulled down her hood. She had never been in the library before, but she was as familiar to me as my own family. That aquiline nose. That resolute jaw. That interrogatory stare. I recognised her from the portrait I had seen every day in the school assembly hall.

"Miss Blaine," I stammered. "I thought you were—"

"Dead? Obviously not. I am neither ghost nor mirage."

There was only one thing I could say. "May I offer you a cup of tea?"

The small upstairs meeting room was free, so I installed her there and went off to brew my home-made blend of Darjeeling and Earl Grey. The Founder, here, in Morningside Library. Neither ghost nor mirage, but what was she? By my calculations, she would be over two hundred years old, but this was a woman in her prime. A woman whom I had almost harangued with views on That Book, which she clearly didn't share. I returned to her with the tea and a plate of Bourbon biscuits.

"Now," she said, "I should like you to explain yourself. Your computer was working perfectly well when I approached you. Are you always that unhelpful?"

"I am the crème de la crème," I protested. "I pride myself on my professionalism, which includes being as helpful as possible."

"And yet you were being positively obstructive."

I couldn't lie to the Founder. "It was the particular volume you wanted. I'm sorry, I can't share your enthusiasm for it."

"My enthusiasm? What makes you think I'm enthusiastic about it?"

"You wanted to borrow it. I assumed—"

Her voice cut across me. "Never assume. When you assume, you make an ass of you and me."

I stored away the epigram for future use.

"What view do you think I would hold of a book which describes me—me!—as the widow of a book-binder?" She grabbed a Bourbon and snapped it in two.

"Blainers do not depend on a man for their identity," I agreed. The school has always been a bastion of feminism.

"It is a deplorable, pernicious fabrication. I cannot imagine how it got published," she said. "I wished to check your loyalty to the school, and I have been reassured. Well done."

Praise from the Founder; I blushed in gratitude. "There's something you should see," I said, taking the key out of my jacket pocket and unlocking the cupboard.

She raised an eyebrow at the copies of *The Prime of Miss Jean Brodie* in all its various editions, which filled every shelf.

"I can't let That Book fall into the hands of readers," I said. "Whenever one comes in, I hide it in here. People keep reordering it—I have to be constantly vigilant."

Her nod of approval was all the thanks I needed.

"Tell me," she said, dunking half a Bourbon in her tea, "what do you know about time travel?"

So Marcia Blaine was a time traveller. At least I assumed she was. It would take some practice to start never assuming. I explained that, thanks to the finest education in the world, I had a good understanding of the basic principles of quantum physics and Einstein-Rosen Bridges.

"What is the chief purpose of a Blaine education?" she demanded.

"To make the world a better place," I responded automatically.

"Correct. I have now established a time-travelling scheme to enable my girls to extend their efforts across the centuries. I believe you would be a suitable recruit."

I felt quite faint at the honour of having been chosen by the Founder herself.

"You can depend on me," I said.

And then I thought. I have a commitment to the library, with late-night opening three times a week. In my spare time, I've currently got Zumba, aquafit and weight training, as well as classes in Etruscan art, contemporary social theory and advanced Mandarin.

"Actually, it's probably best if you don't depend on me. I don't think I've got the time to take on another commitment," I said.

She fixed me with a laser stare. "You told me you understood time travel. You don't need any time—you come back at exactly the same time you left. That is, if you complete your mission by the requisite deadline."

She picked up another Bourbon and bit into it.

"What do you mean?" I asked.

"You are allowed up to one calendar week to complete a mission."

"And if I fail?"

That stare again. "Are you anticipating defeat before you've even begun?"

"Of course not," I assured her.

"Very well. In that case, all you need to know is that there would be repercussions if you fail to meet the deadline. No remuneration attaches to the post, but your travel and accommodation are covered, and reasonable expenses are allowed. I look after my girls—for you are the crème de la crème."

Cremor cremoris. I thought back to that day as I played through the school song again on the Russian pianoforte. I would complete my mission in record time. Whatever my mission was. Miss Blaine had merely told me that it would be obvious.

I closed the pianoforte lid and went to look round the salon. Two spectacular landscape paintings adorned the room. Drawing on my knowledge of flora, fauna and earth sciences, I deduced that one was of the River Volga near Yaroslavl, and the other was of the River Dvina near Veliki Ustyug. I examined them more closely, and was pretty puzzled. Whoever had painted these was exceptionally talented; yet, for all my encyclopaedic knowledge of art history, I didn't recognise the artist.

There had been another painting in the anteroom. I went to check and found a delightful Parisian panorama definitely painted by the same artist, with scenery where you would expect the Eiffel Tower to be. So, painted before 1889—another clue.

I would painstakingly piece them all together until I found out what year it was.

I wandered back into the brightness of the salon and saw at the far end of the room my second samovar of the evening, vaster than the first, big enough to hold boiling water for the largest tea party I could host. It was golden, the pinnacle of the craftsman's art. It had whorls, it had curlicues, it had scallops, it had convolutions, it had involutions, it had dimples, it had excrescences, it had gibbosity, it had indentations, it had crenellations—it was utterly spectacular. And most magnificent of all was the design of the spigot. It was shaped like a ferocious eagle, its wings outstretched, its beak—I was about to run my fingers down it when I backed off. Its beak was razor sharp. I couldn't help tutting. It was an accident waiting to happen. I would have to remember that this was an era before health and safety, and treat the samovar with extreme caution.

And I wasn't too happy that the lighting came from unguarded candles. But even as I thought about going back down the marble staircase, a faint breeze wafted through the salon and one by one, the candles went out.

"Thank you," I said. Politeness costs nothing. I didn't specifically add "Miss Blaine", but I did have the comforting feeling that the Founder was watching over me.

On the ground floor, I discovered my bedroom. It was as though I had walked into a fairytale cottage. It was made entirely of wood, with log walls, and the huge wooden bed was in the shape of a sleigh, with a sheepskin cover.

When I examined the room more closely, I discovered that one wall was actually a fitted wardrobe. Inside was an array of day dresses, afternoon dresses and evening dresses. And a fur coat. I lifted it out, and staggered slightly at its unexpected weight. Of course a fur coat would be heavy, but this was heavier still. When I tried it on, my hands hit a series of unexpected objects before emerging from the sleeves. Unexpected, but not unwelcome. Throwing knives.

"Now that's clever!" I said aloud, to show I appreciated the additions. I couldn't help smiling at the memory they evoked. I had still been in primary school. My mother was furious. "Shona Aurora McMonagle!" she said. "You could have had your father's eye out!" But Dad was understanding as always. "I'm fine, it's only a flesh wound. Try again, sweetpea."

Thanks to his tutoring, I eventually became an expert at knife-throwing. But I certainly wasn't at the start, and I still didn't get it right with that next try. We never did manage to get the bloodstains out of the cushion cover.

Dad instilled in me the importance of practice. Now, in this distant foreign bedroom, it was time for a quick refresher course. I positioned myself in front of one of the wooden walls and took a deep breath. I fluffed the first few attempts because of the density of the fur, but then I started to improve. First, I practised throwing with my right hand, then with my left. Then with both hands simultaneously. Within half an hour, it was as though the coat, the knives and I were one. But the wall would never be the same.

A capacious drawer held accessories: ribbons, necklaces, feathers, earrings. I unfastened the strands of pearls round my neck and added them to the collection. The drawer underneath contained a letter of introduction and money: wads of banknotes and piles of coins. I would be scrupulous in how I used it.

The last drawer was full of underwear. I was being supported, not only financially but with several multiway bras that would work with whatever style of dress I wore.

But it was puzzling that the staff still hadn't emerged.

I wandered back out into the corridor and called "Hello!" again. Still no answer. I walked on further and pushed open a door that turned out to lead to the kitchen and pantry. There was nobody in either of them. I stood very still and listened. There was not a sound in the house and it was clear I was completely alone. But preparations had been made for my arrival. Alongside the formal Sèvres dinner services, cheerful blue and white painted crockery was stacked on wooden shelves. And lying on the kitchen table was a plain wooden platter laden with oatcakes, butter and a knife. Self-catering. Ideal.

I crossed over to the pantry and found everything I could want, including a jug of fresh milk. Marcia Blaine was certainly looking after me. But I felt she was doing so in a supervisory capacity rather than micro-managing: there was something slightly impertinent about associating Miss Blaine with multiway bras.

"Thank you!" I said again into the silence. "This is wonderful. I'll just make myself a cup of tea."

The kitchen samovar was large, brass and barrel-shaped, full of bubbling hot water. I retrieved a white cup with a bold blue floral pattern, poured in some concentrated tea and diluted it before adding milk. It was perfect, Dianhong tea from China's Yunnan province, mellow, with notes of chocolate and dried fruit. I sat sipping it at the broad table, reviewing the past few hours. I had been sent to help Lidia, sweet, nervous Lidia who felt so friendless and vulnerable. And the stunningly lovely Sasha, he was significant as well, I was sure of it, even though I had failed to tingle when he sat on top of me.

I had only a week to complete my mission, whatever it was. The clock was ticking. Hopefully everything would become obvious in the morning.

CHAPTER

3

I woke to a sunny autumn morning and put on a demure mauve day dress. I would have a walk round town after breakfast. Then I hesitated. It had not at all been the done thing to go for walks round town until a certain tsar (but which one?) had started taking a daily constitutional. At that point, it became not only chic but de rigueur.

I looked out of the window to see if any of the upper classes were yomping past. There was no sign of life except for a carriage with a heavily bearded figure sitting on the box.

I raced out of the house.

"Mr Vatrushkin!"

The sun was behind him and I couldn't see his face properly, but I could hear the anguish in his voice. "Please, your excellency, I don't deserve to be addressed as 'Mr'. I'm a serf. So I must be called Old Vatrushkin."

A serf. That was very helpful information. Serfdom was abolished in 1861.

"Never mind," I said. "I'm sure you'll be emancipated soon."

"Your excellency!" he choked. "May that day never come! It would be the end of me. What would I do? Where would I go?"

At some stage, I was going to have to raise his consciousness about his human rights.

"The point is," I said, "what are you doing here? I told you I didn't need you till this evening. You're supposed to be on a day off."

"Your excellency might have changed her mind. I am at all times at your service."

"How long have you been here?" I demanded.

"Not long," he said. "After you came home, the horse and I rested in the stables for almost half an hour before we returned to our post."

And I was going to have to explain employment rights to him. "I don't suppose you've had breakfast," I said. "I'm just about to have mine—come inside and join me."

He lowered his head. "Impossible, your excellency; I could not sully your residence with my presence."

I still found him endearing, but ever so slightly less so than previously. I pride myself on my understanding of human psychology, and this was verging on passive aggression.

"Old Vatrushkin!" I snapped. "Get down, right now, and you're having breakfast with me whether you want to or not."

He responded well to tough love, scrambling down to the pavement and following me into the house to the pantry, where he stopped at the door, twisting his black lamb's wool cap in his hands, his wild straggly hair cascading to his shoulders.

"Sit!" I commanded. I was about to set the table when I saw his face properly for the first time. Most of it was shaggy dark beard and moustache, but there wasn't a single wrinkle on the uncovered bits.

"Tell me, Old Vatrushkin, just how old are you?" I asked.

He calculated. "Twenty-nine years, your excellency."

"Then why on earth are you called Old Vatrushkin?"

He looked baffled. "My father was Old Vatrushkin, and his father before him. If, God willing, I marry and have a son, he will be Old Vatrushkin also."

"You're half my age," I said. "I can't possibly call you Old Vatrushkin. What's your full name?"

"Gregori Gregorievich Vatrushkin, your excellency."

"Great. I'll call you Greg, and you call me Shona. No more of this 'your excellency' nonsense. Agreed?"

Old Vatrushkin's lips trembled. They formed a circle, preparatory to obeying my instructions, then immediately straightened as if to address me formally. Sweat broke out on his brow as he tried to force his lips back to a circle and yet again they shifted back to parallel.

With a cry of anguish, he flung himself across the table and seized the breadknife. "I shall cut out my tongue rather than cause offence," he cried, opening his mouth and grabbing hold of his tongue with his other hand.

He raised the knife and prepared to strike.

I acted instinctively. "What do you think you're doing?" I thundered in the voice that had once struck terror into dozens of first years found smoking in the toilets. "Put that down at once!"

The knife clattered onto the table and Old Vatrushkin's tongue disappeared back into his mouth.

I'm a firm believer in egalitarianism, but it seemed Old Vatrushkin was so convinced of his subordinate position that I was just going to distress him if I insisted on treating him as an equal. In the interests of his well-being, I had to compromise my principles.

"I was testing you," I said. "I wanted to see whether you were capable of over-familiarity. I'm delighted to say you've passed, and shown that you are eminently suitable to be my coachman."

I went into the pantry and retrieved the breakfast ingredients.

"If you've been out there all night, you need a fry-up," I said. "Sorry it won't be a proper one. I've got bacon and eggs and mushrooms and tomatoes and lots of potatoes, but there isn't any square sausage."

"Square sausage?" he said wonderingly. "How can a sausage be square?"

"I've no idea," I said. "But in Scotland, where I come from, it's a delicacy. Sausages is the boys."

He flinched. "In Scotland, you make sausages out of people?"

I reflected that in some parts of Glasgow, they probably did, but there was no need to tell him that.

"No, it's just an expression," I explained. "It was a catch-phrase of the music hall entertainer Jimmy Logan, although the grammatically correct 'sausages are the boys' was previously the catchphrase of the comedian Tommy Lorne, after whom the square Lorne sausage is said to be named."

Old Vatrushkin was listening attentively and nodding, but I felt there was an underlying lack of comprehension. Then it struck me that of course he wouldn't understand since this was probably before the era of the music hall.

"It means that sausages are very good," I concluded. I went over to the stove and started preparing the pans.

Old Vatrushkin sprang to his feet. "You cannot cook for me, your excellency! I beg you, go to the salon and I shall prepare breakfast for you."

I pointed out that he had no idea what I would like for breakfast.

"I shall prepare whatever you want, your excellency. Turtle soup, pickled mushrooms, fermented mare's milk, herring cheeks, goose giblets…"

"Sounds delightful, but I've got all the stuff for the fry-up right here."

Old Vatrushkin reached out to take over the culinary duties and I had to smack his hand away. The pans sizzled and I even managed to rig up a rudimentary toaster in front of the stove.

There was no orange juice to go with the coffee, but I found some black cherries that I mixed with the fermented mare's milk to make a probiotic drink.

Old Vatrushkin approached his plate warily but after a few mouthfuls, he decided that a full Scottish breakfast wasn't bad. I made him some more toast and another couple of eggs, and he wolfed them down.

"If I may be so bold, how long is your excellency staying here?" he asked.

"I'm here on a mission," I said, "and I've been given up to a week to complete it."

Old Vatrushkin swallowed a bit of yolk-covered toast and murmured, *"Le succès de la plupart des choses dépend de savoir combien il faut de temps pour réussir."*

My fork stopped midway towards my mouth. Old Vatrushkin had stopped speaking Russian and was speaking French. And if I wasn't mistaken, which I knew I wasn't, this was an aphorism by the political philosopher Montesquieu, suggesting that the success of most things depended on knowing how long it would take for them to succeed.

He saw me staring at him and immediately started babbling an apology. "Forgive my presumption in using the language of the aristocracy," he said. "I am a fool who must learn to think before he speaks."

"I don't think the definition of a fool is someone who can quote Montesquieu," I said. "Where did you learn French?"

"Paris, your excellency," said Old Vatrushkin, and then returned to his plate, mopping up the rest of the egg yolk with fried potato.

"Come on, work with me here," I said.

"Forgive me for misunderstanding," he said, leaping up and going over to the stove. "I thought your excellency didn't want me to touch anything in your kitchen."

He was simultaneously really sweet and really irritating.

"Sit down and finish your breakfast," I ordered. "It's just an expression—I mean give me a better answer than that. One minute you're telling me you're a serf, the next you're telling me you learned French in Paris. How does that happen?"

"My former master sent me to Paris to study painting because he kindly thought I had some small talent in that direction. Many households think it fashionable to have a serf artist."

"You studied painting in Paris? Do you by any chance know who did those stunning landscapes upstairs? Did you study with them?"

Old Vatrushkin stared down at his plate and mumbled something.

"Pardon?" I said.

Old Vatrushkin mumbled again, but this time I managed to make him out.

"They're really yours? They're totally amazing—the delicacy of the brushwork, the use of impasto, the vitality, the luminism, the psychogeography...Old Vatrushkin, you're a genius."

He was curling himself into a ball of embarrassment, his beard millimetres away from the fried mushrooms.

"And a very good choice of subject, the Volga near Yaroslavl, and the Dvina near Veliki Ustyug."

His head was down, but I caught a twitch of beard that suggested he might be smiling.

"Your excellency is too good, recognising the subject of my poor efforts."

"So what are you working on at the moment?" I asked.

"Nothing, your excellency, my duties as a coachman keep me fully occupied."

That was a scandal. A talent like his needed to be nurtured. At least his former master had had the sense to send him to Paris.

"Isn't your current master interested in art?"

Old Vatrushkin looked up from the fried mushrooms and gaped at me. "But I told you I was here to drive you wherever and whenever you want to go. You are my current master, your excellency. You own me."

My toast fell on the floor, butter side down. Some two centuries later, food scientists at Manchester Metropolitan

University would conclude that toast falls butter side down when the table isn't high enough for it to rotate a full 360 degrees.

"I can't possibly own you," I said. "I'm more than happy to employ you as my coachman, but it's totally immoral for one human being to own another. I could never stand in the way of you being a free autonomous individual. Old Vatrushkin, I emancipate you with immediate effect."

He sprang from his seat and fell to his knees in front of me, his hands clasped in entreaty. "No, your excellency, forgive me, forgive whatever I have done to offend you so greatly—I am unworthy, I know, but I beg you not to cast me off like this!"

I've heard that anybody in Morningside who has a cleaning lady scrubs their house from top to bottom before that lady's arrival. I've always thought it was a rather odd approach to domestic help. But serfs seemed to be a whole new level of problematic.

"You don't want to be free?"

He shook his head. "*Vivo ut serviam.*"

"Old Vatrushkin, if I'm not mistaken, and yet again I know I'm not, that's Latin for 'I live to serve'. And you know Latin because?"

"Because my master before my previous master wanted to translate Virgil's *Aeneid* into Russian, but didn't know Latin. He had no time to study it, so he sent me to study it instead. His translation is very well regarded."

"You mean your translation."

"Oh no, your excellency, I merely told my master what the Latin meant, and how it would sound best in Russian."

"Old Vatrushkin, you're a literate, well-educated man—it's utterly preposterous that you're a serf driving a carriage. It's not what you should be doing. It's like Aristotle being—" I looked for a suitable analogy "—being a chartered accountant."

"I do not know what a chartered accountant is," said Old Vatrushkin.

The Edinburgh Society of Accountants was established in 1854 but it took some time for the trend to reach other countries, so Old Vatrushkin's ignorance of professional accounting bodies didn't help much in pinpointing the date.

"But," he went on, "there can be no comparison between myself and the great Aristotle. He would immediately point out the flaw in your deductive inference, where premise does not link with conclusion. If I may be so bold, perhaps I fit better into the Hegelian tradition of integrating opposites?"

Now this definitely was a clue: Hegel published the third volume of the *Science of Logic* in 1816.

Aloud, I said, "Do I have a garden?"

"Indeed, your excellency, there are extensive grounds behind the house."

"And is there a shed in the garden?"

"There's an orangery," Old Vatrushkin offered.

"In that case, the orangery will be your studio. Shift the oranges out of your way first, obviously."

Old Vatrushkin was gazing at me with the reverent expression that most Scots bestow on square sausage.

"The orangery will be my studio? Your excellency continues to overwhelm me with your beneficence! What do you wish me to paint for you?"

"I don't wish you to paint anything for me," I said. "You're the artist, you choose."

"You don't want my paintings?" said Old Vatrushkin, his lower lip trembling. "No, of course not, how could you? You are a lady of exquisite taste and discrimination, and you see my pathetic efforts for what they are."

"Old Vatrushkin," I said with great deliberation, "you and I are going to fall out if you don't listen to me. You're a wonderful painter, and you must paint what you want—I don't have any right to tell you what to do."

He looked quite scared. "Is your excellency a Liberal?" he ventured.

"I'm not a member of any political party," I said firmly. "I hoe my own row."

"You work alongside your serfs in the fields like Count Bezukhov?"

"I've only got one serf, Old Vatrushkin. And if you don't want to be forcibly emancipated, you'd better start painting whatever it is you want to paint in your new studio."

I retrieved my purse from the dresser and took out a banknote. I was about to pass it to Old Vatrushkin when I looked at it more carefully. It was splendidly multicoloured, featuring the double-headed imperial eagle. But I'd never seen a note of this denomination. "Three roubles? Is that like a nine-dollar bill?"

Old Vatrushkin was gazing at it in awe. "Such riches, your excellency! I've never seen so large a note before!"

"Well, if it's not a fake, take it. Get yourself some paint and easels and stuff."

"This is too much!" he wailed.

"It's fine. Keep the change and buy something else you want."

"What else do I want?"

"I've no idea. A sticky bun. A mug of kvass. An apple for the horse."

Old Vatrushkin pondered. "I could get all of these things, if your excellency wishes."

I heaved a sigh. "Okay," I said, counting on my fingers. "Here's your to-do list. Painting materials, sticky bun, mug of kvass, apple for the horse. But first, have some more tea and tell me all about the countess."

"Alas, there is little I can tell. This is her first time in society."

I processed this. The bulgy-ankled countess, the entrancing Sasha, the beautiful Lidia and me, all newbies.

"How is that possible?" I asked. "Has she only just married the count?"

"On the contrary. They have been married for some twenty years. But following the unfortunate incident, the count has only just returned from exile."

"Siberia?"

"His country estate."

"So what was the unfortunate incident?"

Old Vatrushkin shook his head. "We are forbidden to speak of it."

I considered pressing him further on the incident, but decided it might provoke another attempt at tongue severing. But I couldn't stop myself from asking, "Forbidden by whom?"

"Our Little Father, the Emperor and Autocrat of all the Russias, of Moscow, Kiev—"

"Yes," I said. "Vladimir, Novgorod, etcetera. So is there anything you know about her?"

"Very little, your excellency. She lived on a neighbouring country estate to the count's, and was to come to town for the first time for her own wedding. It was to be the most grand event possible, attended by our Little Father, the Emperor and Autocrat of all—"

"Yes, still with you. And?"

"And then came the unfortunate incident."

"Yes, I see," I said, although I didn't see at all since he was forbidden to speak of it.

"And since she has been unknown in society, that is why she has brought the young gentleman you enquired about," said Old Vatrushkin before drinking some more tea.

This time, I was prepared to say I didn't understand.

"At the countess's advanced age, and with her lack of a waist-line, her entry into society would have gone entirely unnoticed were it not for the exquisite young man," said Old Vatrushkin.

I still found it quite baffling.

"This young man," I said. "Does he have any particular skills, attributes?"

Old Vatrushkin's tea went down the wrong way and it took a while before he could even splutter.

"I mean, can he sing, play the balalaika, tell jokes? It can't be enough for him just to be amazingly handsome."

Old Vatrushkin was looking desperately uncomfortable and I realised I was upsetting him by asking him questions he didn't know the answer to. But I still had one last thing to ask.

"Do you know where he's from?"

Old Vatrushkin shook his head. "The countess brought him with her. The count's estate is near the village of N— so perhaps the people there will know more."

"You've been very helpful," I said to Old Vatrushkin in a bid to cheer him up, although he really hadn't been helpful at all. "Go and make all your purchases, and get on with your painting. I'll see you later."

He got up from his chair, came round to where I was sitting, and gave me a resounding kiss on the shoulder. He never knew how close he came to serious injury. During my schooldays, I saw off innumerable priapic youths from both the state and independent sectors. It didn't matter whether they were solid prop forwards, nippy wingers or simply desperate, I could send them packing within seconds. Not for nothing was I known as Ballbreaker McMonagle. But on this occasion, I fortunately remembered that a serf kissing someone's shoulder was a token of respect, and Old Vatrushkin remained unscathed.

He was just leaving when I remembered. "Oh, one more thing. Does the Little Father, the Emperor and Autocrat etcetera go out walking?"

"Every day, your excellency. It is very fashionable to walk along the boulevards." He paused and beamed. "Walking along the boulevards is the boys."

I was going to explain that "is the boys" applied only to sausages, but he was so pleased with himself that I couldn't bear to see his wee face fall.

"And where's the best place to pick up a newspaper?" I asked, deciding that this would be a good way to find out what date it was.

Old Vatrushkin looked uneasy. "Newspapers have been banned by Our Little Father the Tsar ever since one attempted to report on the unfortunate incident of which we are forbidden to speak. The ban is now presumed to have been lifted following the count's return to town, but Our Little Father's temper is unpredictable and no newspaper proprietor has yet been bold enough to publish."

So it was back to picking up clues. I set out on my walk, and didn't get far before I was surrounded by well-wishers and the inquisitive who recognised me from my appearance at Lidia's party. Yes, Scotland was very beautiful. Yes, there was a strange beast in Loch Ness. Yes, a sheep's stomach. Any moment now, they'd be asking if anything was worn under the kilt, and the traditional response didn't translate well. I switched to unobtrusive mode and shimmered away, leaving behind a mystified group.

I headed off from the busier boulevards, down a tree-lined avenue. Miss Blaine must have been guiding me, since I came to a park where I spotted Lidia Ivanovna promenading with a tiny elderly woman. The woman was even tinier and possibly even more elderly than Lidia's tiny elderly dance partner. But she was surprisingly nippy, and the pair of them were going at quite a rate. I had to break into speed-walking to catch up with them.

"Don't slow down," the old woman commanded her charge.

"Shona Fergusovna!" gasped Lidia, as much from breathlessness as surprise. "Nanny, this is the wonderful Scottish visitor I told you about who made my party such a success. Shona Fergusovna, this is my darling nanny."

The old woman, who had been knitting briskly as she walked, stopped and looked me up and down, although on account of her height, mostly up. I bent in order to shake hands with her, and she then set off again at a brisk pace.

"Thank you on behalf of my little chicken," she said as Lidia and I tried to keep up. I was about to store this away as a new Russian idiom when I realised that it must be Nanny's pet name for Lidia.

"Oh, Nanny, please may we sit down now?" pleaded Lidia. "We have been walking and walking and walking."

"You're the one who wanted to come out," said Nanny. "Now that she has entered society, Shona Fergusovna, she has become ungovernable."

"Not true! If I were ungovernable, we would have sat and rested half an hour ago."

I was baffled. "Why don't we have a wee seat and a chat?" I suggested.

"Oh, a seat, a seat, and have every man for miles around attempt to make my chicken's acquaintance," said Nanny.

Lidia darted to a nearby bench and sat in the middle. "If you and Shona Fergusovna sit one on either side of me, I shall be quite safe," she said.

Grumbling, Nanny followed her and turned to me. "Have you ever known anyone as headstrong as my chicken? It will be the death of me, trying to keep her reputation intact."

Now I understood. Nanny was a totally overprotective chaperone who had been setting a brisk pace to ensure that Lidia was a moving target.

"This is so exciting!" Lidia confided. "I have never been able to promenade before, nor sit on a public bench."

Nanny, who had been rummaging in her capacious apron, sat up. "And now we must go home. I've run out of wool. I meant to bring another ball with me, but you distracted me with all your demands to go out."

I saw Lidia's eyes fill with tears, and felt I had to intervene. "Don't worry about your knitting, Nanny. Just sit and enjoy the view."

Both Lidia and Nanny stared at me the way everyone would back home if I suggested that a wee salad would be much nicer than a fish supper with salt and sauce.

"Nanny knits," said Lidia. "It's what she does."

"What are you knitting, Nanny?" I asked.

"Knitting," she said.

I raised my voice and repeated the question so that the old woman could hear me.

"Knitting," said Nanny more loudly, in a tone suggesting that I was a fool as well as a lunatic.

"Yes, I know it's knitting, but what is it?" I asked. "A cardigan, a shawl, muffatees?"

"Knitting," said Nanny firmly, holding up her work for me to inspect. I had to admit the standard of the knitting was superb, with complex, precise stitches, but it wasn't a cardigan, a shawl, muffatees, or anything else that had a name apart from "a shapeless mass".

"Lovely," I said.

"Well, we can't sit here gossiping all day," said Nanny. "I've got to get on with my knitting. Come along, my little chicken."

Bravely trying to conceal her reluctance, Lidia stood up.

"How far away is your house?" I asked.

Lidia pointed to a mansion on the other side of the park. Nanny's protectiveness meant that they had simply walked round and round in a circle within sight of home.

"Nanny, why don't you go and collect your wool and we'll wait for you here," I suggested. "I'll look after Lidia. I can assure you that I'm well able to ward off unwanted male attention."

Nanny peered at me and then gave a curt nod, apparently satisfied with my ballbreaking skills. She set off for the mansion at a brisk trot.

"She's very concerned about you," I said to Lidia. "I'm surprised she wasn't at your party last night."

Lidia blinked. "But nannies do not attend evening functions. That would not be *comme il faut*."

"More *comme il faux pas*," I said, but Lidia didn't seem to pick up on my Gallic witticism.

"Nanny stayed in her room," she went on. "Knitting. But she was close enough to intervene had anything untoward occurred. And she had counselled me thoroughly on correct behaviour beforehand. For weeks."

A gentleman walking past raised his hat to us. I knew my duty. "On your way," I said.

Another stopped to pass a comment about the weather. "Yeah, yeah, beautiful," I said. "Go and enjoy it somewhere else."

Within a few minutes, word had got around and we were left undisturbed. Lidia and I beamed at one another. She really was lovely—I couldn't blame the blokes for wanting to chat her up.

"So this is your first day out?" I said.

"Not at all—I've been out before," Lidia assured me. "Probably to this very park, although I don't remember it very well. I was brought out in my baby carriage every day, and then once I could walk, I came out either with Nanny or my saintly mother. That was until I was five. Twenty years ago."

"And what happened then?"

"We had…" Lidia's voice faded into silence. She swallowed a few times. Then, with an obvious effort, she said, "We had a family tragedy. A terrible loss. It was very distressing. We do not speak of it."

Her eyes filled with tears yet again, and she retrieved a cambric handkerchief from her reticule. Someone with less insight into human nature might have tried to cajole her into saying more. But I was sensitive enough to know that first, I must gain her confidence.

The best way of doing that was to confide in her myself, to explain who I was, and why I was here. But the time-travelling issue was going to be problematic. H.G. Wells's *The Time Machine* didn't appear until 1895, and I had already established that it wasn't yet 1861. So there was little chance that Lidia would be able to grasp the concept, however simple I made it. I would have to use terms she could understand, avoiding any mention of Lorentzian traversable wormholes.

"Can you keep a secret?" I asked. "I'm not who you think I am."

She sat up attentively, her hands clasped in her lap.

Where to start? My surname often causes confusion, and I always have to stress that I have an impeccable east-coast pedigree. The Edinburgh McMonagles are on no account to be confused with anything you might find in Glasgow. Our family approached the Lord Lyon King of Arms himself and it was ascertained that our name dates from the thirteenth-century Auld Alliance between Scotland and France. It is derived from *mon aigle*, my eagle, and was subsequently Scotticised with the addition of Mc. The family crest is a horizontal blue eagle on a silver background or, as the Lord Lyon himself puts it, "Azure an eagle volant argent". And underneath is the family motto, in which the Scotticisation has been re-Frenchified into *Moque Mon Aigle*, Mock My Eagle, an expression indicating the futility of being jealous of us. It was very appropriate that I had found a razor-beaked eagle on my samovar: it would take a brave person to mock it.

I was about to explain all this to Lidia, but I wasn't sure how conversant she was with Scottish heraldry or the tensions between Scotland's capital and the conurbation to the west.

"I don't come from here," I continued.

"I know," said Lidia. "You come from Scotland, a faraway country about which I know little."

"More faraway than you think," I said. "This may be difficult for you to understand, but I'm not from your world. I've been sent here to help you and look after you. Does this make any kind of sense?"

Lidia's eyes were shining. "You're an angel," she gasped.

This was embarrassing. I was, after all, just doing my job, and wasn't looking for compliments or gratitude.

"Away you go!" I said.

Lidia stood up. "If you bid me go, then of course I obey."

"It's just an ex—" I began, overlapping with Lidia saying, "But first—"

She knelt in front of me, and grasped the hem of my mauve day dress. I realised to my horror that she was preparing to kiss it. My dress had been trailing in the dirt and could have picked up all sorts of pathogenic bacteria. Whatever year it was, antibiotics were still decades away and tetanus was discovered only in 1884. If Lidia kissed my dress and had any sort of problem with chapped lips, she might be infected with *Clostridium tetani* and could very well end up dying of lockjaw.

"Let go of that!" I thundered. "You don't know where it's been!"

Lidia sprang back. "No—I can only imagine," she stammered. "Now I see through a glass darkly, and all I know is that it comes from a glorious realm beyond my comprehension. To think I was about to defile it with my lips!"

I suspected there had been a misunderstanding. "Let me put this as simply and clearly as I can," I said. "I'm no angel. I am Shona McMonagle from Edinburgh, librarian and former pupil of the Marcia Blaine School for Girls. Got that?"

Lidia nodded vigorously. "You have come among us in human form. Nobody must know that in reality you are a celestial messenger. Just as I have complete faith in you, you may have complete trust in me to keep your secret. Although perhaps I may tell Nanny?"

"Absolutely not," I said. "You tell nobody anything."

Lidia looked slightly disappointed. "But she is so devout. She would love to meet an angel."

I spoke very slowly and distinctly. "There are no angels here. There will be no talk of angels. There will be no talk of angels to anybody, Nanny included."

I managed to extract a promise from her only seconds before Nanny re-joined us, puffing.

"Lidia Ivanovna!" she said, fixing her little chicken with a soul-searching stare. "I hope you haven't been talking to any men."

"Of course not, Nanny," said Lidia. "Shona Fergusovna frightened them all away."

Nanny gave me an approving nod.

"We have merely been talking about—about nothing in particular, utterly insignificant chit-chat, which I can now scarcely remember. Shona Fergusovna, would you like to come home with us and we can continue our delightful yet utterly insignificant chit-chat over some tea?"

"Backwards and forwards, backwards and forwards," grumbled Nanny.

"Just like Scottish country dancing!" cried Lidia as we set off. "Oh, Nanny, it was so beautiful seeing everyone so happy and lively, just like the old days. Do you remember how you would let me peep through the balustrade as the guests arrived in all their finery? And sometimes you would even let me stay up to watch my revered father and saintly mother waltzing together."

"Ah yes," sighed Nanny. "He was always the most handsome man and she the most beautiful lady. And then—but we do not speak of it."

A single delicate tear trickled down Lidia's cheek.

I definitely had to find out more about the family tragedy. But a breakneck march across the park wasn't the best place to do it. I would try later.

"Last night's party was marvellous," I said. "I heard a number of your guests complimenting you on the champagne. Was it local?"

Lidia looked vague. "Nanny sorts out everything."

"I ordered it from a French lady," said Nanny. "The poor thing's widowed, so I thought I'd put a bit of business her way. I can't remember what she's called—these French names are so complicated. Madame something or other."

"Madame Veuve Clicquot?" I asked, and Nanny nodded. Another clue. The Widow took over the business in 1805 and went to the great vineyard in the sky in 1866.

"It must have been popular," Nanny said, "because I ordered ten bottles, and there wasn't a drop left."

"Only ten bottles?" I asked. They get through more than that at the Morningside Heritage Association Christmas party.

"They were quite big, I think, weren't they, Nanny?" said Lidia.

"Yes, they had some fancy name—Nebuchadnezzars."

Ten Nebuchadnezzars. The guests had got through 150 litres of champagne. Even allowing for a bit of spillage while they had been getting the hang of the dancing, that was straying into Glaswegian levels of drinking.

"How much did you have, Lidia?" I asked.

"Not a drop," she said. "I have never tasted alcohol. Nanny has forbidden me to drink until I am safely married. She says that at this point, I must keep all my wits about me."

"There's no better drink than tea," said Nanny, and I felt myself bonding with the grumpy old soul. I enjoy a wee Baileys when a celebration is called for, and Christmas wouldn't be Christmas without a Snowball, but now that I was on a mission, I wasn't going to risk any impairment to my sight, hearing and muscle coordination.

"Speaking of widows," I said, "I've been hearing about someone called Madame Potapova who throws the best parties in town." Little did I know that only a few hours later, I would see the black-clad widow hurtle to her death down her own staircase.

Nanny sniffed. "A dreadful woman. Throws her money around trying to impress people. Foreign muck on golden platters and three footmen to every guest. For those who like that sort of party, that is the sort of party they like."

I felt myself bonding with her even more.

We went into Lidia's mansion via the grand entrance, but instead of going to the ballroom, we ascended the broad staircase to a drawing room where a samovar was already bubbling. Footmen noiselessly set out glasses for the tea and arranged three armchairs, then stood at the back of the room, immobile as statues. Lidia and Nanny ignored them as though they actually were statues. I gave them a friendly nod and was a trifle narked when they completely ignored me.

Nanny sat down and retrieved her knitting while Lidia prepared to pour out the tea. But my attention was immediately caught by an exquisite wooden model battleship, displayed on an occasional table.

"The *Viva Catherine*!" I said.

Lidia gave a shy, delighted smile. "You recognise it?"

"How could I fail to, with those innovative fore and aft sails? Not to mention the sixty-six guns. The pride of the Black Sea Fleet—launched in 1783, wasn't it?"

Lidia nodded.

I circled it, marvelling at the delicacy and detail of the workmanship. "It's fabulous. Is it a family heirloom?"

"I made it," said Lidia. "With the leftovers from the floor. I made the table as well."

"The table as well? The whole thing, including the tulip baluster? That's a nice in-joke, by the way, making it in tulipwood."

"I had to order it from China," said Lidia. "The walnut came from Persia."

"And a pretty kopeck they cost you!" said Nanny.

"Well worth it," I said. "You just couldn't get that quality of veneer with wood from elsewhere."

Nanny sighed and laid down her knitting. "Please don't encourage her, Shona Fergusovna. You've no idea the mess she makes. I tell her, it's not an appropriate occupation for a young lady, why don't you take up a nice tidy hobby, like water-colouring or embroidery, but oh no, it's woodwork or nothing. Hours she spends on that parquet, hours and hours. You'll ruin your fingernails, I say, not to mention your eyesight, but does she listen to her nanny?"

I blinked. "The parquet floor in the anteroom?"

Lidia nodded again.

"I was admiring the floor when I was—" I was about to say, "—pinned to the ground by the countess's backside" but swiftly changed it to "—having my cup of tea in the interval."

"It does not bear close examination," murmured Lidia. "Two of the parallelepipeds are not quite exact, and now that I have become more proficient, I see I should have used Karelian birch instead of ash in the quadrates. I'm much happier with the results in the ballroom. The texture is so greatly improved with oak, alder and maple, and I'm rather pleased with the way the leaf intarsia turned out."

"You made the ballroom floor as well? All by yourself?" I asked. The room was the size of a football pitch.

"I had to find something to occupy me during these years of seclusion," said Lidia apologetically.

"Anteroom floor, ballroom floor," complained Nanny, starting knitting again. "That's the least of it. Name me a floor she hasn't had a go at. You never know what rooms are going to be closed, what corridors are going to be blocked off, because my little chicken's at work with her chisels and owls."

"Awls," said Lidia. She reached into the pocket of her dress and produced a lethal-looking instrument. "This is my favourite," she said to me. "I always have it with me in case I need to make small repairs."

Nanny heaved a theatrical sigh. "And yes, Shona Fergusovna, she does it all by herself. Nobody could stand working with her when everything has to be just so, and if it's not, it all gets ripped up and she starts all over again."

"I just want it to look nice," Lidia faltered.

"Give us a bit of peace, I beg her, and then she has the impertinence to say she. wouldn't need to stay indoors doing woodwork if I let her go out. Maybe now she's out in society we'll be able to walk around uninterrupted in our own mansion."

"Lidia, you can't possibly give up your woodworking," I said. If we had been in Edinburgh, I would have said, "You've got a flair for it." But I felt the Scotticism would lose something in the translation, so I just said, "You've got a real talent."

"That will depend on her husband," said Nanny brusquely. "Not many men will put up with living on a building site."

"Her husband?" I asked.

"That is why I've entered society," Lidia explained. "In order to find a husband. My prospects are poor because I am so old."

Nanny cackled. "Your prospects are anything but poor because you are so rich. But I won't let you marry just anybody. It must be the right person."

My mission would be obvious, Miss Blaine had said. Now all was clear. I had to help Lidia to get married. To the right person. Even if that person wasn't Nanny's choice.

I was a tad disappointed. Being sent on a mission had sounded exciting. I had hoped to pit my intellectual wits and physical prowess against some master criminal, perhaps solve a murder or two. Playing matchmaker wasn't exactly a stretch. But I would still carry out my duties with rigour and precision and make Miss Blaine proud.

I thought back to the gentle voice and respectful demeanour of the beautiful Sasha. If he were to be Lidia's husband, I couldn't imagine that he would stand in the way of her vocation. And the party at Madame Potapova's would be an ideal opportunity to get them together.

"Maybe you'll meet someone nice at the party tonight," I said.

Lidia toyed with the lace edging on her cambric handkerchief. "I shall not be attending," she said in a low voice.

"Why ever not?"

"Since I have only just entered society, I was too late to be put on the guest list. Perhaps I would not have been put on the guest list anyway. Only the elite are invited."

I could see now why Miss Blaine had chosen me. Lidia was far too self-effacing, but I had the necessary doggedness, diplomacy and acumen to sort things out.

"Don't you worry," I said. "I'll go round now and get us an invitation."

"Is that how people behave in your Scotland?" asked Nanny. "They just turn up on the doorstep without a by-your-leave when they don't even know you?"

"They do if they're Jehovah's Witnesses," I said. "But it's all right, Nanny. I have a letter of introduction."

Nanny sniffed. "Good luck with that."

"Please, dear Shona Fergusovna, don't put yourself in an embarrassing position on my account," said Lidia.

"I don't embarrass easily," I said. "And I guarantee that once I explain to Madame Potapova that I'm the crème de la crème, we'll be invited." It never crossed my mind that there would be no opportunity to explain anything to Madame Potapova.

"Nanny—please let me go!" cried Lidia, running over to the wee old woman and giving her a hug, expertly avoiding the knitting needles.

Nanny fixed me with a stare not unlike Miss Blaine's. "You must chaperone her. No scandal must attach to her. If scandal attaches to her, she will be unable to marry."

"Obviously I'll try to minimise the incidence of scandal," I said. "Although, is marriage really the be-all and end-all?" Try as I may, the feminism will keep breaking through.

"Of course it is," said Nanny. "That is why she hosted the party yesterday evening. That is why she has entered society. It is her duty. She is an heiress with unimaginable wealth. What is she supposed to do with her fortune other than attract a suitable husband?"

"Travel the world?" I suggested. "Engage in chemical experimentation? Become a professional floor-covering technician?"

Lidia's eyes glistened. "A professional floor-covering technician? Is such a thing possible?"

"Yes," I said, just as Nanny said, "No."

Nanny laid down her knitting to underline the seriousness of the issue. "Only one profession is open to women and that is not one fit for discussion."

Lidia turned to me.

"That may be the case at the moment," I said. "But there must always be trailblazers and pioneers."

Nanny resumed her knitting, unimpressed. "She can have no sort of public life if she is unmarried. If she does not marry soon, she will either have to live in seclusion here at home or enter a convent."

"What about me?" I asked. "I'm not married."

Nanny sniffed and tugged more wool out of her apron. "You're a foreigner. Nobody cares about you."

I raised my tea glass to her. "Cheers, Nanny," I said.

Lidia clutched my arm. "I care about you, dear Shona Fergusovna. You are my true friend. I would love to go to Madame Potapova's ball, if you would be kind enough to be my chaperone."

"I'll come and get you at eight," I said. "And if you're absolutely set on finding a husband, we'll see what we can do."

"But he is already found," said Nanny. "My little chicken has told me everything about the ball last night and it is clear that there is only one man suitable to be her husband."

I have to say I was surprised. If Nanny already knew about the divine Sasha and approved, this was going to be the fastest mission ever.

"I thought he was a little short," said Lidia in a small voice.

"Really?" I said, disappointed that she would be so picky. "I thought he seemed just the right height."

"Lidia Ivanovna, you should not be concerned with his height but with the fact that he is a general."

"He's a general?" I said. I knew that plenty of families pulled strings to get their sons prestigious jobs in the military, but it was still startling that such a young man could have risen so high in the ranks. And why on earth did he and the countess feel the need to conceal his status?

"Yes, a general. And so fortunate that he is newly widowed," said Nanny.

"Widowed?" I echoed. This was even more unexpected. He only looked about twenty.

"You must do everything you can to bring them together," said Nanny.

"Absolutely," I said. "That's exactly what I was trying to do yesterday, get them together as dance partners, but it didn't work out."

"It did," corrected Nanny. "It was a most successful dance."

"Not at all," I said. "Lidia only had one dance…" I stopped, horrified. "The wee old man? That's the general? The new widower?"

Lidia nodded sadly.

"Nanny, you can't possibly want her to marry him—he's half her height and three times her age."

Nanny shrugged. "He's the only suitable match."

"What about the gorgeous young man?"

Nanny's knitting needles clacked to a halt. "What gorgeous young man?"

"Lidia, you must have seen him?"

Lidia lowered her eyes. "I don't recall," she murmured. I couldn't tell whether that meant yes or no.

"So who is he?" demanded Nanny. "What is his name and position in society?"

"I'm not exactly sure," I admitted. I wasn't going to join in the old prince/blue-eyed baroness charade.

"And you think this—this indefinite person is a better match for my little chicken than a newly widowed general?" said Nanny.

I bit my lip and stopped myself saying that absolutely anybody would be a better match than the newly widowed general. I needed to keep Nanny onside.

Lidia drained her glass of tea and tossed her head in an unexpectedly headstrong gesture. "Perhaps I shall not get married," she said. "Perhaps I shall become a trailblazing pioneer instead."

Nanny turned on me. "This is your doing, filling her head with nonsense," she hissed. "Lidia Ivanovna, you will go to your room and choose a suitable dress to meet the general tonight."

Lidia's brief spark of rebellion was quickly extinguished. "Of course, Nanny," she said. "What do you advise? The one I got for my twenty-third birthday? Or perhaps the one I got when I was twenty-two?"

"The navy blue is a less provocative colour than the rose," said Nanny. "But it's still rather décolleté. I'll knit you a fichu to cover yourself up."

"Nanny darling, you are too good to me," said Lidia as she rushed off. She had seemed to capitulate, but as she left, I detected a revolutionary glint in her eye. Nanny was right, it was my fault. I was in danger of sabotaging my own mission.

I refilled Nanny's glass with tea by way of apology.

"I really do want to help," I said. "I'm sure I could do more if I understood Lidia better. I believe there was a family tragedy? A terrible loss? Which was very distressing?"

Nanny shot me a sharp look, glanced at the immobile footmen, then gathered up her knitting and packed it away in her capacious apron.

"We will go to my room. Bring the tea," she said. A footman opened the double doors for us. I picked up the two glasses and followed Nanny along a thickly carpeted corridor.

"I put down the carpet to prevent Lidia hammering bits of wood outside my room at all hours of the day and night," Nanny said.

She opened the door and I found myself in a fibrillous cocoon. Nanny's room was bursting with knitting and its accoutrements. Dominating everything was a large wooden yarn winder, which she obviously used to transform the spun yarn into the many hundreds of balls of wool that covered every surface, including the floor. They were a rainbow of colours, which I noted all came from natural dyes. This was another possible clue: the first synthetic dyes, mauveine and fuchsine, were developed in the 1850s. Then again, I could imagine that Nanny was a traditionalist who would have no truck with scientific innovation.

Alongside the balls of wool were varying lengths of shapeless knitting. Nanny removed some fraying cochineal-coloured yarn off two Nanny-friendly, and therefore extremely low, armchairs. The chairs were upholstered in woad-coloured worsted, and the curtains were pendulous camomile webbing. The plain wooden bed was covered in a quilt made up of multicoloured strands of knitting tacked together.

Above the bed hung an icon of a particularly fractious-looking female saint wrapped in a long shaggy cloak. Nanny scrambled up to it with the help of handy skeins and gave it a devout kiss.

"My patron, Saint Volosiya. I dedicate all my knitting to her."

"How thoughtful," I said. "Not that she needs any knitting with that cloak to keep her warm."

Nanny's brows drew together. "That's not a cloak, it's her hair. You are not familiar with Saint Volosiya?"

I confessed this was an atypical gap in my education.

"Sit!" she ordered.

I plonked myself down on one of the low chairs, narrowly avoiding banging my chin on my knees.

Nanny sat opposite me, closed her eyes, and began reciting a story she had obviously told time after time. "The hagiography of Saint Volosiya. Volosiya was a young girl of extreme piety whose hair had miraculous strength. Every day, she would attach her hair to barges and haul them along the Volga, a task that otherwise required eleven men. One day, iniquitous Kipchaks who had taken a wrong turning arrived at the river-bank and demanded that she tow them and their horses to their kurultai."

"Terrible," I said. I wasn't entirely sure what a kurultai was, but from Nanny's tone, it didn't sound like a desirable destination.

Nanny, her eyes still closed, held up her hand, indicating silence. "Volosiya was an obliging girl, and would have been delighted to help, but unfortunately failed to do so since she could not understand the Kipchak language. The Kipchaks, infuriated by this, decided to tie her by the hair to the tails of three horses and have her torn limb from limb."

I forebore to mention that she would simply have been scalped. It's unwise to apply logic to the stories of the saints.

"But her hair had such miraculous strength that, instead, it tore the tails from the horses. The Kipchaks tried with another three horses, and another three, but each time with the same result."

"Poor horses!" I burst out. I absolutely cannot abide cruelty to animals. "Sorry, Nanny, didn't mean to interrupt again. On you go."

"They brought their last three horses, and this time, instead of tying her hair to their tails, they knitted her hair and their tails together."

"So this time, she was torn limb from limb? She became the first martyr of knitting?"

Nanny opened her eyes and glared at me. "No," she snapped. "There was an apotheosis. She was raised up to glory, taking the three horses with her as she ascended, the horses neighing in praise as they hung from her miraculous tresses."

"And to think people say animals don't go to heaven," I said. "That's a lovely hagiography. Thank you, Nanny. Now, about this family tragedy."

Nanny resumed her knitting as though nothing had been said.

"The terrible loss," I said, not bothering to raise my voice since I was perfectly aware that Nanny wasn't deaf. Nanny continued knitting.

"Which was very distressing."

Nanny knitted two and purled two.

"Oh, come on, Nanny, help me out!"

Nanny struggled to her feet. "Honestly, Shona Fergusovna! A young thing like you needing an old woman like me to help you out of your chair. I don't know. Young people today."

"It's just an expression," I explained. "I mean I want you to talk to me about Lidia."

Grumbling, Nanny sat down again.

"You invited me in here," I went on. "What was the point if you're not going to talk to me?"

"I'm considering," said Nanny. "You want to know about my little chicken. But what do I know about you?"

"You already know everything there is to tell about me. I'm Shona from Morningside in Edinburgh, the capital of Scotland."

"And why have you come here?" asked Nanny.

"To help Lidia," I said.

Nanny increased the tension on the wool.

"Why?"

I was getting completely exasperated. "Because that's my job," I snapped. "I'm not here on holiday, you know, I'm working."

The knitting dropped to the floor. "It's your job? You're not just here out of nosiness?"

I was about to tell Nanny that I had never been so insulted in my life when I remembered that that wasn't true. But the appalling reminiscence was interrupted by Nanny demanding to know why I was trying to destroy Lidia's marriage prospects.

"I misspoke," I said. "If Lidia is to get married, I will be assiduous in bringing it about." I didn't mention that I would be getting her married to Sasha rather than the general. "So tell me about the tragedy."

Nanny shook her head. "We do not speak of it," she said. "But since you are here to help my little chicken, I shall tell you what I can. She has only just emerged from mourning."

"Following the terrible loss?" I asked.

"No, I told you, we do not speak of that. She has only just emerged from mourning another terrible loss entirely, the demise of her revered father."

"So that terrible loss wasn't distressing?" I persisted, anxious to gain as full a picture as possible.

"The loss of her revered father was extremely distressing, almost as distressing at the loss of her saintly mother shortly after the terrible loss of which we do not speak," said Nanny. "We speak of these two other losses, which is why I am speaking of them. Lidia's revered father and saintly mother were a most virtuous couple and vastly wealthy. They were anxious that the great name of Chrezvychainodlinnoslovsky should not die out. When Lidia Ivanovna was born, their happiness would have been complete, if she had been a boy."

My hackles were on the rise again.

Nanny, oblivious, continued, "Five years later, their happiness would have been complete, but then came the tragedy of which we do not speak. Lidia's parents removed themselves from society and never left the house again. Since they no longer spent any money on lavish entertainment, they became even more vastly wealthy. Following the loss of Lidia's saintly mother and later the loss of her revered father, my little chicken has inherited everything."

"What did they die of?" I asked.

"Grief and melancholy," said Nanny. If they had never left the house again, I suspected it was more likely that they had succumbed to vitamin D deficiency.

"Now, I shall give you your instructions for this evening," Nanny went on. "Lidia is to dance with nobody except the general. Lidia is to talk to nobody except the general and the ladies. Lidia is to keep her knitted fichu across her bosom at all times." She rooted around and retrieved a ball of yellow wool.

OLGA WOJTAS

"The dye comes from onion skins," she said. "This will go beautifully with her blue dress."

I took a breath. "Nanny, I think you're being a bit unreasonable. Isn't it better for her to meet a few men before she makes any long-term decisions?"

Nanny made a slip knot from the onion-coloured wool, attached it to a knitting needle and began casting on.

"If you're not able to follow my instructions, then Lidia Ivanovna is not able to go to Madame Potapova's party," she said, yellow wool flowing from her needles. "Which is a pity, since I know she would enjoy wearing this fichu."

I sighed. "All right. I agree."

"You swear?"

"Never. I believe it's the sign of a limited vocabulary."

Nanny went and took the icon off the wall. "Kiss the image of Saint Volosiya to cement your oath and then if you break it, you will go to hell."

"You know I'm not of your faith?" I said.

"That's good," said Nanny. "Better that a heretic should go to hell than one of the faithful."

I pressed my lips to the icon. So now I had hell to worry about as well as everything else. But I couldn't waste time worrying about it. It was now afternoon, and I had to charm two invitations out of Madame Potapova for her party that evening.

Old Vatrushkin was waiting outside in the drozhky.

"How did you know I was here?" I demanded.

He looked puzzled. "I asked a brother coachman." Then his face creased with anxiety. "Did I do wrong?"

Lidia was my first priority, but I would try to make time for a crash course in assertiveness for Old Vatrushkin.

"Perfect timing," I soothed him. "Take me to Madame Potapova's."

At least I didn't have to feel guilty about keeping Old Vatrushkin waiting. I had scarcely arrived in search of my party invitation when the widow tumbled to her doom, and I was back out again.

"Take me to Lidia Ivanovna's," I said.

This wasn't good. One day in, and I was already meeting with failure.

"Lidia's going to be so disappointed when I tell her she can't go to the ball," I said to Old Vatrushkin as we sped along.

"But your excellency, she already knows."

Lidia had many excellent qualities, but I was pretty sure she wasn't psychic. I was also pretty sure that even though the Russian diplomat Pavel Schilling had designed an electromagnetic telegraph in 1832, it wasn't yet in general use.

"Why do you say that?"

"Because she was there, visiting Madame Potapova."

CHAPTER

4

I wondered how I could ever have thought that Old Vatrushkin needed assertiveness training. He could have run master classes in it. He remained as polite as ever, but he was utterly unshakeable.

It all started when I told him he must be mistaken. "Lidia didn't go out. She went off to her room to sort out what she would wear this evening."

"Your excellency's drozhky was sitting next to the young lady's carriage."

I had never heard such firmness in his voice.

"It probably wasn't Lidia's. I'm sure one carriage looks much the same as another," I said.

There was a heartbeat's pause, which I found a little intimidating. Then, without raising his voice, Old Vatrushkin said, "I know my carriages."

"Lidia's carriage doesn't mean Lidia," I argued. "She might have wanted to maximise our chances of an invitation by sending Madame Potapova a bunch of flowers, or a spare Nebuchadnezzar of champagne."

Old Vatrushkin's tone reminded me of a teacher explaining the bleeding obvious to the class numpty, and it wasn't a tone I was used to.

"In that case, the young lady would have sent a small open carriage, not the large formal closed one."

"Did you actually see her?" I demanded.

He turned and gave me a small smile that seemed almost pitying. "I did not have to, your excellency."

I was going to have to bow to his expertise. But this was extraordinary. Lidia, who never went out anywhere? Who couldn't go out unchaperoned? Why on earth was she visiting Madame Potapova anyway? Had I really seen a shadowy figure behind the widow before she fell?

"And the carriage was still there when we left?"

"Yes, your excellency."

"Well, we'll know she was visiting Madame Potapova if she's not at home when we get there."

"The young lady could easily get home before us," said Old Vatrushkin. "Her driver could take a shortcut that I judged too jarring for your excellency." This wasn't helpful.

When we arrived, I was ushered into a reception hall. Some moments later, light footsteps pattered down the hallway. Lidia entered, smiling radiantly. I studied her keenly. Did she look slightly flushed? Out of breath? Jarred?

"Dear Shona Fergusovna, what a joy to see you. I ran all the way to greet you when they told me you were here."

A perfectly acceptable reason for someone to look as she did. I was about to ask her how she'd been spending the afternoon when Nanny turned up.

"Back again?" she said. "What is it this time?"

"I'm afraid I've got some very bad news," I said, still studying Lidia, whose expression changed to respectful attention.

At that moment, there was a knock at the reception room door. A footman crossed to open it, revealing another footman, and they had a short whispered conversation. Then the first footman announced, "Her excellency's coachman!" and Old Vatrushkin came in, clutching his lamb's wool cap.

"Forgive the intrusion, your excellencies," he said. "But I have news through my brother coachmen that I thought you should hear as soon as possible. The countess is inviting everybody to a ball at her palace this evening."

"The countess?" said Nanny. "But that will clash with the dreadful Potapova woman's party."

I prepared to watch Lidia closely as I revealed the news about Madame Potapova, to see whether she knew it already. But before I could speak, Old Vatrushkin intoned, "Madame is defunct."

Nanny shrieked, making me jump and taking my attention away from Lidia. "God forgive me for speaking ill of the dead!" she cried, crossing herself.

"*De mortuis nihil nisi bonum*," whispered Old Vatrushkin, nodding glumly as he agreed that speaking ill of the dead was to be discouraged.

By the time I got round to looking at Lidia, her head was bowed and she was murmuring a prayer for the departed.

"I'll come round for you about eight," I said when she finished. She gave me a smile so luminous and guileless that it was inconceivable that she would be engaged in clandestine expeditions.

No, for once Old Vatrushkin had got it wrong. No doubt Lidia had sent the large closed coach because the small open one was away having its wheels balanced or something.

But Old Vatrushkin remained an excellent coachman and got us safely to the countess's palace that evening. The long driveway was illuminated by hundreds of flambeaux.

"Now I see how things should be done," said Lidia in a small voice.

"Nonsense," I said. "This is a vulgar new-build. Your mansion has Slavic class. Mine has Scottish solidity. I always reckoned the countess would go for baroque excess, but this isn't even Rastrelli-garish, it's sub-Rastrelli garish. Old Vatrushkin, when exactly did this monstrosity appear?"

"A few months ago, to mark the count and countess's return from exile into town."

"I thought so. They didn't have time to get anybody reputable, so they hired some architecture student who wanted to create something edgy for their portfolio."

"Your words are unfamiliar and yet I think I understand your meaning," said Lidia. "These caryatids—"

I looked into the distance at the columns of storey-high unclothed female statues fronting the palace.

"—I think they are the countess?" Lidia continued.

"The countess when she was a few decades younger and many stone lighter," I said.

Above the caryatids was a frieze of vast medallions depicting the countess in profile, albeit with a substantially firmer jaw line and fewer chins. I was just wondering what egotistical eyesore would come next when I realised the carriage had stopped. The entrance was still a considerable distance away.

"Why aren't we moving, Old Vatrushkin?"

"There is such a press of guests. This is the first party the count and countess have held, and everyone is anxious to see the palace and the—" He was overtaken by a fit of coughing.

"Did you say protégé?" I asked, but he was still coughing.

There was a massive queue of carriages in front of us. "It's going to take hours to get to the entrance. You two stay here, and I'll go and check the lie of the land."

"It is predominantly flat with a slight slope to the right," said Old Vatrushkin.

"It's just an expression," I said. "I mean I'm going inside."

"Of course, I quite understand that you wish to make your entrance unencumbered by me," said Lidia humbly. "But when the carriage finally reaches the doorway, may I enter?"

"Lidia, I wouldn't dream of making my entrance without you," I said. "I'll be back shortly."

I jumped lightly out of the carriage, gathered up my evening gown to knee level and jogged my way to the front door, all in unobtrusive mode. The major-domo, resplendent in uniform, recoiled slightly as my shadow fell on him, but gave no other reaction.

The tubby countess was everywhere. She was a set of golden nymphs holding torches. She was a series of plaster cherubs on top of every pilaster. She was a large marble neo-classical statue (though still not as large as the original) on the half-landing. The only place she wasn't was in person at the top of the stairs, greeting her guests. The count, cadaverous, forbidding and unsmiling, stood alone.

"So very kind of you to step into the breach after Madame Potapova's party was called off," chirped an elderly guest. "But where is our dear countess?"

"Not here," said the count. "Champagne?" He indicated a footman with a tray just inside the ballroom and the elderly guest toddled away.

"I hope she is not ill," said the next guest.

"No," said the count. "Champagne?"

I glanced into the ballroom to see even more gilt and alabaster representations of the countess, reflected to infinity in the vast floor-to-ceiling mirrors, but still no actual countess. I edged along the corridor and went through the first door I could find, which turned out to lead into the count's study. Even here, there was no escape from his formidable wife. On the desk was a vast marble bust of the countess, presumably the nineteenth-century equivalent of a framed photo. She was in the pose of a bashful maiden, which I was prepared to bet money she had never been. The eyes were modestly downcast, the lips had the trace of a shy smile. It was possible to be sure that it was the countess only because of the dimensions of the bosom, which kept the bust firmly anchored to the desk. I tried to move it to see if there was any clue to the sculptor who had so totally compromised his artistic integrity, but it wouldn't budge. The count was lumbered with a perpetual reminder of his other half.

I have remarkably acute hearing, and I picked up a distant sound that I identified as the countess shrieking. I crept out of the count's study and tiptoed down the servants' stairs towards the noise. I found myself in a drab corridor and sensed that the countess and the person she was shrieking at were just round the corner. It was too dangerous to go any further: being unobtrusive is fine when there's a crowd or some other distraction, but I was pretty sure the countess would see me if I came any closer.

"You slut! You hussy!" the countess was screaming. "You think because you're an insignificant nobody that I don't notice you?"

"No, madam," whimpered a female.

"I see the way you concoct reasons to come into the room when he's there, the way you try to catch his eye, the way you flaunt yourself in front of him! How dare you, when you know he belongs to me!"

How odd, I thought, that anyone should be after the count. He wasn't a looker and he seemed to have a pretty grim disposition. Perhaps the guilty party had a thing about father figures, and had had a rubbish father.

"You will leave immediately and you will not pack your bags, since your bags and everything they might contain belong to me," the countess went on. "You have nothing."

"Madam, you can't mean—" came a disbelieving wail.

"I can and I do. From this moment, you are no longer my maid. You are emancipated."

There was an outbreak of heartrending sobs. "Madam, madam, please—if you emancipate me, there is only one road open to me, and that is not one that any decent girl could take."

"And what would you know about decent girls?"

"Madam, you can't mean to send me away without anything at all!"

"Indeed I don't. Here!"

There was the sound of a vigorous slap, and a renewal of the wailing.

"Get out! You have delayed me long enough," hissed the countess. "Tonight I take up my rightful role, unjustly postponed for twenty years, as a leader in society."

I fled, just before the countess appeared round the corner. I sprinted up the servants' stairs, dodged past the count, and raced back to the carriage, which had scarcely moved.

"Slight change of plan," I gasped. "Old Vatrushkin, do you know where the servants' entrance is?"

He jumped down from the carriage to join me. "It should be at the back of the palace. I shall find it for you."

We headed off round the back, where there was not a flambeau to be seen, and wandered around in the darkness in search of an insignificant door. It was so insignificant that we failed to see it until it creaked open and a tear-stained figure stumbled out.

"Hello," I said. "I believe you're looking for a job."

The figure raised its head to look at me with a mixture of suspicion, gloom and surliness. Never, despite a lifetime in Scotland, had I seen anyone who so perfectly merited the description of dour.

"I know your sort," said the countess's erstwhile maid. "You want to sell me down the Bosphorus as an odalisque."

"In fact I don't," I said.

A look of annoyance crossed the maid's face. "Are you saying I'm not good enough to be an odalisque?" she said.

I was about to embark on a discussion of whether being an odalisque was a desirable career choice but I had doubts as to whether the maid's feminist consciousness was sufficiently raised to make the conversation meaningful. What was important was keeping her in gainful employment and saving her from inappropriate decisions.

"I can offer you a job as a serf, in the capacity of a lady's maid," I said.

"What did you do to your last lady's maid?" she demanded mistrustfully.

"Nothing. I'm new here, and I'm in the process of hiring staff. Perhaps you'd like to hear from one of my current employees? Old Vatrushkin, tell the lady what it's like working for me."

"It is like living in paradise," breathed Old Vatrushkin. "Her excellency is the kindest and most munificent owner one could hope to have; she is compassionate, gracious—"

"I was thinking more of terms and conditions," I interrupted. "It's a five-day week, free board and lodgings, and twenty kopecks an hour for evening and weekend work."

"You'll give me money?" said the maid, looking animated for the first time.

Old Vatrushkin gasped. "No, no, no, your excellency, you must not give her money—she will only spend it."

"Old Vatrushkin, that's not your concern. So, is my job offer acceptable?"

"Yes, your excellency."

"Splendid. What's your name?"

The maid shrugged. "Don't have one."

"What does the countess call you?"

"'You.'"

"What does your family call you?"

"Nothing pleasant."

I felt it would be too presumptuous for me to give the maid a name. "All right, we'll work round it," I said. "With or without a name, you're hired."

Old Vatrushkin glared at her. "Express your gratitude to her excellency, you ingrate."

"Don't you dare talk to me like that, you unkempt lout! You're just a coachman, I'm a lady's maid."

Old Vatrushkin began to make a retort, but I interrupted in my prefect's voice. "Not another word from either of you. There is no hierarchy in this household. We're all Jock Tamson's..." I stopped, unsure of how to Russify "bairns".

"We are all the children of Jock Tamson," I said. "That's an expression. The Reverend John Thomson was the minister of Duddingston Kirk until 1840. In fact, for all I know, he may be minister of Duddingston Kirk at this very moment."

I paused and waited for confirmation or denial of the date from my audience, but my order not to say another word was being taken seriously.

"Anyway, he said of his congregation—" I paused again, unable to translate *They're a' ma bairns.* "—'They're all my children.' Or it's also possible that he had a number of children with his first wife, then married a widow with children, and had more children, and other people would say, 'They're all the children of Jock Tamson'. But that's by the way. What's important is that it has come to be axiomatic of the Scots' support of social equity. So we all treat one another with respect. And if you don't, you know what I'll do."

Panic in his voice, Old Vatrushkin whispered, "On your knees, girl! Beg her excellency's pardon!"

"Why?" she whispered back. "What will she do?"

Old Vatrushkin gulped. "She will…she will emancipate us."

The maid sank to the ground, moaning. "No, I couldn't survive being emancipated twice in one day." She clutched at my pelisse. "Forgive me, your excellency, forgive me," she gabbled. "I promise you will have no reason for complaint."

"Old Vatrushkin?"

"Nor from me, your excellency," said Old Vatrushkin, twisting his lamb's wool cap in his hands.

"Great. Old Vatrushkin will take you home and show you where everything is. I expect I'll be home late, so don't stay up. We'll have a proper chat tomorrow."

I led them back towards the palace's grand driveway where we found various horses whinnying and stamping, and coachmen shouting. The queue in front of us had disappeared, and the guests in the carriages behind us were getting restive. We rushed back, Old Vatrushkin leaping up to the driver's seat and setting off at speed as I hauled the maid inside.

"Lidia, this is my new maid. This is Lidia Ivanovna," I said, and congratulated myself on my skill in navigating round the maid's lack of name.

A few moments later, flanked by Lidia, I made my official entrance, announced by the major-domo.

The chubby countess, now standing beside her husband at the top of the staircase, raised her eyebrows as we approached.

"Ah, little Lidia Ivanovna and the foreign lady who tried so hard to turn her evening into a success."

I always try to see the best in everyone, but the countess was making it very difficult.

"You're just in time," she went on. "I would like you to lead us in some of your quaint Scottish dances in half an hour."

"Would you indeed?" I said. "I'm terribly sorry, Countess, but I'm afraid I can't do that. Last night was a personal favour to my friend Lidia Ivanovna. I'm not an itinerant dance instructor."

From the countess's expression, I deduced that she liked my tone just about as much as I liked hers. "I cannot—" she snarled, but what she couldn't do remained unspecified as she caught sight of the next guest and gave a shriek of excitement.

"Princess!" she gasped, sinking into a deep curtsy. "You honour me with your presence!"

An elderly lady dressed in a mass of chartreuse silk and lace, her grey hair in elaborate coils and loops, gazed somewhere over the countess's left shoulder. Her expression was even more contemptuous than the count's.

"Get up," she said irritably. "I'm not here to see you."

The countess turned puce and stayed where she was. I was quite impressed that she was prepared to disobey a princess. But as the moments went past, I realised her change of colour stemmed from effort rather than annoyance. She hadn't got up because she couldn't.

Since nobody else was doing anything, especially not the countess, I took charge.

"You grab her right arm," I told the count. "I'll grab her left arm, and Lidia, you push from the back." With some difficulty, we managed to propel the countess upright.

The princess surveyed us through her lorgnette. "Who are these people?" she drawled.

Lidia went into an even deeper curtsy than the countess, but since her knees were fine, she had no problem getting up again. My egalitarian principles prevent me from bending the knee to someone who's considered superior purely because of an accident of birth. But I believe in politeness, so I nodded in a friendly enough manner.

The countess waved a dismissive hand. "Do not trouble yourself with them, Princess," she wheezed. "They are nobodies."

"How extraordinary. I wouldn't dream of inviting nobodies to my soirées."

"I scarcely invited them, Princess. They simply arrived."

"Even more extraordinary, to allow anyone entry—they could be anarchists."

I was about to reassure the princess that I firmly believed in the supremacy of the ballot box when it struck me that she probably didn't.

"But you're wasting my time, Countess. Where is the young Adonis?"

With a ghastly ingratiating smile, the countess indicated that the princess should follow her, and lurched in the direction of a sofa that contained the handsome Sasha surrounded by a gaggle of young wives.

He was even more delicious than I remembered, the floppy fair hair, those dark-fringed eyes, that perfectly straight nose, that luscious mouth. And then the mood was destroyed by the countess clapping her hands as though she were shooing away stray cats. The young wives sprang up, curtseyed to the princess, and vanished.

With panther-like grace, Sasha got to his feet and bowed low. The princess walked round him, then took hold of his chin, tilted it, and made a detailed study of his face.

"Most acceptable," she said over her shoulder to the countess, who simpered. "Now, sweet creature, what is your name?"

"Sasha, your imperial highness," said the young man, his musical voice respectful.

"Call me Princess." She sat down on the empty sofa and patted the place beside her.

Lidia had been completely oblivious to the exchange. She was gazing round the ballroom, eyes shining, her hands clasped in delight.

"How grand it all is, how magnificent! How I wish I could dance here! But I cannot see the general."

"Yes, he's pretty tricky to spot," I agreed. "Oh, look, there he is, almost hidden by that Ming vase."

I signalled to him to join us. He formally asked Lidia for a dance and she formally accepted. Then they set off, Lidia politely stooping so that the general could get hold of her.

I parked myself on a spare sofa, my gaze drawn yet again to Sasha. Even though the princess had requisitioned him, I could see his eyes were fixed yearningly on Lidia as she whirled round the ballroom. He was obviously smitten, which was perfect; I would have no problem with him once I got them together. But tonight I couldn't do anything, not after my vow to Nanny. I couldn't allow Lidia to talk to or dance with any man apart from the general. I also had to make sure her fichu stayed in place. Fortunately, because the general could take only small steps, she wasn't dancing vigorously enough to dislodge it.

This was a wasted evening as far as my mission was concerned, and I had a deadline. I was going to have to stop making vows to Nanny, or at least cross my fingers behind my back.

The dance ended. Lidia charmingly thanked the general and, oblivious to Sasha's wistful look, went to sit by an old lady whose voluminous dress was made of scarlet silk.

Even as I watched Lidia, and watched Sasha watching Lidia, I became aware of an odd recurring noise, a scrabbling followed by a hastily stifled squeal of pain. I looked round to find a number of guests surreptitiously rubbing their lower legs. Then I saw an animated floormop creep up behind an elderly officer and sink its teeth into his ankle. Unlike the others, the officer had masterly self-control and didn't make a sound. He merely shook his leg until he managed to dislodge the floormop, then began limping stoically in the direction of a drink.

"Whatever is the matter with you, Colonel?" called the countess.

"Afraid the old war wound's playing up," he said.

I leaned over towards the guests on the next sofa. "What's that thing on the floor?" I asked.

"It is the countess's darling little lapdog," someone trilled. "Such an amusing little creature! We all love it so much!"

The countess might be new to the social scene, but nobody seemed in any hurry to challenge her. She had attracted a princess to her party, after all.

The darling little lapdog shuffled closer, and I could see its malevolent little eyes focus on me.

"Not a chance," I said. "Shuffle along."

The creature locked gazes with me, its eyes glittering balefully, and with a sudden bound, it landed on the sofa beside me.

"Bad dog," I said, grabbing it and plonking it back on the floor. There was a horrified silence from the guests around me, broken by piteous whining. With a cry, the countess rushed over and scooped the floormop up in her arms, cooing at it and petting it.

"My darling, what happened to you?" she screeched.

The silence spread in ripples across the ballroom, reaching even the orchestra, which lurched to a discordant halt. Everybody was looking at me.

"Nothing happened to it. I merely shifted it from the sofa to the floor," I said evenly.

"My poor Tresorka, what did the nasty foreign lady do to you? Never mind the nasty foreign lady. She doesn't like dear little doggies."

"On the contrary," I said. "I'm a regular St Francis of Assisi. But I believe there's a place for everything and everything in its place. And a dog's place is not on the soft furnishings."

"Ah yes, one's place." The countess's voice reverberated round the hushed ballroom. "And where is *your* place, Shona Fergusovna? You have already informed me that you are not an itinerant dance instructor. In that case, I am quite at a loss to know who you are."

I stood up, smoothed down my dress, took a deep breath and addressed the gathering.

"You want to know who I am? Very well. I come from the capital of Scotland, where I attended the Marcia Blaine School for Girls and gained the finest education in the world. May I say that I believe what is important is not our social position, but the use we make of our talents."

"Good God!" an officer exclaimed. "The woman's a Decembrist!"

I carefully noted this latest clue to the date. The Decembrists, a radical political reform group, had had a failed uprising in 1825.

"I'm not any kind of -ist," I retorted. "Except a feminist, obviously."

"What is a feminist?" I heard someone whisper to their neighbour.

"It must be someone who upholds the highest virtues of womanhood: humility, obedience and flower arranging," came the reply.

I decided to let that one go.

"As I told you yesterday evening, I am the crème de la crème," I went on. "It was no idle boast."

Even as I said the words, there was a tightening in my chest and a pounding in my temples at the thought of That Book.

"Yes," I said, "every single Blainer is the crème de la crème by virtue of our outstanding education. But a depraved novelist claimed that this epithet applied only to a small coterie, the pupils of one particular teacher. And in a salacious misrepresentation of our beloved school and its irreproachable staff, she portrayed that teacher as a promiscuous adulteress who was prepared to prostitute her pupils. Pupils whose prepubescent sexual fantasies she described in sordid detail."

I had to clutch a nearby gilt salon chair for support, and to let my pulse slow down. I pride myself on my self-control, but this is a wound that will never heal.

A lady sitting nearby leaned forward eagerly: "Please, Shona Fergusovna, may we have the name of this book and its author? In order that we may avoid it, of course."

That Book, here! It was a dreadful thought. But who knew what wrinkles there were in the time-space continuum? After all, here I was, without any idea how I'd got here. What if That

Book should suddenly turn up in nineteenth-century Russia and people mistook it for an accurate representation of the Scottish education system?

"A wise precaution," I said. "The title of this depraved novel is *The Prime of Miss Jean Brodie* and the writer is a Mrs Spark."

There was a rustling as the ladies all opened their reticules, took out pencils and paper and carefully wrote down the details.

"We shall seek out every copy in order to prevent them falling into innocent hands," said the young lady, and they all nodded.

This was heartening. "I'm most grateful to you," I said. "The sooner we can rid the world of this farrago of lies, the better."

Now that I had averted danger, I could resume my theme. My self-control and my pulse were within acceptable levels. I looked steadily at the countess.

"But it seems that some of you here still believe in the importance of social status. In that case, I'm proud to inform you that there is not a single person in Scotland who can boast a finer or a higher lineage than my own, or claim precedence over me. For I, Countess, am one of the children of Jock Tamson."

There were wondering gasps and then someone began to clap, swiftly followed by the others. Everyone, I noticed, apart from the countess. I also noticed that the person who had started the applause was none other than the guest of honour, the elderly princess. That startled me, because she had seemed very status-conscious. But I had been speaking from the heart, and must have touched her with my eloquence.

Her clipped patrician tones cut through the continuing applause. "My dear Princess Tamsonova! Pray come and sit by me."

The daft woman had got the wrong end of the stick entirely. Inbreeding has a lot to answer for. There I was, making the case for social equality, and she thought I was saying I was Caledonian royalty. The very definition of ironic. I was going to explain her mistake, and then I thought it was unwise to antagonise her unnecessarily. Also, I couldn't really be bothered.

"Delighted, Princess," I said.

She gave Sasha a dismissive shove and he disappeared into the crowd. I had the distinct impression that he was escaping. Another signal from her, and the orchestra struck up again.

"It is an unexpected pleasure to meet another princess," she said in perfect English and gave a dry chuckle at my reaction. "Ah yes, I speak your language. I had an English governess —indeed, I should say a Scottish governess, for she was most particular on that point. A Miss Menzies from Aberfeldy— perhaps you know her?"

"Sorry, I don't think so," I said.

"No matter—she was, as you say in your picturesque language, a nippy sweetie." Another arid chuckle. "Ah yes, I know Scots as well as English. And I am well acquainted with your beautiful country—or should I say *bonnie land?*—through the works of Sir Walter Scott. I am at present reading *Rob Roy*, and it would be a pleasure to speak with you of Scotia's glorious braes and glens."

Excellent. Another clue. *Rob Roy* was published in 1817. "The pleasure will be all mine, Princess," I said. "I never tire of talking about my dear, my native soil."

The princess flourished her lorgnette enthusiastically. "A quotation from your national bard, dear Rabbie! I adore his enchanting verses. Simple. Inspiring. Profound."

"Left—" I began and just managed to prevent myself continuing: "—wing." That wouldn't go down well with royalty. "—us a wonderful legacy," I concluded, glancing round to see what was going on elsewhere. Quite a few guests were gawking at us in open-mouthed awe, albeit at a discreet distance so they couldn't be accused of eavesdropping. Not that they would have gleaned much, since the princess was holding forth in a fine Perthshire accent. But the countess was giving me evils, a snarl on her face that would have done credit to the animated floormop. She seemed, in the words of dear Rabbie, to be nursing her wrath to keep it warm, to the extent that I feared her stays might spontaneously combust.

Lidia was now chatting to another old dear who was brandishing an ear trumpet and wearing an eye patch, while Sasha had ended up sitting beside the lady in red who had been Lidia's previous companion. As I watched, Sasha helped her to her feet. She was completely cylindrical and looked remarkably like a pillar box.

This was exciting—another possible clue. Every Blainer knows that the great Victorian novelist Anthony Trollope invented the British pillar box in 1852. The Post Office had sent him to Europe on a fact-finding mission. Had he got as far as Russia and been inspired by Pillar Box Lady?

And then I had to smile at my jejune error. The original pillar boxes had been green.

"Tell me," I said to the princess, "does that lady over there have an olive-coloured dress?"

The princess shook her head. "She is known for only ever wearing scarlet. Her late husband found a financially advantageous deal on a bale of silk from the Indies."

A pity. But it was a timely reminder that I must never take anything for granted. Had I forgotten that it was twenty years before pillar boxes were painted red, I could have made an erroneous assumption. I must always check and double check, and deal in facts, not suppositions.

Pillar Box Lady was making her way to the door with the help of Sasha and a walking stick. My super-acute hearing picked up their conversation.

"You will not forget?" said Pillar Box Lady.

"How could I?" said Sasha. "I shall be counting the minutes until I see you tomorrow morning."

She stroked his cheek. "Sweet child! My coachman will bring you straight to me."

What a sweet young guy, I thought, offering to visit lonely wrinklies. But the princess was demanding my attention.

"So you have come from high Dunedin's towers. Do you reside in the castle itself or in the picturesque Palace of Holyroodhouse?"

It would do my mission no harm if she thought I was a fellow princess, but I was reluctant to tell an outright lie.

"Neither," I said, thinking of the topography of Morningside. "I actually live on a brae."

"Delightful!" said the princess. "Such a wise choice. A town palace can be so dreadfully enervating with the constant bustle of common people nearby. It is much more pleasant to remain on one's country estates. And do you rin aboot the braes and pu' the gowans fine, as dear Rabbie suggests?"

"Frequently," I said.

"I've always wondered," said the princess, "what exactly is a gowan? I assume it is a Scottish serf?"

"More like a small gerbera," I explained, and the princess gave a sigh of disappointment.

"You must tell me about that intriguing item of male clothing, the kilt. It must be very splendid to see the brawny thighs of your serfs when the snell wind blaws."

I wasn't going to get drawn into a conversation about serfs. "Kilts are a Highland tradition, and Edinburgh is a lowland city."

"Then when I visit, you must take me to the Highlands."

Did time travelling work in both directions? It would be quite awkward if she turned up. I would have to take time off to show her round properly. And since she was a princess, I would probably have to give up my bedroom and sleep on the bed settee. But I didn't say any of this to her, just smiled in a non-committal way.

She patted my arm. "I came here with few expectations, but young Sasha is bonnier than I could have imagined, and it is a muckle joy to find such a braw lassie as my fellow princess."

"Sir Walter couldn't have put it better," I said politely.

The princess waved a bejewelled hand at the countess, who scuttled across as fast as her fat little feet could carry her.

"My carriage," ordered the princess in Russian as though to a hearing-impaired doorman.

"But you can't leave already!" the countess protested.

The princess stared at her, gimlet-eyed. "Do you presume to command me?"

"No, Princess, of course not—what I mean is, it would be so disappointing for all the other guests."

"I am not a dancing bear, here to provide entertainment. You seem to have an extraordinary capacity for thinking that royalty is a source of diversion. And can you explain why you told me that Princess Tamsonova was a nobody?"

The countess spluttered. "Dearest Princess, you must have misunderstood!"

"I? Misunderstood?"

"No, no, of course not, what I mean is that I must have been unclear. Of course I would never describe our dear Princess Tamsonova as a nobody. I was referring to the other people present at the time, whose names I forget."

I felt I should be helpful. "There was only one other person present, my friend Lidia Ivanovna," I said.

The princess's eyes widened. "Not little Lidia Ivanovna, who has been locked away for all these years?"

"That's the one," I said.

"How fascinating! It is beyond me, Countess, why you should describe her as a nobody when she must be one of the richest heiresses in the land. Princess Tamsonova, my dear, I shall call on you tomorrow."

"Excellent. I'll make sure I'm in all day," I said.

The princess kissed her hand to me, then descended the staircase without a further word or glance for the countess.

There was a scrabbling noise. The animated floormop was baring its teeth at me.

"Hello, doggy," I said. Tresorka growled and scuttled under the countess's voluminous gown.

"Lovely party," I told the countess, beaming. "Always nice to meet a fellow princess."

The countess's smile was fixed like concrete. "But how wicked of you, Princess Tamsonova, to remain incognito yesterday."

"Yesterday wasn't about me," I said. "It was about Lidia Ivanovna taking up her rightful place in society, which I'm glad to see she's doing very successfully."

Lidia was now dancing a quadrille with the general, thoughtfully steering him out of the way of the other couples since he couldn't see through her.

"Anyway, must go and circulate," I said. "Noblesse oblige." I watched the countess carefully to see if she recognised the phrase, which had been coined by Honoré de Balzac in 1835. The rictus smile remained intact. But as I turned to go, my super-acute hearing picked up a faint whisper: "I shall destroy you."

I couldn't be sure whether the countess didn't know the Balzac expression, or just really hated me. Whichever it was, it hadn't helped to pinpoint the year.

I approached a gaggle of young wives who all reverently jumped to their feet and installed me in their midst.

"This is your first visit here, Princess Tamsonova?" ventured one. "What are your impressions?"

"Very much as I imagined," I said. "I reckoned it would be a bit of a fashion backwater, so I got my dressmaker to make me up some of last year's designs which I see make me fit right in. But I couldn't believe it when I saw Lidia Ivanovna—what a style maven! Retro is so totally on trend in Scotland this season, but she's the only one to pick up on it. And she's got the dare-to-bare look absolutely right—everybody in Edinburgh is using no-make-up make-up. And her hair! It must take her hours to get that simple, natural, just-washed-in-the-loch effect. Honestly, you think all these years she's been shut away, missing out on all the social life, and it turns out she's been keeping up with high fashion all the time. That yellow wool fichu matched with the navy cotton is so totally this season's colours and textures—I just can't wait to try it out."

I shook my head in admiration.

At that moment, the quadrille ended. The young wives twittered with excitement and called Lidia over to join them, making a space for her. I spotted Sasha on the other side of room, sitting by the old woman with the ear trumpet and the eye patch. He showed every sign of listening attentively to her, but his eyes were on Lidia. I tuned out the young wives' conversation and tuned in to Eye Patch Lady and Sasha.

"I shall be waiting for you tomorrow afternoon," she was saying.

"And I shall be counting the minutes until then," Sasha replied.

He was such a sweet guy. When he married Lidia, she would have to be careful that he didn't exhaust himself doing good works, and left some time for her.

An irritatingly squeaky-voiced young wife interrupted my thoughts. "Dearest Lidia Ivanovna, may we send our dress-makers to you to copy your charming on-trend gowns?"

"And please tell us where may we purchase a woollen fichu," said another.

A third begged for the secrets of Lidia's beauty regime.

"Lidia Ivanovna will tell you that the key thing is to insist on performing a wide range of domestic duties: chopping logs, scrubbing clothes, peeling potatoes," I said. "It really gets the circulation going and tightens up the pores, leaving you with a smooth complexion. It's also great for toning up those flabby upper arms. If your serfs complain that there's nothing for them to do, don't back down, just remind them who's boss."

"But—" said Lidia.

"You're quite right to correct me," I said. "But most impor-tant of all, as Lidia was about to tell you, is one's beauty sleep. So if we're all to be up at the crack of dawn tomorrow to get those stoves and samovars heated up, we really should go."

As Old Vatrushkin settled us in the drozhky, Lidia said, "How kind and welcoming they are to me."

I didn't want to disillusion her. The lesson on pretentious social climbers could come later.

"You're enjoying being out in society, then?" I asked.

She hesitated. "It's not quite as I imagined it."

"It's much more exciting than you imagined?" I suggested.

"I was so looking forward to dancing," she said. "The general is a charming and valiant gentleman but I find stooping to dance with him slightly uncomfortable. His conversation is very lively, about carnage on battlefields, but I'm afraid I know very little about carnage or battlefields and cannot contribute much."

This would all be solved when I got her together with Sasha.

"And the ladies," she went on. "It is so good of them to include me, but I fear I cannot contribute anything to their conversation either, since I know nothing about fashion and beauty regimes."

You and me both, sister, I thought.

"Society seems…" She hesitated again. "I'm not sure if I can find the right word."

"Just say what comes into your head," I encouraged. "I'm sure I'll work out what you're trying to say."

She smiled gratefully. "I know I can always depend on you, dear Shona Fergusovna. I find society trivial, petty, worthless and inconsequential. Forgive me if I haven't expressed myself clearly."

"No, that seems clear enough," I said.

"Nobody in society does anything that is not trivial, petty, worthless and inconsequential," she went on. "And so I have decided to withdraw from society and return to my woodwork."

I clutched the side of the drozhky in alarm. If Lidia withdrew from society, I would never be able to get her married to Sasha, and I would have failed in my very first mission. Which probably meant I wouldn't get sent on a second one. This was all my fault, bigging up her woodwork when I should have been extolling the virtues of marriage and motherhood like a Stepford Wife.

"Promise me you won't do anything hasty," I said. "Give it until the end of this week."

She gave a delighted laugh. "I see, it is a test," she said. "I shall not disappoint you. My resolve to lead a life of seclusion will be even firmer by the week's end."

CHAPTER 5

I awoke knowing that there was someone in my room. Someone who was sneaking around. Someone who didn't want me to know they were there.

I kept my eyes closed and breathed in heavily as though deeply asleep. No scent of cologne, tobacco or leather boots. A faint whiff of cabbage.

I sensed the figure approaching me and held myself in readiness. Martial arts is one of my hobbies and while I wouldn't claim to be as expert as a Shaolin monk, I've got more than enough knowledge to be effective. As the intruder leaned towards me, I leaped up and pinned them to the wall.

The maid screamed.

"I'm terribly sorry," I said, loosening my grip and helping her into a chair. "I thought you were somebody else."

The maid scowled. "It is very hard working for you. The countess beat me all the time, but she never tried to kill me."

"I wasn't trying to kill you," I said. "I was just trying to find out who you were and what you were doing in my bedroom. Incidentally, what are you doing in my bedroom?"

"I came to dress you," she whined.

"Do you dress yourself?" I asked.

The maid rolled her eyes. "Of course, madam."

"Do you find it difficult?"

"Of course not, madam."

"Well, neither do I, so in future, there's no need for you to come into my room in the morning."

"It's not right," muttered the maid. "It's what I'm supposed to do." And then, apparently noticing my attire for the first time: "Saints in heaven, madam, what are you wearing?"

"Pyjamas," I said. "Black Watch tartan. Very cosy. Would you like a pair?"

The maid shuddered. "It's not decent. You should wear proper nightclothes, madam."

"It's what I was given, and I'm very happy with them," I said.

"I hope the rest of madam's clothes are appropriate," sniffed the maid.

I decided against showing the maid my underwear drawer, guessing that the multiway bras would cause particular upset. But I opened the wardrobe to display my dresses and evening gowns.

"Do these meet with your approval?"

The maid nodded, a glint of acquisitiveness in her eye as she surveyed the elegant muslins, chintzes, satins and silks.

"Tell you what," I said. "To make up for giving you a fright, why don't you borrow my clothes if you're going out somewhere special? We're about the same height and build."

I had assumed that this would be a bonding exercise, but the maid simply gave a shrug. "I suppose there are a few I wouldn't mind being seen in. Of course madam is substantially wider than myself in the—" She gestured in a disparaging way. "But I'll try to make the necessary adjustments."

I was going to point out that my glutes were solid muscle, but she was already rummaging through the wardrobe. She requisitioned three of my most expensive-looking gowns and a couple of velvet bonnets.

"These will do for the moment," she said disdainfully. She turned to leave the room with her haul, and screamed.

"What is it now?" I asked.

The maid pointed a trembling finger at the log wall that was covered in deep gouges and splintered planks where I had been doing my knife-throwing practice. It did look pretty bad. I would have to leave some money for repairs when I left.

"What happened?" she whispered.

"I was having a bit of trouble with the sleeves of my new fur coat," I said.

Her eyes wide in terror, the maid fled.

"Breakfast in ten minutes," I called after her. But when I reached the kitchen, I discovered that was where she had fled to, so that she could complain to Old Vatrushkin.

"Madam tried to kill me!" she was saying. "You should see the wall—she tore it to pieces with her nails because she didn't like her coat. I've never known anyone to have a temper like madam's. You mark my words, it's only a matter of time before she tries to tear us to pieces."

"Her excellency may do as she wishes," said Old Vatrushkin. "It would be an honour for us to be torn to pieces by her."

I cleared my throat warningly. "If you repeat these preposterous, inaccurate and defamatory allegations one more time," I said, "you know what I'll do."

The maid screamed. "No, don't tear me to pieces!"

"Oh, for heaven's sake," I said. "Stop being such a drama queen. I was referring to emancipation. Anyway, I'm expecting a visit from the princess some time today, so we'd better get the place tidy and organise some tea and cake for her."

The maid gave a petulant sniff. "I'm a lady's maid," she said. "These are not my duties."

"What exactly are your duties?" I asked.

"To dress and undress you, madam."

I sighed. Still, life would probably be simpler with her doing as little as possible.

"Your excellency, it would be a privilege to be allowed to clean the mansion for you," said Old Vatrushkin. "I shall also start making some epicurean delicacies. And if in my poor unskilful way, I could serve them with some tea to your imperial visitor—but no, that would be unimaginable."

"I'm imagining it right now and it would be perfect," I said. "So that's the staffing situation sorted."

"To think that a princess is coming to visit and you don't have a major-domo," the maid sneered.

"The princess will just have to take us as she finds us," I said. "I'm not getting involved with any more serfs."

"No need, your excellency," said Old Vatrushkin. "I am conversant with the duties of a major-domo."

Proof yet again that coachmen know everything.

When the princess arrived, Old Vatrushkin performed his major-domo duties to perfection. But as she ascended the stairs, she remarked, "Your major-domo has a very odd uniform," and I wondered whether he should have changed out of his jerkin and the shabby long coat with its turned-up collar, not to mention the scruffy black lamb's wool cap. But I decided it ill became the princess to criticise anyone else's clothes since she was wearing a bright emerald satin dress that made her look like a particularly lurid spear of asparagus.

The princess installed herself in the best seat in the salon and Old Vatrushkin set about serving the tea.

"Your footman has a very odd uniform," said the princess. "It looks very similar to that of your major-domo."

She obviously suffered from aristocratic myopia when dealing with the lower orders, and had no idea that she had seen Old Vatrushkin before.

"They're one and the same," I said.

"You can't mean that your footman is your major-domo?" demanded the princess. I nodded.

"Just a wee Scottish thing. Saves on staff costs."

The princess clapped her hands in delight. "Oh, Princess Tamsonova, what a splendid idea! There is so much we can learn from Caledonia, stern and wild. The moment I get home, I shall instruct all the major-domos in my palaces to become footmen immediately."

"But you won't get rid of your existing footmen?" I said, petrified that I might have been instrumental in a round of forcible emancipations.

"Of course not," said the princess. "One can never have too many footmen."

Old Vatrushkin went over to the golden samovar to pour the tea. The princess turned her lorgnette on it.

"What an exquisite samovar! And what an exquisite serf! I quite understand why you have him as both your major-domo and footman."

Startled, I peered at Old Vatrushkin. He looked the same as always, timid dark eyes peeping out of a tangle of wild black curls. I would never have described him as "exquisite". "Cute", tops.

He served the princess with her tea, and she playfully pinched his cheek, yanking a quantity of beard. As he handed me my own glass of tea, he swivelled his eyes meaningfully towards the door and looked back at me with a pleading look. I understood immediately.

"We can manage very well on our own from here," I said. "Return to your major-domo-ing."

Swiftly, to prevent the princess countermanding my order, I said, "I'm intrigued by the countess. Do tell me more about her."

The princess yawned. "I have no interest in her. Yesterday was the first time I made her acquaintance. Even if her wedding to the count had taken place in town, I doubt I would have attended. But of course it took place in the country as a consequence of the unfortunate incident of which we are forbidden to speak."

"We can't even speak about it a bit?" I asked.

"No indeed." The princess leaned forward confidentially. "An artillery officer spoke of it in the hearing of his imperial majesty and the tsar tore off his epaulettes with his own hands."

"Nasty," I said. "That would definitely put you off speaking about it. So tell me about the count."

The princess yawned again. "I have no interest in him. He is not amusing and he is certainly not handsome. We have missed nothing over the past twenty years through his absence." Then she perked up. "But have you ever seen anything more delightful than the young Sasha?"

"The countess's protégé?" I asked cautiously and the princess erupted in gales of laughter.

"Yes, yes, her protégé—oh, Princess Tamsonova, there is no man in town more exquisite than Sasha and no man or woman more amusing than yourself! I shall certainly describe him as her protégé from now on."

I couldn't see anything remotely funny in what I had said. It was how Old Vatrushkin had described him and it seemed perfectly innocuous. But I laughed companionably so that the princess didn't feel awkward.

"And speaking of Sasha," I asked, "what do you know about him?"

"I believe he is the first cousin of the old prince. And I am certain he is related to the blue-eyed baroness, because of the unmistakable family resemblance."

Interesting. Even the princess had been fooled by Sasha's fake CV.

She had a faraway look. "But it is absurd the way the countess dresses him so drearily! She has no sense of style. I shall send my late husband's tailor to him. I have a fancy to see him in some of the more snug Parisian fashions."

I didn't like the direction the conversation had taken.

"Princess..." I cleared my throat. "Your interest in Sasha. I presume it's...maternal?"

The Princess's laugh put me in mind of Sid James.

Feminism is nothing if it does not liberate both women and men. It is equality that we seek. "Princess," I went on, "I think you might be being a wee bit sexist."

"Sexist?" said the princess. "I do not know this word."

"You're sort of…objectifying."

"Objectifying? My dear Princess Tamsonova, what language are you speaking? I have met none of this vocabulary in the delightful works of Sir Walter Scott."

I explained that Scott often used archaic language for stylistic purposes, and that mine was more up to date.

"What I mean is that you're treating Sasha as an object, thinking of him purely in terms of your own gratification rather than seeing him as a person in his own right."

The princess clapped her hands again. "Exactly so! My dear princess, it is as though you can see directly into my soul! So I am sexist and I objectify—how marvellous. I had no idea I was doing anything so profound."

"Yes, but…" I gazed helplessly at the ceiling and found myself completely unable to appreciate its exceptional stucco work. "You see, it's not necessarily a good thing. We don't like it when men behave like that to us, so it's not very fair if we behave like that to them."

There was silence. The princess was obviously pondering the justice of what I had said and would resolve to behave herself. Then I realised that she had stopped breathing and was turning bluish purple, clashing unpleasantly with her emerald dress.

I had to make an instant decision, and I made it, thumping her hard on the back. There was a small chance that this would cause arrhythmia, and the more cautious strategy would have been to go through her reticule in search of sal volatile. But that would have lost vital seconds. I thumped again, harder. The respiratory arrest continued. I thumped again. No response. I thumped again, really, really hard.

There was a faint breath and I managed to make out some words.

"…no…more…"

"I'm so sorry," I said. "I wasn't trying to hurt you, but it was an emergency."

"Not…that…" the princess wheezed. She lay back in her seat, eyes closed, fanning herself until she revived. "No more, I beg you, Princess Tamsonova, of your wicked Scottish wit! I might have died laughing. 'We don't like it when men behave like that to us, so it's not very fair if we behave like that to them.'" She began to cackle again but restrained herself with an effort. "Princess, I'm sure you won't object to my repeating your epigram at my next social engagement."

"Not at all," I said, suspecting that the princess was still missing the point. But if she repeated it often enough, I was sure the wisdom of my words would eventually percolate through the Russian female consciousness.

"And I want to hear about the little Lidia Ivanovna, now that she is no longer a hermit," she said. "The last time I was in that house must have been over twenty years ago. They had quite a reasonably sized ballroom, as I remember. Her late father would never dance with me. An extraordinarily handsome man but a dreadful prude. His wife was always very wary of me—she probably imagined I was planning an *affaire* with her husband. Which of course I was, but one cuts one's losses and moves on."

I would have to explain the concept of sisterly solidarity to her.

I gave a glowing description of Lidia's party, not forgetting to mention the ten Nebuchadnezzars of Veuve Clicquot.

The princess raised an eyebrow. "A successful party indeed. I was not invited but I forgive her. She didn't know I was in town, since I came only when I heard about the countess's—what was it you said, protégé?" The princess began cackling again and I kept a close watch on her in case more first aid was needed.

"The vulgarity of the countess's so-called palace. It was a relief to find the youth was so well-bred. I've decided to throw a proper party tomorrow evening to help people recover. You must come, of course, and bring the little Lidia Ivanovna with you. She was a sweet, pretty thing as a child. Has she aged well?"

Aristocratic myopia had again taken its toll, I reflected, since the princess had seen her the previous evening when we helped the countess to her feet. But of course she hadn't paid any attention to her because at that point, she believed her to be a nobody.

"Extremely well. She's lovely. Very lovely indeed. In fact, every bit as attractive as—young Sasha." I had been going to say "the countess's protégé" again, but I was getting a bit fed up with the way the princess cackled every time I said it, particularly as my French pronunciation is flawless.

"I should like to meet her," decided the princess. "I should like to see how she has turned out when she has scarcely seen the light of day for twenty years."

"Yes, about that," I said. "Why did the family lock themselves away like that?"

The princess's eyes lit up. "You don't know about the scandal?"

"Scandal?" I said. "Just a minute, let me get you another wee glass of tea."

In my haste, I nearly did myself a mischief with the samovar eagle's razor-sharp beak as I poured out the water. It really wasn't acceptable to have something so dangerous in what was, after all, my place of work. Just as I had sent out a "thank you" where it was appropriate, I sent out vibes of complaint. And I got the distinct impression that my vibes were being blocked.

The princess settled back with a fresh glass of tea and a plate of Old Vatrushkin's melt-in-the-mouth pastries. "Lidia's mother was said to be the most virtuous of women, devoted to her prude of a husband. It made her downfall all the more delicious."

"I had no idea there was a downfall; I just knew there was a tragedy, a terrible loss, which was very distressing."

The princess barked with laughter. "A terrible loss? Indeed there was! The loss of the virtuous lady's reputation!"

"That's not the impression I had," I said. "I thought Lidia's mother was a living saint."

"Do living saints dispose of their infants as soon as they are born? No, no, Lidia Ivanovna's saintly mother was guilty of an indiscretion and never dared show her face in public again."

"Hang on," I said.

"Hang what on what?"

"It's just an expression," I said. "I mean, please will you go back to the beginning and tell me what happened? And how do you know?"

The princess rearranged the cushions to make herself more comfortable. "My coachman, of course. Coachmen know everything. And mine is under firm orders to pass everything he knows on to me. Lidia's parents called the priest to make the arrangements for the christening, but no christening took place. Instead, they claimed the child had suddenly died. The child had been hale and hearty. So tell me what happened?"

"It's probably better if you tell me what happened," I said.

"The lady had been able to fool her husband into thinking the child was his, but she could not fool the man of God. It is my belief"—she leaned forward confidentially—"that the child was *ginger*."

I have to say I took this as something of a racial slight. Some members of my own family are ginger (fortunately nobody that close), so I understand the importance of tolerance. But I was never going to get any information out of the princess if I intervened every time she needed her consciousness raised.

"Lidia Ivanovna's father could not face the world knowing that he had been betrayed, so there was no question of divorce. But he never allowed his wife to leave the house again. She died of shame a few years later."

"And this is all fact?" I said.

"Of course not," said the princess, tapping me with her fan. "This is all gossip. Marvellous fun! Lidia's father refused to let Lidia mix with society in case she turned out the same as her mother. And look! He's scarcely cold in his grave and she's throwing champagne-fuelled parties, the hussy."

"From what I know of her, she seems a very nice girl," I said firmly. "Is any of what you've told me possibly true?"

"All of it could be," said the princess robustly. "I knew the couple who were going to be godparents, and they never said a word about it. That proves it. They were obviously sworn to secrecy."

"I'm not sure that—"

"The family pretended that there was a funeral, but if there was a funeral, you tell me where the infant's grave is."

"Where?" I asked.

"Nowhere!" crowed the princess. "That child was smuggled out of the house in the dead of night."

"You mean Lidia's got a brother who's still alive somewhere?"

The princess nodded. "Exactly!"

"Shouldn't somebody look for him?"

"I can't imagine who would want to."

"Lidia?"

"Princess Tamsonova! Even with her sheltered upbringing, she could not be so foolish. These family scandals should be left where they belong, to add excitement to conversation in the salons of the upper classes. I'll invite the girl to my party, but I'd like to meet her in a more intimate situation first. I won't trouble myself to call on her, in case I find her boring. But you are never boring, Princess Tamsonova. Perhaps you would arrange a little gathering for tomorrow and invite her?"

Once the princess had wafted off home, I sought out Old Vatrushkin in the pantry. He was slumped against the wall and his face had a ghastly pallor.

"You don't look too clever," I said.

He hung his head. "Indeed, your excellency, I can make no claim to intelligence."

"It's just an expression," I said. "I mean you look a bit ill. Anyway, I apologise for the princess's dreadful behaviour. I had no idea how bad she was. Thank goodness you signalled to me that you wanted to get away. She's sexist and she objectifies."

Old Vatrushkin shook his head. "It wasn't that, your excellency. If you had required me to entertain her highness, of course I would have done my best to give satisfaction."

I gaped at him. If only I didn't have a mission to deal with: there was serious consciousness-raising work to be done on everyone. "I can assure you, Old Vatrushkin, that sort of thing will never be part of your job description."

Old Vatrushkin bowed. "As always, your excellency is too good to me. But I was anxious to leave as quickly as possible, since I had stupidly sustained a small cut on the samovar and was afraid I might stain something."

I nodded in agreement, thinking of the bloodstains on the cushion cover back home when I inadvertently stabbed Dad with the throwing knife. "That thing's a menace. Take it down to the pantry and bring up the other one for tomorrow—I'm having a girls' afternoon tea."

Old Vatrushkin gave a moan of distress. "In this one instance, your excellency, I must contradict you. The samovar in the pantry is of mediocre quality, intended only for serfs. These ladies will all be curious to see your home and it is essential they recognise that you are a great lady. I must serve them from the samovar in the salon."

I shook my head at him. "Old Vatrushkin, have you not paid attention to anything I've told you? To paraphrase the national bard's hymn to egalitarianism, *the samovar's but the guinea's stamp, the man's the gowd for a' that.* Gowd means gold."

"But it's the samovar that's gold," protested Old Vatrushkin. "Please, your excellency, let it stay. All I need do is file down the beak a little."

He was flapping his hands with anxiety, and I noticed a massive bandage on his right hand, with blood oozing through it.

"This is the slight cut?" I asked.

"It is nothing," he said. "I found a needle and thread and sewed the skin back together."

"Old Vatrushkin, you can't possibly have done it properly one-handed, especially not left-handed," I said, unwrapping the bandage to reveal a confusion of knots in a gaping wound. "See? This is a complete mess."

Old Vatrushkin's bottom lip trembled. "Forgive me, your excellency. I did my best. I'm sorry it was not good enough."

"Why on earth didn't you ask the maid to do it?"

"I did," said Old Vatrushkin. "She said it wasn't part of her duties."

My mouth set in a firm line. "She's having a laugh," I said.

"Forgive me again, your excellency, for contradicting you, but I don't think so. I have never seen her laugh. In fact, when she saw the blood, she screamed."

"It's just an expression," I said, summoning the maid with some asperity.

She lounged in the doorway, looking sulky.

"Listen, missy, I've had just about enough of your airs and graces," I said. "I've told you already, this is an egalitarian household. I may not be completely conversant with the demarcation between household staff, but I'm pretty sure a lady's maid gets involved in a little light needlework. You must have to mend torn frocks from time to time."

The maid opened her mouth to protest but I continued regardless. "That, however, is not the point. The point is that another member of the household asked you for help. You will now get your sewing-case and you will give that help. Understood?"

She dropped a small reluctant curtsy and set off as instructed.

"Your excellency," said Old Vatrushkin urgently. "If I am to be resewn, I would much rather it was by you than by that incompetent creature."

"Don't worry," I soothed him. "I'll supervise, and if she doesn't get it right, she'll just have to rip the stitches out and start again. I won't let her get away with shoddy work, however long it takes."

"Your excellency is, as ever, too good to me," said Old Vatrushkin.

The maid returned and produced a threaded needle.

"Right," I said. "Make sure the two flaps of skin are slightly overlapping before you start."

Old Vatrushkin stretched his hand open to allow the operation to begin, setting off another gush of blood. The maid screamed and, for good measure, fainted.

With Old Vatrushkin's help, I propped her against a table leg.

"Honestly, I'm sure she did that on purpose," I said. "Your wish has come true, Old Vatrushkin, and I'm performing the procedure after all."

"I was being selfish," he said. "I cannot put your excellency to this trouble. Please ignore it. After all, what is the worst that can happen?"

We both thought.

"It could become gangrenous and your hand would have to be amputated?" I suggested.

"I'm sure I could learn to drive one-handed," said Old Vatrushkin. "I shall go and practise immediately."

He was such a conscientious, determined soul that I was sure he'd manage, but I was actually quite keen for an opportunity to try out my surgical skills. In the absence of anaesthetic, I poured Old Vatrushkin a large glass of vodka and then made him take off his leather belt and bite on it. I sutured the wound, and I have to say my precise, delicate stitching would have done credit to Edinburgh Royal Infirmary's finest. Embroidery tends to be a despised, outmoded skill these days, but I like reclaiming so-called feminine pastimes and reshaping them for modern needs.

"Are you fit to go back to work?" I asked.

Old Vatrushkin spat out fragments of leather. "Better than ever, thanks to your excellency. May I now go and file down the eagle's beak on the samovar?"

I pondered. The beak was an undoubted health hazard. But the samovar was also a work of art, which I couldn't allow to be vandalised.

"No filing," I said. "Just try to be more careful during my girls' tea."

I went to my writing desk and began composing the invitations in graceful Cyrillic script. "The Princess Tamsonova has great pleasure in inviting you to a traditional Scottish afternoon tea," I wrote, carefully adding "Tea" in the bottom right-hand corner, where other occasions might demand "Drinks" or "Cocktails". Then I wrote "Ladies Only" in the bottom left-hand corner.

Once I had completed a stack of invitations, I handed them over to Old Vatrushkin. And then I had a thought.

"Old Vatrushkin, is it all right just to call in on people unannounced in the afternoon?"

"That would be a sign of very poor breeding, your excellency."

"Pity," I sighed. "I wanted a wee chat with Nanny, and I thought I could see her if I delivered Lidia's invitation personally."

"Then you should go now," said Old Vatrushkin. "You will be there in time for lunch."

"I can't do that. I haven't been invited."

"But it is the custom among our noble families to welcome anyone to join them at mealtimes. Some people have not eaten at home for years—they simply go to other people's houses. Of course, nobody will think of going to Lidia Ivanovna's since her home has been shut for so long, but now that she has entered society, she will be prepared to take up her public duties."

"So anyone can join them?" I said, a new and improved scheme developing in my head. "Right, let's go."

I arrived just before lunch to be told that Nanny was down in the kitchens, supervising the preparations. There was no sign of Lidia and I occupied myself admiring the detail on the wooden model of the *Viva Catherine*. Suddenly Lidia burst in, looking flustered and slightly dishevelled.

"I forgot the time," she apologised. "Forgive me for keeping you waiting."

"No apology necessary. Far be it from me to distract you from your woodwork."

"But I wasn't—that is, I am very happy to see you."

She distractedly ran her fingers through her fair hair.

"I'm having a wee party tomorrow, which is girls only, so I'm sure Nanny will let you come," I said.

"How kind of you. I should have loved to join you, but I'm afraid I have some business to attend to."

"The princess is particularly keen to meet you," I said. "Can't you rearrange? She has very fond memories of your father."

She clasped her hands. "My revered father. I shall do my utmost to rearrange things as you request."

"And keep tomorrow evening free as well, since the princess has invited us to a party at her place. I'll give you some back exercises that will help for dancing with the general."

In fact, my preferred solution was to ensure that Lidia danced with Sasha instead. It was already the third day of my mission: I really should be further ahead with getting them together.

"Ah yes, the general," she said with a heavy sigh. She certainly didn't sound like a woman in love, which was a good thing. "Nanny thinks I should marry him because of his status." Then flinging her arms wide, she burst out passionately, "But what does that matter? It is trivial, petty, worthless and inconsequential. If I fell in love, it would not matter to me if he were a prince, a boatman or a serf."

She was always so docile that I was completely taken aback by this outpouring of feeling. And then I had one of these blinding revelations where you wonder how you could have been so stupid not to have seen it before—something that happens to me very rarely. With those words of Lidia's the mystery of Sasha's background was solved. He was the countess's serf. And since Lidia subscribed to a notion of romantic love that transcended all boundaries, she wouldn't find his lowly status a bar to marrying him.

There was a knock at the door, and a footman came in with a note for me on a silver salver.

"The young gentleman is currently at lunch with a lady on the countess's instructions but will leave before dessert and join you at Lidia Ivanovna's. Your excellency's humble serf, G. G. Vatrushkin."

I was hurtling towards my mission's goal.

"By the way," I said, "the princess was telling me about your family tragedy, the terrible loss of your wee brother. I just wanted to offer you my condolences."

"How kind you are!" said Lidia. "Nobody ever speaks of it, so it's a comfort for me to hear your words."

"And it must also be a comfort to you to be able to go and visit his grave," I said.

Lidia blinked. "Goodness! I never thought of that. I pray for him every day, of course, but I have never noticed his tomb in the family mausoleum. How strange."

"Very," I agreed. "Perhaps you should ask Nanny about it."

Nanny was already in the dining room, simultaneously presiding over a tureen of soup and frantically knitting a form-less length of wool.

"I have another three fichus to finish by this evening," she complained. "Lidia Ivanovna, there is surely someone else in this town who can knit."

"But nobody who knits as beautifully as you, Nanny. The ladies said they wanted ones just like mine, and it will make them so very happy."

"And you, Shona Fergusovna? Do you require one as well?" said Nanny, serving the soup with one hand and casting off with the other.

"If I were thirty years younger, I wouldn't be seen without one," I said. "But I'm at an age where it's best to leave high fashion to the youngsters."

I gave Lidia an encouraging smile to prompt her to ask Nanny about the missing tomb, but she misunderstood my meaning.

"Oh, Shona Fergusovna, you could wear anything—you are ageless!" she said. Then she flushed. "No, of course you are not ageless. You have an age. Just like everybody else who is made of flesh and blood, rather than if you were an incorporeal spirit who transcends our hours and days."

"Speaking of hours and days," I said, "how long exactly did your wee brother live for?"

Nanny's spoon clattered into her plate, spattering soup all over the emergent fichu.

"Alas," said Lidia, "a matter of hours only. I remember hearing his cries, and then the priest came, and after that there was silence. Nanny, I was chatting with Shona Fergusovna on this very matter just before lunch, and I realised he is not buried with the rest of the family. Perhaps you know why?"

"Yes, Nanny," I said, "we thought it was really strange."

Nanny had dipped the end of her apron in her water glass and was busy dabbing at the soup stains on her knitting.

"Strange?" she said. "I'll tell you what's strange. I put two new balls of wool in my apron this morning and one of them's completely disappeared."

"Dear Nanny!" said Lidia, jumping up, and running to kiss her on the cheek. "It's disappeared because you've knitted it into a fichu! Look!"

"What? But it was blue, and this one is—"

"—blue as well," supplied Lidia. "There, do you see now? It was a ball of wool this morning, and now it is knitting."

"Saints have mercy, it's all so confusing for a poor old woman like me," sighed Nanny. "I must go and get another one."

She tottered out of the room. But I had the distinct impression that she wasn't confused at all, and had created a fuss about the wool in order to change the subject.

I heard the sound of approaching footsteps, two sets. A footman and a lunch guest. And Nanny couldn't accuse me of breaking any promises, since my promise had applied only to last night's party. The door opened, and I smiled in greeting at Sasha.

Only it wasn't Sasha. It was the general.

"General!" said Lidia. "How kind of you to join us. And of course you know Shona Fergusovna, our distinguished foreign visitor?"

"We have not yet been formally introduced. A very great pleasure," he said, bowing and practically disappearing from view.

Nanny returned, her apron stuffed with wool.

"And this is my darling nanny," said Lidia. "Nanny, this is the general who has been so kind as to dance with me."

Nanny nodded at him. "So glad you could accept Lidia Ivanovna's invitation to lunch," she said.

Lidia's eyelashes fluttered in bewilderment, and I realised that the invitation had come not from Lidia, but from Nanny herself. I had been feeling slightly guilty about my surreptitious invitation to Sasha, but I was going to have to up my game.

Nanny was fussing around the general. "Sit here," she said, placing him next to Lidia. "Let me get you some soup. My little chicken has told me all about you."

The general looked startled.

I leaned over to him. "Yes, it confused me as well to begin with," I said. "Don't worry, it's nothing to do with haruspices and hepatoscopy."

The general looked even more startled and I reflected that while a military man might well be expert when it came to sieges, fortifications and pincer movements, he was unlikely to have had the finest education in the world. I seized the opportunity to expand his horizons.

"In Ancient Rome, priests—haruspices—foretold the future by inspecting chicken entrails—hepatoscopy," I explained. "But Nanny's not really talking about an actual chicken. She means Lidia Ivanovna."

"Lidia Ivanovna inspects chicken entrails?" said the general.

I was tempted to say yes in the hope that it would put him off, but since he had already engaged her in conversation about carnage on the battlefield, he would probably approve of a wife who wasn't squeamish.

"Dear Nanny!" said Lidia affectionately. "She misses the country so! That is why she calls me her little chicken, because it reminds her of the beloved companions of her childhood. She has never really taken to the town."

"That's a shame," I said. "So how long have you been here, Nanny? About twenty-five years?"

"Oh, many, many more years than that!" scoffed Nanny.

"She was my revered father's nanny, and then when he grew up, she took over managing the serfs," said Lidia. "By the time I was born, she was so expert at it that she could look after me and manage the serfs simultaneously."

I was well impressed. Serf management was complicated enough with only two to deal with, and I reckoned that a vast mansion like Lidia's would require a good few more.

The general, who, as prospective husband, had a personal interest in the matter, asked, "How many serfs do you have?"

Lidia looked vague.

"Eight hundred and twenty-six," said Nanny promptly. "That's just here, of course. There are another three thousand, four hundred and seventy-three on my little chicken's country estates. I say country, but they are just on the outskirts of town. And where are your own estates, General?"

"I have no property in town," said the general. "I do not like the town. But I have been obliged to come here and live in rented accommodation while I look for a bride, since there are no suitable candidates in the country."

"The luxury apartments by the river?" asked Nanny. "I believe they're very nice."

"Charming," agreed the general. "But unfortunately, still in town. Thankfully, my estates are very isolated and distant from here. The nearest habitation is the village of K——."

"The village of K——!" cried Nanny. "Why, I was born not three versts from there. Oh, Chicken, it is the most beautiful place in the world. Flat as a blin, not a single hill to spoil the view. And the quaint ramshackle hovels! I remember how the goats would eat their way through the wooden walls, and the wind would whistle through, straight from Siberia. We would fill the holes with grass, and then the sheep would eat the grass. It was a losing battle, something I'm sure you know all about, General."

The general politely bowed his head to her. "Indeed, I have had the honour of losing many battles."

Nanny's childhood home sounded ghastly. "I'm sure it's improved a lot since you were last there, Nanny," I said.

"No," said the general. "Most of the time, I live in my campaign tent in the garden. It is warmer and drier than indoors."

"Don't you have a big mansion?" I asked.

"An extremely big mansion," said the general. "It's very draughty because of the holes in the walls. The roof is also full of holes."

"Grass," said Nanny firmly. "That's what you need for the roof. The sheep don't usually manage to get on the roof."

"Sound advice, I am sure, dear lady, but we have no access to grass because of the mud."

Nanny's eyes closed in blissful reminiscence. "Ah, the mud," she murmured.

"The goats are a terrible problem," the general went on. "We attempt to tether them, but they simply eat through whatever we tether them with."

And then Lidia's voice rang out, firm and decisive, in a way I would never have imagined possible. "The problem is neither the sheep nor the goats. The problem is the wood. Tell me, what kind of wood is being used?"

Nanny gave an indulgent chuckle. "Just plain ordinary wood, Chicken."

Lidia gave what would have sounded like a snort from someone less diffident. She turned to the general with an enquiring eyebrow.

He gave a helpless shrug. "Brown wood?"

The piece of bread between Lidia's fingers exploded into fragments but her tone remained polite. "Thank you, General, that's most helpful. Although your description could apply to several types of wood, and a site visit by a professional may be necessary to determine the precise variety. Tell me, is the wood affected by anything other than goats?"

"Where do I begin? The floorboards in the upper storeys are rotten with mildew. And most of the verandah has disappeared because of an infestation."

Lidia's cheeks flushed, and she clasped her hands to her bosom, dislodging her fichu. "A rundown verandah! Oh, how

I should love to restore a verandah! The footings, the joists, the bevelling!"

"Lidia Ivanovna!" gasped Nanny. "How dare you be so forward! And kindly readjust your fichu. Please excuse her, General. I assure you, she is a modest, well-brought-up girl. I have never known her to yield to extreme emotions like this."

"There is no need to excuse her," said the general. "I am overjoyed to find that there may be a happy coincidence between Lidia Ivanovna's desires and my own."

"Lidia!" said Nanny. "Thank the general for being so understanding."

"Thank you, General, for being so understanding," said Lidia obediently.

I shuddered. The general's estate, decaying, dilapidated, in the back of beyond, sounded like East Kilbride. Was Lidia to be consigned to a life of misery in a swamp just because she liked woodwork?

"So, so beautiful, Chicken," Nanny reminisced. "I will never forget the mud. It was a true pleasure to walk on, not like the nasty hard pavements you get in town. Tell me, General, is there still as much mud?"

"Even more," said the general. "The Volga burst its banks last year. My wife was swept away in the flood."

"How terrible!" exclaimed Lidia.

"Thank you for your concern, but I'm soldiering on," the general said, and Nanny gave a peal of laughter.

"You're quite the wit, General," she said.

"I like to keep cheerful," he said. "And of course, were I not now a widower, I would not have had the opportunity to take lunch in such pleasant company."

"Lidia!" said Nanny. "Thank the general for his gallant compliment."

"Thank you, General, for your gallant compliment," said Lidia obediently.

"And there is still a great deal of mud in the environs?" Nanny enquired.

"More than I have ever seen," said the general.

"Do you hear that, Chicken? You would love it!"

Nanny was going to have Lidia betrothed to the general by the end of lunch if I didn't take action.

"What was your favourite battle, General?" I asked.

It was a masterstroke. The general commandeered plates, silverware, crystal glasses, candlesticks and napkins to illustrate the battleground tactics. Nanny tried to encourage a conversation between him and Lidia, but I kept bombarding him with questions, much as the enemy batteries had done to his entrenchments. And then my reinforcements arrived.

Not for the first time, I marvelled at Sasha's beauty. The long eyelashes, the blond curls over his smooth forehead, the perfect curve of his ear lobes: everything conveyed integrity and sincerity.

I sprang up, offering him my seat opposite Lidia. "I need to sit closer to the general," I explained. "That decanter is stopping me seeing what direction the artillery's firing in. Do you mind introducing yourselves?"

I have a great ability to multi-task, so while I insisted on getting a minute-by-minute account of the battle from the general, I could also keep tabs on the adjacent conversation.

That light, attractive voice: "Forgive me for the intrusion. My name is Sasha. I was kindly invited to join you by Shona Fergusovna."

Nanny glared at me. "How very hospitable of Shona Fergusovna to invite people to lunch when it is not even her own home."

I tried to look suitably contrite and, after a pause, Nanny signalled to a footman to reset the place. "Well, sit down. I'm Nanny and this is Lidia Ivanovna. Would you like oysters, soupe printanière, turbot with sauce Beaumarchais, poularde à l'estragon or a bit of all of them?"

"You're very kind," said Sasha. "I've just had lunch, but a small coffee would be most welcome. I hope I'm not inconveniencing you."

Nanny waved a peremptory hand at the butler. "Just coffee for the gentleman. And no, you're not inconveniencing us. We know our social duty. It's open house at mealtimes, even to guests of our guests." She glared at me again.

"I believe," said Sasha, his soft voice contrasting with Nanny's unfriendly rasp, "that until recently, it has not been open house."

"Oh really? You seem to know a lot about us and we don't know anything about you. Where are you from and what's your family?"

I froze. From what I had heard while I was jammed under the settee, Sasha and the countess had just assumed that everyone would believe he was an aristocrat, and hadn't actually concocted a cover story for him.

"All in good time, Nanny," I interrupted. "Let the poor boy drink his coffee in peace. Lidia, why don't you tell Sasha about dovetail joints or something?"

When Sasha had sat down beside her, Lidia had shifted her chair so that her back was to him. Her insistence on behaving modestly wasn't helping her get to know him, but I appreciated that when you were facing him, there was a real temptation just to sit staring at him with your mouth open, drooling slightly.

Without turning, Lidia said, "I particularly favour the secret mitred dovetail when building cabinets. It is both challenging and time-consuming, but it provides strength and a superb finish."

She spoke so softly that Sasha had to lean towards her, practically breathing down the back of her neck. I was still feigning fascination with the general's strategic retreat, but simultaneously marvelling yet again at how perfect Sasha and Lidia looked together.

Nanny was similarly observing Lidia and Sasha from her place at the other side of the table. "Young man!" she suddenly grated. "How old are you?"

"I'm twenty," he said.

She scrambled off her chair, shoving her knitting into her apron.

"Lidia Ivanovna!" she said. "You can't sit here gossiping all day! You have that picture frame to finish off."

Lidia, her mouth falling open in surprise, stood up uncertainly.

"Come on! Come on!" Nanny exhorted, standing at the door like a prison warder escorting Lidia back to her cell.

"Excuse me," Lidia murmured. "Thank you all for coming."

Nanny grabbed her by the elbow and propelled her down the corridor, Sasha gazing after them with the gentle, wistful expression he always had when Lidia was near. Some men in the benighted nineteenth century might object to a wife five years older than them, I reflected, but Sasha was so evidently enthralled by Lidia that age was clearly not an issue.

Now Lidia had gone, he joined me in providing an audience for the general's war stories, attentive and respectful as the wee guy droned on.

We were interrupted again by a footman carrying a note on a silver salver, which he presented to me. In careful block capitals, it read: "Shona Fergusovna, I must see you alone as soon as possible on a matter of the gravest importance. I shall be in my room. Nanny."

The salver had been placed between me and Sasha. He glanced at it involuntarily, the way you do, and then gave me the sweetest apologetic smile, before turning away and catching sight of the clock.

"Please excuse me—I had no idea it was so late," he said. "The countess has instructed me to call on another of her acquaintances, whom I must catch before her afternoon nap." He gave us both the most graceful bow and left.

I had been going to answer Nanny's summons, but the general had just poured himself another glass of wine and I felt it would be rude to abandon him. Also, this was a useful opportunity to garner more information. If Nanny's message was really urgent, she would send another footman, or come and get me herself.

"Would you like to hear about my second-favourite battle?" the general asked, picking up the condiments.

Miss Blaine's Prefect and the Golden Samovar

"That sounds great," I said, "but I think I need a bit more time to absorb the tactics of your favourite battle. I wouldn't want to confuse the two. Anyway, about your late wife."

To my astonishment, he burst into tears. "She's not entirely dead."

I had a hideous vision of his mansion being terrorised by a marauding zombie. No wonder he preferred to live in a tent in the garden.

"When you say not entirely…?"

He hiccupped. "Not at all."

"So she wasn't really carried away in the floods?"

"She was," he said. "But she was rescued by a miller when she got entangled in his watermill. She sent me a letter saying she much preferred him to me, and that I should consider her gone forever."

He didn't seem to have a strong grasp of legal matters, so I explained about bigamy, and how he couldn't marry anybody while he was still married to the Mrs General.

And then he explained that he had immediately divorced her, but to avoid the social scandal of being a divorcé, he was passing himself off as a widower.

By this time, his sobs were diminishing. "I thought we were happy together," he said. "I was always away on manoeuvres or at war and we never saw one another. Then when I retired, she said I just got under her feet and stifled her individuality."

My sympathy was with the wife. I didn't imagine he had done any pre-retirement planning. But I felt a twinge of sympathy for him as well. He looked so forlorn, blowing his little nose on the starched linen napkin.

"I just want companionship in my old age," he snuffled. "And a draught-free mansion."

"There must be plenty of ladies who would love to marry a war hero," I said.

He shook his head. "Lidia Ivanovna is the only suitable lady on the market at the moment. And I'm certain she's the only one who can do woodwork." He paused and shot me a hopeful look. "Unless…"

This time I shook my head. "Not bad at woodwork. But not on the market."

He sighed. "A pity. But I must go. That young man reminded me, it's time for my afternoon nap as well."

I was more determined than ever to keep Lidia away from him if he thought she was merely interchangeable. I walked him down to the grand entrance. As he left, there was the weirdest trick of the light—I could have sworn I saw Sasha disappearing down the end of the driveway. But that was impossible, since he had left ages ago.

I went back indoors and made my way to Nanny's room.

When I knocked on the door, there was a gasp of alarm from inside. "Who is it?" she quavered.

"It's me, Nanny," I said and then, for the avoidance of doubt, "Shona Fergusovna from Scotland."

There was no reply, so I opened the door and went in. Nanny was huddled in a pile of knitting in the corner. There was something different about the room, I thought, something missing, but I couldn't work out what it was.

"You wanted to see me?" I said.

"No!" she said.

I produced the note from my pocket. "Didn't you send me this?"

"Yes," she said. "No."

"Yes you didn't or no you did?"

"Stop trying to bamboozle a poor old woman!" she moaned. "Why don't you just leave me alone?"

"Nanny, are you cross with me?" I asked. "Are you cross because I invited Sasha to lunch?"

She started rocking as she sat in her cocoon of knitting. "Stop pestering me with questions!" she wailed.

"I just wanted Lidia to see that the general wasn't her only option," I explained. "He's a nice old guy, but you have to admit he's not a patch on Sasha as a fiancé."

Nanny was still rocking and wailing, and now she threw her apron over her head. I was beginning to realise she was a sore loser.

"I'm sorry, Nanny," I said, "but as we agreed, I'm doing my best to help Lidia and I'm a bit disappointed that you're being so pig-headed about it."

"You don't understand!" she howled.

"Then explain it to me," I said.

"I can't! I can't!" she moaned. "Just go away and stop bothering me!"

But after my conversation with the princess, there was still something I wanted to clear up.

"Nanny, Lidia's mother. Am I right in thinking that—" I tried to put it as delicately as possible "—she was no better than she should be?"

Nanny sat up, dislodging countless balls of wool. "Exactly!" she said. "No better than she should be!"

I was surprised by how readily she had agreed. It suggested that Lidia's allegedly saintly mum had been a bit of a one.

"So the tragedy, the one we don't speak of, the baby—"

I stopped, abruptly. It's tricky to keep talking when you've got a mouthful of yarn. She had lobbed a ball of wool at me, and her aim was impressive.

"I can't say anything, but isn't it obvious?" she yelled.

I removed the wool. "Isn't what obvious?"

She lobbed another ball of wool at me, hitting me on the nose.

"You're useless! Get out! I told you, get out!"

"I'm going," I said with dignity. "But I'm inviting Lidia to a wee afternoon tea tomorrow. Girls only. No boys. No Sasha, no general. I hope that's all right."

I tried to hand her the invitation but she turned her back on me and looked out of the window instead. Then she gave the most pitiful wail, the sort you might give if your team had just lost to Partick Thistle.

"Oh, Chicken," she groaned, "what have you been doing?"

I looked out of the window over her head, which wasn't difficult, and saw Lidia emerge from a large closed carriage. Nanny shoved past me and scuttled off down the stairs. I left the invitation on the nearest pile of wool and followed her.

Nanny ran towards the carriage, shouting, "Where have you been, Lidia Ivanovna?"

Lidia recoiled, colour draining from her face.

"I asked you where you had been," Nanny persisted.

"Nowhere," Lidia faltered. "That is, I just went for a little drive."

"Have you been speaking to any men?" demanded Nanny.

It was fleeting, but I was sure a look of relief crossed Lidia's face. "No," she said. "No, I haven't."

"You shouldn't have been out at all. Now get inside and stay there."

"Bye, Lidia," I called as she fled into the house. "Don't forget afternoon tea tomorrow and then the princess's party."

Nanny turned on me. "This is all your doing, Shona Fergusovna," she hissed. "You fool, you don't understand the danger—" She clapped her hand over her mouth.

"Danger?" I said. "No, I don't understand. What are you talking about?"

"I can't tell you!" she screamed. "Just go!"

So I went.

CHAPTER 6

I'd given up asking the maid to do anything. She spent most of her time swanning around town in my dresses and sneering at other maids.

But I couldn't load all the work on Old Vatrushkin. He was always hanging around in case he could help, and it was taking me all my time to get him to paint for an hour a day.

"Old Vatrushkin, can you go out for some messages?" I asked.

"Your excellency is expecting messages? Will the couriers not come here?"

I really had to stop translating directly from the Scots. I explained I wanted him to do some shopping for the traditional Scottish afternoon tea. I sent him off with the list I had written for him, using the appropriate weights and measures. Peter the

Great had standardised everything on the eighteenth-century English system, with futs and dyuims for feet and inches and funts and untsyas for pounds and ounces.

Old Vatrushkin set off with my list: *4 plain loaves; 3 funts plain flour; 2 funts cheese; 1 kruzhka pickle; 3 cucumbers; 1 dozen eggs; 1 funt sugar; 2 funts butter; 1 vedro milk; 1 kruzhka condensed milk; 2 garnets raspberries; baking powder if available, otherwise, leavening agent such as unpasteurised beer with live yeast.*

I set about cleaning the public rooms. I was just doing a bit of last-minute tidying up when my super-acute hearing picked up the sound of faint sobbing outside. I went to investigate and found Old Vatrushkin huddled on top of the box on the drozhky, his dark beard soggy with tears. He hid his face when he saw me.

"Oh, your excellency," he said brokenly, "I was unable to fulfil all your instructions about the messages. I don't know what condensed milk is. And there was not a cucumber to be found so I had to improvise with gherkins. Emancipate me now."

"Don't be silly, Old Vatrushkin. What did you manage to get?"

He choked back a sob and started ticking things off on his fingers. "I have the bread, and the cheese, and the pickle, and the flour, and the sugar, and the butter, and the raspberries, and the milk, and the eggs, and the beer."

"Well, that's perfect. As long as we've got cheese and pickle sandwiches."

"Your excellency's tolerance of my ineptitude is beyond anything I deserve," hiccupped Old Vatrushkin as he carried his purchases to the pantry and began setting them out on the table.

"What's that?" I asked, pointing at some peculiar-looking packages.

He beamed. "Cream cheese and cabbage pickle for the cheese and pickle sandwiches. And I have four of the plainest rye loaves I could find."

I managed to say "Excellent", but for once my heart wasn't in it as I contemplated the buckwheat flour, buffalo milk and massive sugarloaf. It was going to be dreadful. The only good thing was that they wouldn't make snarky comments about deep-fried Mars bars because they wouldn't have heard of them. I set Old Vatrushkin to snipping bits off the sugar loaf, while I boiled up buffalo milk to make cream.

A few hours later, we had finished. Though I say it myself, the results were fabulous. The buckwheat scones and Victoria sponge hadn't quite risen, but with cream and raspberry jam, they tasted brilliant. The cabbage pickle and cream cheese on rye was excitingly tangy. And the tablet made with sugar loaf and buffalo milk was sublime. Old Vatrushkin and I arranged everything artistically on the Sèvres porcelain.

Lidia was the first to arrive, not realising that she was supposed to be fashionably late.

"Glad to see you," I said. "I wasn't sure whether you would be able to come."

"That's why I went out yesterday, to leave me free today," she said. "Nanny was so angry with me. But I really didn't do anything wrong, Shona Fergusovna—you must believe me."

I only had to look into those limpid guileless eyes to believe her. I got her to send her coachman away, giving him some time off, since Old Vatrushkin could take her home. I was determined to do what I could to improve the working lives of the serfs. But I stopped after that. It wasn't going to improve Old Vatrushkin's working life if he had to take everyone home, besides which I wouldn't get rid of my guests for hours if they all had to wait their turn.

Nobody was as fashionably late as I had expected, presumably through nosiness. Lidia distributed the newly knitted fichus to the young wives, who cooed over them and jealously checked whose was the best. Fortunately, Nanny had ensured that they were all equally shapeless.

The princess commandeered Lidia to sit beside her and pronounced her charming, which set the young wives off in a new fashion frenzy, trying to untangle their carefully primped and ringleted hair to duplicate Lidia's plain style.

"Now, my dear," the princess continued, "I am hoping for some wonderful gossip from you."

Lidia's limpid guileless eyes widened. "From me? I'm afraid I don't—"

The princess wagged a playful finger at her. "Now, now. My coachman has just informed me of the field-marshal's widow falling downstairs and breaking her neck. God have mercy on her soul." They all crossed themselves.

This was embarrassing. The princess had seemed quite on the ball but she was having a seriously senior moment.

"That was two days ago," I reminded her. "That's why the countess threw her party."

The princess stared at me and one of the young wives gave a shriek of laughter, hurriedly stifled when the princess turned and stared at her.

"My dear Princess Tamsonova, I am not speaking of little Potapova, but of the field-marshal's widow. We discussed her at the countess's atrocious party. I remember your particularly remarking on her scarlet gown."

Pillar Box Lady.

"She fell downstairs and broke her neck?" I asked.

"Yesterday morning," said the princess. "And my coachman informs me that dear Lidia Ivanovna had just been visiting her."

This was the first I had heard of it. Lidia had been out yesterday afternoon, but she hadn't said she had been visiting anybody.

"So, my dear." The princess patted Lidia's hand encouragingly. "Were you there when she fell? Did you see everything? Was it dreadfully shocking?"

Lidia's hands were clenched tightly in her lap. "I…no…that is…I…"

The princess's smile was fading.

A young wife seized her chance to shine. "Princess, by a remarkable coincidence, I have some gossip to share with you."

"Then convey it in a loud, clear tone so that I miss none of it," commanded the princess.

"My coachman," began the young wife in a loud clear tone, "informs me that yesterday afternoon, the admiral's widow fell downstairs and broke her neck too."

"God have mercy on her soul," said the princess and they all crossed themselves again.

"The admiral's widow?" I asked.

"You must know her," said the princess. "Everybody knew her. She was as deaf as a post, couldn't hear a thing without her ear trumpet. And she always wore an eye patch in memory of the admiral, who lost an eye in the battle of Kronstadt."

Eye Patch Lady.

"Enemy fire?" I asked.

"Too much vodka. Fell on a sextant."

"But that is not the only remarkable coincidence," chirped the young wife. "My coachman also informs me that Lidia Ivanovna had just been visiting her."

I knew Lidia had been out yesterday afternoon. And I had seen her chatting to Eye Patch Lady at the countess's party.

"Disgraceful!" bellowed the princess and Lidia quailed. "This happened yesterday afternoon, and I am hearing it from some young flibbertigibbet? Why did my own coachman not inform me? I'll have the fellow flogged!"

"Don't do that," I said hastily. It must be a nightmare for the princess's poor coachman trying to keep up with all the news. "I'm sure he was just spreading things out to create a bit of dramatic tension."

Old Vatrushkin was still being the doorman. I went to find him, on the pretext of getting him to hand round the tea things, so that he could warn his brother coachman to think up a plausible defence before the princess got hold of him. And as I went downstairs, pondering Lidia's presence at the homes of Pillar Box Lady and Eye Patch Lady, I remembered Old Vatrushkin's insistence that Lidia had been visiting Madame Potapova, the first of the plummeting old dears. It looked as though I owed him an apology.

But before I could talk to him, he ushered in two more guests. The countess, accompanied by Sasha. I caught my breath at the sight of him—he looked lovelier than ever. But the countess was a cheeky bizzum for bringing him, and I had no intention of putting up with her nonsense.

I descended the staircase towards them. "I'm sorry, Countess," I said, "I think I made it perfectly clear that this was girls only."

I was expecting at least a show of embarrassment, but instead, the countess's expression was a mixture of slyness and smugness. If I had being paying more attention, I should have been worried, but I was too busy admiring Sasha.

"What an unfortunate misunderstanding," she said, now displaying nothing but bland regret. "But I'm sure you will have no objection to our darling Sasha joining us, now that he is here."

"I apologise for the error," said Sasha quietly. "Of course I shall leave immediately."

The countess turned on him. "You shall do no such thing," she snapped.

I was going to make an issue of it when I realised this was the ideal opportunity to get Lidia and Sasha together.

"Don't worry about it," I said to Sasha. "You're most welcome."

The countess's bosom heaved alarmingly under her pelisse. She rootled around among layers of satin and lace and produced her ghastly lapdog.

"Perhaps you'd like to leave your fur in the cloakroom," I suggested.

The countess puckered her lips and mimed a kiss at the matted bundle. "Naughty Princess Tamsonova, always teasing poor Tresorka."

"If you're bringing that thing upstairs, it stays on the floor."

The countess began to protest.

I raised an admonitory hand. "My house, my rules."

Despite her bulk, the countess raced past me up the stairs and by the time Sasha and I came into the salon, she was draped melodramatically over a sofa next to the princess.

"Oh, Princess," she wailed. "I am so distressed. Princess Tamsonova has been scolding and scolding me for bringing our poor Sasha, even though I did so at your express instruction. I couldn't bear to disappoint you, but she is so very angry and I don't know what to do for the best."

I should have paid attention to that look she gave me downstairs. She was stitching me up like a Loch Fyne kipper. She had promised to destroy me, and apparently she was going to do it socially, pitting me against the princess in a battle only the genuine blue-blood would win. The young wives reared up like meerkats to see me get my comeuppance.

But the countess hadn't reckoned on me having been trained in the psychological warfare of the prefects' room.

"Impossible," I said, in the voice I had used to play Lady Bracknell in the 6th year production of *The Importance of Being Earnest*. "We princesses adhere to a strict code of conduct. It's quite beyond the realms of possibility that the princess would have taken it upon herself to invite anyone to a social gathering organised by another princess, far less to invite someone of the male persuasion to an all-female get-together. How you have the temerity to try to involve the princess in your machinations, I do not know, but I cannot allow you to slander one of my guests, indeed my most distinguished guest, in this way. I'm afraid I shall have to ask both you and the young man to leave."

The meerkats turned as one towards the spluttering countess, whose bosom was rippling in rage.

The princess nodded gravely. "Of course one would never dream of interfering with another princess's social arrangements," she confirmed. "The countess is clearly delirious. But surely, Princess Tamsonova, the poor creature deserves compassion rather than censure."

"That's one way of looking at it," I said.

"Indeed I am looking at it," said the princess. By now, the whole of the countess was quivering like a barely-set blancmange. "And I fear she might become even more unstable if she were forced to face up to the consequences of her extraordinary behaviour. Therefore, I propose this solution: the young man and I will retire to a *chambre séparée* where I can prevent him incommoding the other guests."

"Princess, your unselfish suggestion is just what I would expect from a fellow member of the aristocracy, but I wouldn't dream of letting you sacrifice yourself like that," I said. "It wouldn't be the same without you. No, let the young man stay here with us, but since it's a girls' afternoon, he'll have to be a footman."

The young wives giggled delightedly.

"Now," I said, "we're going to have a Scottish afternoon tea. Sasha, you can help Old Vatrushkin to hand round the comestibles."

The countess smiled maliciously. "Dear Princess, our darling Princess Tamsonova is so very unconventional—did you know that her coachman is actually her major-domo? And even more amusingly, her major-domo is her footman? This fellow—" She flapped a pudgy paw at Old Vatrushkin, who was approaching with a tray of sandwiches, "—fulfils all these roles at once."

The princess peered at Old Vatrushkin through her lorgnette. "No! Beyond belief."

The countess smirked and the young wives reared up again, ready to see me crash and burn.

The princess's lorgnette swivelled in my direction. "What a splendid idea! Princess Tamsonova, you are ahead of me at every turn. I have only just transformed all my doormen into footmen, and now I must reallocate my coachmen. I try to imitate you and I find you inimitable."

"I'm sure you're inimitable in your own way," I said.

The countess glowered and subsided in her chair, the animated floormop scrambling up to sit beside her.

"And that thing's going on the floor," I said, seizing Tresorka. It did its best to sink its gnashers into me, but I was particularly careful how I gripped it, given the absence of anti-tetanus injections.

The countess was about to protest when the princess launched forth. "My coachman informed me that the field-marshal's widow is not known to have left a will. But since the imbecile failed to tell me about the admiral's widow's demise, I do not know about her testamentary circumstances."

I shot a meaningful look at Old Vatrushkin, who gave me a quick nod: the princess's coachman would be warned to have his story ready.

The wife who had broken the news to the princess chirped, "Like the other ladies, she has no family, and nobody has heard of a will. So her estate will go to Our Little Father the Tsar."

"Ridiculous!" snorted the princess. "That man has more than enough already."

There was an uneasy murmuring. The princess and the tsar were family, so she could say what she liked, but nobody else wanted to be accused of treason and summarily executed.

"Have you made a will?" I asked to change the subject.

There was more uneasy murmuring.

"Indeed I have, as is well known. My estates will go to the deserving rich. Each palace will go to the first aristocrat to complete a year of self-flagellation in my memory in the nearest monastery or convent. In case my cousin the tsar gets religion, I have added a codicil that he is excluded from the competition."

"Won't the tsar challenge it?" I asked.

The princess's eyes flashed. "Let him try. My will has been drawn up by Kirill Kirillovich, the best lawyer in town."

The guests were getting increasingly agitated by the anti-tsarist sentiments, so I signalled to Old Vatrushkin to start serving the tea. In an undertone, he instructed Sasha on what to do, rather brusquely, I thought.

The princess examined the trays being presented to her.

"Ah, my dear Princess Tamsonova! There is no need to tell me what these are," she said. "I know all your traditional Scottish dishes through the great works of Sir Walter." She pointed at a plate of flat scones. "Ladies, these are bannocks."

She introduced the cheese and pickle sandwiches as kebbock and cockaleekie, the gherkin sandwiches as bashed neeps, and the Victoria sponge as sheep's heid. The young wives dutifully parroted the unfamiliar words. But whatever they called it, Old Vatrushkin's fusion cuisine was a sensation. I would have to replicate these recipes when I got back to Morningside.

"A cup of tea with your bannock?" I asked the princess. "Would you like the milk in first or afterwards?"

The young wives squawked in alarm. "A cup?" quavered one. "Milk?" squealed another.

The princess drew herself up. "I have been reading about your Prince Charles Edward Stuart in Sir Walter's enchanting novel *Waverley*. Did the bonnie prince take his tea in a cup?"

"Certainly," I said.

"And he added milk to his tea?"

"Never drank it any other way," I said.

"And did he add the milk first or afterwards?"

"First, every time."

"A princess must follow the lead of a prince."

Sometimes I doubted if I would ever make a good feminist of her.

The young wives watched in alarm as I poured some milk into a cup, added tea and passed it to the princess.

"It's the wrong colour," said one.

"It's a different colour," I corrected.

The princess, with the air of a French aristocrat approaching the guillotine, lifted the cup to her lips.

"And if you want something to sweeten it, how about a wee piece of tablet?"

I proffered a plate of buffalo milk and sugarloaf squares.

The princess popped the tablet into her mouth and took a sip of tea. There was a pause.

"Sublime," she pronounced.

Once the young wives saw she had suffered no ill-effects, they each demanded a cup of tea with the milk in first, and seized squares of tablet to drink it through.

"These bashed neeps are delicious," said one. "What is your secret, Shona Fergusovna?"

"I always cut the skins off the gherkins first," I said, and they got out their pencils and notepads and wrote it down.

The only problem was that in turning Sasha into a waiter, I had undermined my own plan to get him sitting beside Lidia. I grabbed a plate of blinis à l'écossaise from him. "You've done very well, thank you. Have a seat over there, and I'll bring you a cup of tea."

The princess's voice cut in. "No, no, no—sit here, by me." She shifted very slightly from the middle of the sofa and Sasha obediently wedged himself in beside her. "I should like you to read to me. Princess Tamsonova, do you have some reading matter available? Ah, I see a book over there. Perhaps it is the educational novel you mentioned to us at the countess's?"

I pride myself on my self-control, but I don't mind admitting that I panicked. This was the first time I had ever seen the leather-bound book the princess was indicating, which lay on top of the pianoforte. What if it was indeed That Book? All I could think of was to trip as I brought it to the princess, and rip it to shreds as I fell. My muscles tensed in preparation as I picked it up.

I really should have had more faith. The spirit of Marcia Blaine moves in mysterious but helpful ways.

"I think you'll like it," I said, handing it over. "It's the Russian edition of Sir Walter Scott's *The Bride of Lammermoor*. A tragic love story."

It couldn't have been better. The tale of a manipulative older woman who was determined not to allow a perfect young couple their happiness. Sasha would be more than capable of applying it to his own situation.

He dutifully opened the book, and began reading to the princess in a quiet voice, not loud enough to disturb other conversations, but providing a pleasant obbligato to them. Periodically, I saw him snatch a longing gaze at Lidia, then return to his reading with an obvious effort. I had to get them together.

The room was full of contented chatter, tea slurping and scone scoffing when I heard another sound. Scuffling on the parquet. The animated floormop was slinking towards a set of ankles.

"No!" I said sharply.

The floormop flattened itself against the floor, but a few moments later began edging towards me.

"I'm warning you," I said.

It gave me a contemptuous display of its fangs and leaped onto the sofa.

"Well, you can't say you weren't warned," I remarked in the tone that had chilled the blood of hundreds of misbehaving third years. I picked Tresorka up by the scruff of the neck, deposited it on the floor, and plunged on top of it.

"Help! Murderer!" shrieked the countess. "The evil foreigner is crushing my darling Tresorka! Seize her!"

There was consternation. Evil foreigner I might be, but as a princess, I outranked the countess, and the young wives didn't dare lay a hand on me. They squirmed around in their seats for a while and then took the only action they could under the circumstances: pretending they'd fainted from shock. I bet one or two of them also hoped that they would end up in Sasha's arms while he administered sal volatile.

"Stop your caterwauling," I said to the countess as I got up and went back to the sofa. The young wives revived slightly from their swoon, disappointed not to have been resuscitated by Sasha, but anxious to see what happened next.

"I wasn't injuring the creature. I was using a recognised training technique," I went on. "Dogs are pack animals and they have a strict hierarchy. All I was doing was showing Tresorka that it is not the pack leader. I am."

"Most laudable," said the princess.

There was renewed scrabbling on the floor. The animated floormop crawled up to my chair, and began quivering at one end. I deduced that this was his tail wagging.

"Good doggy," I said. "Give me a paw."

A small tangled mass extended towards me.

"Very good. Other paw."

Another small tangled mass extended towards me.

"Now beg."

Tresorka leaped up and balanced precariously on what were possibly his hind legs. I rewarded him with a piece of skinless gherkin, which he swallowed whole.

"And now, die for his Imperial Majesty the Tsar."

Tresorka rolled over on his back and lay motionless.

The countess shrieked again. "She will rest at nothing until she has killed my precious darling!"

"I'm only teaching an old dog new tricks," I said patiently. "Stop worrying. Dogs like this sort of thing. It gives them a purpose in life. They're miserable when you only use them as fashion accessories."

The animated floormop rolled the right way round, and scuffled over to my feet where he lay down, tongue lolling.

The countess, incensed, struggled out of her chair. "My poor Tresorka must be exhausted by all these terrible ordeals. We shall leave now." She wobbled in the direction of the door and then realised that her little darling was still lying at my feet. "Tresorka!" she shrilled. "Come, precious, away from this dreadful place!"

Tresorka looked up adoringly at me. "Go on!" I urged. "Go to mummy!"

A small pink tongue emerged and licked my hand. I was so, so tempted to keep the wee creature. He wasn't a bad dog, he just hadn't been trained properly. But I had to accept that he didn't belong to me.

"Offski!" I said firmly. He scampered across to the countess, who snatched him up as if to shield him from further harm.

"Darling princess," she said, which surprised me until I realised she was talking to the other one. "I hope we shall see you at the concert before your party this evening. How we are all looking forward to seeing you grace the imperial box."

"I may be occupied," said the princess. "You don't mind if I keep your...protégé for a little longer."

It was a statement, not a question, and when she said "protégé" I definitely heard Sid James again.

"Of course not," the countess fawned.

"My coachman will see you out," I called after the countess as she left and the princess gave a delighted cackle. "What a splendid idea! The moment I return home, I shall give instructions for all my coachmen to see my guests out. And now, my dear Princess Tamsonova, I too must depart, taking this charming young man with me so that he can read me a bit more of the story."

Nice try, I thought. But since she had hogged him during the afternoon tea, she wasn't going to rob me of my last opportunity to get him together with Lidia.

"Sorry, Princess," I said. "The price of him gate-crashing our girls' get-together is that he has to do the clearing up. You can hear more of the story another time."

The princess shot me a look of what I could have sworn was admiration. "So you have requisitioned the young man for yourself. Yet again, my dear Princess Tamsonova, you are one step ahead of me. It is not only the small dog who is learning that you are the leader of the pack."

She stood up and kissed me on the cheek in farewell.

"I can't be bothered going to the concert if the wretched countess is going to pester me. And it's some modern German composer. I prefer classical music. If you're not otherwise occupied, feel free to take my place in the imperial box. And I look forward to welcoming you to my little party tonight."

The young wives were all open-mouthed. "Right, girls," I said, "don't you have husbands to go home to?" and they jumped up from their seats, thanking me profusely for the wonderfully exotic refreshments.

Old Vatrushkin was back at his major-domo-ing, and had organised Sasha to do the clearing up, so Lidia and I were alone.

"No need for you to rush," I said. "After all, you don't have a husband to go home to yet. Enjoy the freedom. You must come to the concert with me before the princess's party, by the way. We can't pass up the opportunity of being in the imperial box."

And then I remembered what I'd been meaning to talk to her about. "Tell me," I said. "Madame Potapova, the field-marshal's widow and the admiral's widow. Did you really visit them all on the days they fell downstairs?"

"I didn't kill them!" she said.

I thought it was an odd thing to say.

"Of course you didn't. They were just a bunch of doddery old wifies. But what were you doing there in the first place? Nanny didn't even know you were out."

"I didn't tell Nanny," said Lidia. "I thought it was all right to go because you had encouraged me."

It was news to me. I hadn't encouraged her to do anything. Except get together with Sasha. Sasha, who had been sent by the countess to call on Madame Potapova. And who had made arrangements to call round on Pillar Box Lady and Eye Patch Lady.

I looked at her with new eyes. "You and Sasha have been using the old dears' houses for secret assignations?"

Lidia gasped. "No! How can you think such a thing? I never met Sasha. I never met anybody. When I got to Madame Potapova's, she already had a visitor. I waited in an anteroom, but before I could speak to her—God have mercy on her soul." She crossed herself. "I was also waiting to see the field-marshal's widow, and the admiral's widow, but they too already had a visitor and I never had the opportunity to speak to them either. God have mercy on all their souls."

"But if you weren't meeting Sasha, why were you there?"

"I was following your inspirational advice that I become a professional floor-covering technician. I wished to seek out parquet floors in need of repair. To ensure that I did not damage my reputation, I approached only elderly ladies who lived alone. Of course, I did not do anything so improper as to approach them as an unannounced visitor—I went to the tradesmen's entrance. But I realise now that their untimely deaths are a sign."

I was about to agree that it was a sign that we should all do muscle-building and balancing exercises every day, but she went on: "I have been guilty of the sin of pride, and cannot expect to become a professional floor-covering technician immediately. So I have decided that when the general asks me to marry him, I shall accept, and hone my floor-covering technical skills on his dilapidated home. Then when, God willing, he dies, I shall return to town as a respectable widow and ask if anybody requires some woodwork."

At this critical moment, Sasha emerged from the pantry where he had been washing up. He looked particularly enticing after his exertions, with a healthy glow and slightly damp hair. I had to move fast to stop Lidia getting engaged to the general.

"Why don't you sit and relax with Sasha, and he can read you a wee bit of *The Bride of Lammermoor*? I'm sure you'd find it an interesting story."

Sasha's smile was like the radiance of the sun after a spring shower. "I will read to Lidia Ivanovna with the greatest of pleasure," he said.

But Lidia had retrieved her shawl and was moving towards the stairs. "Thank you so much for a wonderful afternoon, dear Shona Fergusovna," she said. "But I must go and change my dress for the concert."

I rushed after her. "Can't you stay for another half-hour?" I said in an undertone. "Sasha reads very well, you know." I could almost detect a Sid James timbre in my own voice.

Lidia put a hand on my arm. "Please, Shona Fergusovna, it would not be proper. I must go."

I summoned Old Vatrushkin to drive her home. That left me and Sasha. I marvelled at his lustrous blond hair, his beguiling eyes, his tantalising mouth. If only I had got him sitting beside Lidia, the magic would have begun. But at least this was a perfect opportunity for me to find out more about him.

"Let's go and relax in the salon," I said.

"There is no further work for me, Princess Tamsonova?"

"Please, don't bother with that princess nonsense. Call me Shona."

As soon as I'd said it, I panicked. Since he was a serf, was he going to try to cut his tongue out the way Old Vatrushkin had?

But instead, he breathed "Shona" in such a thrillingly hushed way that I felt slightly light-headed. "Shona," he breathed again, and then "Sasha," lingering on the unvoiced fricatives. "Our names are so strangely similar, as though there were a mystical union between us."

I think I might have blushed a bit. "Come and have a seat," I said. "I'd like to get to know you better."

"I would like that too," he murmured.

But rather than sit down, he came round behind me and kissed my shoulder. This was definitely not the deferential kind of kiss Old Vatrushkin had given me. And now he was kissing my neck, my ear...He smelled fabulous, heady male pheromones mixed with a light citrus cologne. I found myself melting against his muscular torso, my eyes drawn inexorably to those dark-lashed eyes, those chiselled cheekbones, those kissable lips...

And then I heard Miss Blaine's voice as clearly as if she was in the room. "You're on a mission, girl! You're not there to enjoy yourself."

This was utterly wrong. I jabbed an elbow in Sasha's ribs. He gasped, then imprisoned me in his arms and bore me down onto the floor. It was like being in the coils of a hyperactive python. Every time I wrenched one of my limbs free, it was immediately recaptured. My martial arts expertise is pretty impressive, but Sasha seemed even more proficient. We rolled over and over, crashing into the pianoforte, knocking over occasional tables, the fine Sèvres porcelain shattering around us.

I managed to free an arm and was in a perfect position to deliver a left hook, but one glance at Sasha's beautiful bone structure and I thought *not the face*. And the next thing I was trapped again. I was reaching the appalling conclusion that he might actually overpower me when he suddenly let go and lay there, wheezing.

"Forgive me, Shonetchka, my little Siberian tigress, but I cannot match your energy. Perhaps you would give me a few moments to recover?"

I leaped up, grabbed the nearest weapon, which turned out to be an overlooked pastry fork, and shouted, "Are you completely insane?"

Sasha scrambled to his feet, still breathless, and steadied himself against the pianoforte. "This...this is not what you wanted?"

"Are you kidding me?" I didn't even attempt to keep the fury out of my voice. "I'm old enough to be your—" I thought. He was twenty. I was technically old enough to be his grandmother. But there was no way I was going to say that. "—your older sister!"

Very slowly, he straightened up, his blue eyes unreadable.

"Why do you say that?"

"To impress upon you that your behaviour was completely inappropriate and not to be tolerated."

He closed his eyes and when he opened them again, they were pained and misted. I had an urge to give him a consoling cuddle but decided against it.

"I would plead for you to forgive me, but I do not deserve forgiveness," he murmured. "But perhaps I can give, if not a defence, an explanation. It seemed to me you ensured that we would be alone together. You told me you would like to get to know me better. You sent away the other guests and you sent away your—"

Simultaneously, he said "major-domo" and I said "footman".

"You invited me to lunch with you at Lidia Ivanovna's, you—"

"And you thought that was me sending out some kind of message?" I said with as much sarcasm as I could muster.

"Of course," he said with such obvious sincerity that I reflected these were different times, different manners. But that certainly didn't make it all right.

"You must never assume," I said severely. "When you assume, it makes an ass out of you and me."

Sasha looked faintly confused, and I realised that the Russian translation didn't quite convey the witty wordplay of the original.

"Since you made an honest mistake, we'll say no more about it," I decided. "So let's start again. Tell me about yourself, your family, where you're from."

The dark lashes lowered to hide his eyes. "I am forbidden to speak of it."

"By the tsar?"

He shook his head. "By the countess."

Then he gazed straight at me, making me catch my breath slightly because his concerned look was even more attractive than his ashamed look.

"The countess is a very dangerous enemy. I beg you, be careful."

"Don't worry about me," I said. "I'm not scared of her."

"Perhaps you should be. You have twice humiliated her publicly in front of the princess. She does not forget and she never forgives. Even now, she will be plotting your downfall."

He was speaking so earnestly that I could only imagine the terrible hold the countess must have on him. I was here to help Lidia, not him, but if I was going to get them married, I had to free him from the countess's pernicious grasp. If he was forbidden to tell me anything about himself, then I would just have to go to the village of N— to find out for myself.

"Anyway, don't let me keep you," I said. "I have to go and change for the concert and then go and collect Lidia. She's nice, isn't she?"

I watched him closely. That familiar yearning look came into his eyes.

"I feel there is a very great bond between Lidia Ivanovna and myself," he said.

It was all going well.

"See you later, then," I said.

"You are so magnanimous, so merciful," he said in a broken voice. "I have no right to ask, but might you give me a token that we part, if not as friends, at least not as enemies?"

The wee scone. He had made a terrible mistake, true, but he obviously felt really bad about it.

"What do you have in mind?" I asked.

"This." He picked up the copy of *The Bride of Lammermoor*, which had escaped the general destruction. "Would you be so generous as to inscribe it for me?"

"Of course," I said. I led him into the anteroom, where there was pen and ink, and wrote *To Sasha. Best wishes, Shona.* "There."

"Thank you a thousand times. I have no right to ask more, but your full name is so very beautiful, Shona Fergusovna McMonagle."

I was quite touched that he liked my name. I added *Fergusovna McMonagle*.

"You are the quintessence of kindness," he said. "I shall cherish this always." He gave me a luminous smile.

It must have been the smile that affected my concentration. I accompanied him to the top of the staircase, intending to see him out. But suddenly I slipped and found myself falling through thin air. Even though it would have been a perfect opportunity to focus on Newtonian physics and Einstein's theory of general relativity, I found myself completely unable to do so. All that flashed through my mind was "terminal velocity".

The stairs and entrance hall were marble, and I was about to die. I did wonder what would happen to my body. Would my crumpled remains be found back in my flat, baffling Police Scotland's finest? Or would I simply never reappear in Morningside, and how would they manage in the library without me?

I continued to hurtle towards the unforgiving marble. I had failed in my first mission.

"Forgive me, Miss Blaine," I whispered.

And then I thought (quickly, because I was falling at quite a rate), the crème de la crème don't give up in the face of adversity. Are we downhearted? No!

My martial arts expertise includes knowing how to break-fall. I closed my eyes and imagined myself in the dojo. A swift breath in, then a breath out as I landed, slapping my arm on the unyielding floor. I was badly winded, and my head had suffered a nasty crack, but no bones were broken. I was still alive.

And then there were fingers on my throat, pressing into my windpipe till I began to lose consciousness.

CHAPTER 7

As though from a great distance away, I heard Old Vatrushkin yell, "You devil!"

The pressure on my windpipe disappeared, and there was the sound of a thud.

"If you ever come near her excellency again, I'll rip your head off your shoulders!" roared Old Vatrushkin.

With an immense effort, I half-opened my eyes and imagined I saw Sasha slumped against the wall, his head spinning round and round. Lack of oxygen was making me hallucinate, subconsciously latching on to the mention of heads.

Old Vatrushkin picked Sasha up as though he were a bag of gherkins and hurled him out of the front door before slamming it shut and locking it.

Babbling incoherently, he rushed over and propped me up in a sitting position. My head felt as though it were spinning even faster than I had imagined Sasha's was. I tried to speak but no words emerged from my damaged throat.

Old Vatrushkin was weeping now.

"I should never have left you!" he sobbed. "I suspected, who could fail to! But I never thought…"

Dazed though I was, it was crucial that I ascertained what had just happened. I swallowed with difficulty and managed an approximation of speech.

"Old Vatrushkin…"

His sobs redoubled, but he was beaming. "Oh, your excellency! God be praised, you can speak! May the angels protect you, since I have signally failed to do so."

"Old Vatrushkin." It still hurt to talk, but this was important. "Did you just throw Sasha out the front door?"

"Thanks be to heaven, I did."

"Old Vatrushkin," I croaked, "that was very rude of you."

He blinked.

"Your excellency?"

"Sasha was a guest in my house."

"But, your excellency!"

My head was throbbing and I was going to have the most spectacular bump. I closed my eyes and took a long breath. "What don't we do? We don't throw our guests out the front door."

"I obey your excellency in all things," said Old Vatrushkin. "Except this." His brow was creased in anxiety and determination.

"Old Vatrushkin," I said, "how can I possibly invite anybody round again if you're likely to throw them out the front door?"

"I am talking only of that devil! He tried to kill you!"

His words made no sense. I must be dreaming. But the way my head ached suggested I was conscious.

"He had thrown you to the ground and was strangling you!" wailed Old Vatrushkin. "If I had been a minute later, you might have been—you might have been…" He began sobbing again.

I leaned back against the wall and tried to override the pain. "You have the most extraordinary imagination," I said. "I keep warning people against making assumptions. Sasha hadn't thrown me to the ground. I was daft enough to miss my footing at the top of the stairs, and he was rushing to help me. He was obviously checking for a pulse, but just didn't know how to do it properly. Which is why first aid courses are so important."

Old Vatrushkin's mouth was set in a firmly defiant line. "He was trying to kill you," he said.

"Okay, one question," I said. "Why would he want to kill me?"

"Because he is a devil!" Old Vatrushkin burst out.

Why was he saying these crazy things, bad-mouthing Sasha? One answer suggested itself. I felt a surge of unease. "Old Vatrushkin," I said, "are you in love with me?"

"I would not dare, your excellency!" he said. "You are as high above me as the summit of Mount Elbrus is above the depths of Lake Baikal. And, speaking with the greatest respect, you are slightly too old for me. You are also a little too—that is to say, I prefer ladies who are more slender."

I managed to keep my tone even. "That's good," I said. "This is solid muscle, by the way."

If he wasn't in love with me, why was he making these extraordinary allegations against Sasha? Of course—he was jealous of the prestige and adulation his fellow serf was enjoying. "Anyway, let's have no more nonsense about murder plots," I said. "All I did was slip at the top of the staircase, although I've never noticed it being particularly slippy before."

Old Vatrushkin leaped up the staircase and let out a great cry. "That accursed pickle!"

"I know it wasn't Branston, but it wasn't that bad," I said. "They all seemed to like it."

But there was no getting through to him. He was beating his breast and blaming himself for almost killing me by dropping pickle on the landing. I distracted him by telling him to clean it up, which also stopped him wittering on about murder plots. But when somebody tried the front door, found it locked and started hammering on it, he sprang up, his face pale.

"Stay there, your excellency! I shall protect you, with my life if necessary."

He opened the door to an extremely disgruntled maid.

"What's the idea, locking me out?" she demanded.

Old Vatrushkin was about to speak, but I silenced him with a shake of my head. I couldn't bear the thought of her histrionics if he convinced her there was a mad strangler on the loose.

"Come and help me change for the concert," I said in the hope that doing her job would cheer her up. But now that she didn't do anything except put on airs and my clothes, she got quite grumpy at being asked to help. Serfs really were the limit. I couldn't begin to imagine how Nanny managed four thousand, two hundred and ninety-nine of them.

The maid looked critically at the dove-grey silk gown I had chosen. "It would suit me better," she said.

I ran my fingers through my hair in frustration, and winced as I made contact with the tender bump on my head. It was as though the sudden pain was a direct message from Miss Blaine. I was four days into my week-long mission and I hadn't even started my background checks on Sasha. I had to get moving.

"Tell me," I said to the maid, "would you be prepared to do something ever so slightly illicit?"

"I knew it," she said. "I knew you were planning to sell me down the Bosphorus as an odalisque."

"You're completely fixated, aren't you?" I said. "I don't want you anywhere near the Bosphorus. Before you came here, you worked for the countess on her estate near the village of N—?"

"Yes, I hated it," she said. "A horrible, boring place. I'm never going back."

"Ah," I said. "Would you go back for, say, three roubles?"

A glint of greed appeared in her eyes. "It depends. Why would I go back?"

"I fancy seeing the countess's estate. Am I right in thinking nobody there knows you're no longer in the countess's service?"

"How could anyone know?" she scoffed. "It is a long way —the count and countess would not bear the expense of communicating with the estate unless it was a matter of life and death."

"So we could go together, and I could tell them I was a friend of the countess's, and that she had given me her personal maid to accompany me."

The maid rolled her eyes. "They would never believe that. The countess has no friends."

"But she might have made friends in town. Especially if that friend was a princess."

The maid reluctantly acknowledged that this could sound plausible. "I still don't ever want to go back to that miserable dump," she said.

"Not even to show off your fine clothes?" I said. "They'll never have seen you dressed in anything so amazing. Especially this dove-grey gown. They'll be really jealous."

She was definitely swithering, but she still wasn't quite prepared to capitulate.

"If I pretended the countess had sent me with you, that would be a lie," she said primly. "And lying is a sin."

"Indeed it is," I said. "I wouldn't want to imperil your immortal soul, so we'd better just forget the whole thing."

"But I'm your serf, madam, and I must do as you say," she announced. It was the first I'd heard of it. "Although it would ease my conscience if you were to give me another three roubles."

I produced a single note from my reticule and handed it over. "Three roubles now, three roubles once we get there and you convince them I'm a mate of the countess's."

"That's not fair!" she whined, and I was obliged to point out that nobody said life would be fair. The deal was duly agreed.

"And not a word to anyone," I warned. "This trip is secret."

The maid pouted. "You want me to keep my mouth shut? That's worth another twenty kopecks."

It was verging on blackmail, but I was depending on her silence. I dropped a coin into her outstretched hand. And then another thought struck me. "Do you know how to get in touch with Sasha, the countess's protégé?"

She sniggered. Nobody seemed to appreciate my perfect French accent. "Of course."

"Great. Could you go and give him my best wishes for a speedy recovery?"

She gasped. "Why, what's happened to him?"

It was better not to mention Old Vatrushkin. There was enough strain between him and the maid already. I explained Sasha had been in a bit of a collision with a wall. The maid screamed.

"I must go to him!" she yowled as she rushed off. It was quite refreshing to see her doing what she was told for once.

I changed my clothes by myself and then went to find Old Vatrushkin. That was the next problem. He didn't want me to go out. Not ever. He wanted me to stay behind locked doors while he stood ready to protect me. And he was still distraught at not having protected me earlier and begged my forgiveness. First, I told him that there was nothing to forgive, but he wouldn't accept that. Then I told him I forgave him, but he wouldn't accept that either. Eventually, I just had to shout at him, and he relaxed a bit.

"But please, your excellency, be careful," he said as we set off. It struck me that he was the second person that day to have told me that.

I geared myself up to avoid making rash promises about Lidia not dancing with anyone but the general, but when we got to Lidia's, there was no sign of Nanny.

"She's behaving very strangely," sighed Lidia. "She told me she couldn't talk to me, and when I told her she could always talk to me, she said I was the stupidest chicken she had ever met, and ran off to her room."

So that had worked out well. And when we got to the concert hall, the posters announced that the avant-garde composer whom the princess had been avoiding was Beethoven. Not only that, but he was conducting this performance of his Fifth Symphony. I felt quite faint with excitement. I'm a total fangirl when it comes to

Ludwig van—have been since I learned to play *Für Elise* at the age of five. Any thought of my mission went clean out of my head. All I wanted to do was immerse myself in sublime music.

"This is going to be really brilliant," I told Lidia as we made our way to our seats. "You'll love Beethoven. He's got great hair." When we walked through the door into the imperial box, it was like emerging on to a film set. The light from the auditorium was practically blinding, and the hubbub from all the concert-goers was practically deafening. Everybody turned to see who had arrived.

Lidia shrank back, daunted by the exposure, and grabbed a chair by the door where she was concealed by the curtain. As a stalwart of the school dramatic society, I was unfazed, and pulled my chair to the front of the box. The young wives waved and nudged their husbands, who bowed respectfully. In a box straight across from me was the countess, who shielded her face with an ostentatious flourish of her fan so that she didn't have to acknowledge me. And there, sitting beside her, was not the count, but Sasha, thankfully looking none the worse for his encounter with Old Vatrushkin. He deftly shifted his seat behind the countess and gave me a discreet nod, along with a gloriously forgiving smile. Equally discreetly, I waggled my fingers at him as though I was adjusting my coiffure.

A formally dressed gentleman appeared on stage and the noise died down.

"I am the bearer of bad news," he said. "The orchestra will no longer be conducted by Maestro van Beethoven. He has failed to arrive, and although we sent messengers to his rooms, there was no reply."

What did you expect, I felt like shouting. *He's deaf—he can't hear them.* I would have offered to go myself and climb through his window, but the orchestra was already filing in. I was thrilled to see contrabassoons, whose first symphonic use was in the premiere of Beethoven's Fifth in 1808.

I settled down to enjoy the concert, but I was the only one. Everybody kept on chatting, paying no attention to the glorious music. Well, maybe not that glorious since I felt the conductor's artistic interpretation was very pedestrian, and he'd got the second violins too loud. But I still wanted to listen to the symphony rather than other people's conversations.

"What are you doing?" asked Lidia in a perplexed tone.

"Ssh," I whispered. "I'm listening to the music. Don't talk until they stop playing."

The next thing she did was stand up and wave her arms about. This was definitely the last time I was taking her to a concert if she couldn't behave. I turned round myself to remonstrate with her and found Sasha standing there, holding the thick yellow curtain cord.

Other people might be philistines but there was no way I could bring myself to natter during a concert. I shepherded Lidia and Sasha out into the corridor and closed the door behind us. I was going to miss the contrabassoons, which perform only in the Finale, but that couldn't be helped.

"Shona Fergusovna!" Sasha gave me his most radiant smile. He really was stunning. "And Lidia Ivanovna! Excuse me, Lidia Ivanovna, I did not know you were here with Shona Fergusovna. I took advantage of the music to slip away from the countess in order to reply to Shona Fergusovna's kind enquiry about my health."

Of course he had been obliged to do it surreptitiously. The countess would be livid if she thought he was talking to me.

"I hope you're feeling better," I said.

"All the better for seeing you," he said, bowing to us both to indicate he wasn't just referring to me. This was encouraging.

"I'm sure you're even happier to see Lidia Ivanovna since the princess never gave you a chance to chat to her earlier," I said. I gave her a nod, encouraging her to join in the conversation.

"What were you doing?" She pointed to the curtain cord.

He looked down at it as though seeing it for the first time. "Oh, this? When I came into the box, I saw it had fallen down from the curtain, and I picked it up in case someone tripped over it. There have been too many accidents today."

"There certainly have," I said. "That was very thoughtful. Since we're all out here, why don't we go and beat the crowds for an interval drink?"

"I think I would like to go home," said Lidia. "I am not used to all these crowds."

"Don't be silly," I said. "We've got a party to go to. Sasha, would you like to come with us?"

That heart-stopping smile again. "I can think of nothing I would rather do, but of course I must escort the countess."

"We'll see you there," I said. We might as well move on. The concert was a wash-out with all the chatting. Not to mention the second violins.

When we were settled in the drozhky, I slyly asked Lidia what she thought of Sasha. She grimaced.

"Are you all right?" I asked in concern. "Some bad borshch?"

She shook her head. "I am quite well, thank you."

"That's good. So, what about Sasha, then?"

"There's something about him," she said slowly.

"Yes, isn't there?" I agreed. "He's so handsome. And I'm sure he thinks you're very beautiful." I glanced at her perfect profile, her alabaster skin. Their kids would be adorable.

"Shona Fergusovna," she said, "I didn't notice the curtain cord on the floor."

"Neither did I," I said. "Thank goodness Sasha did. He's very observant. He notices you, you know. I wouldn't be surprised if he asks you to dance this evening."

"Nanny would not wish me to dance with him," she said. "I may only dance with the general. Perhaps tonight he will ask me to marry him."

"Please don't do anything rash," I begged. "If the general asks you, tell him you want some time to think about it. And if anyone else asks you to dance, it would be rude to refuse."

She squeezed my hand affectionately. "I do not understand why I should delay accepting the general. But I know your celestial wisdom far exceeds mine and of course I shall obey."

The princess's palace was full of footmen. It was impossible to avoid them. They followed you with chairs, in case you needed a sit-down between the door and the staircase, or on each stair, or between the landing and the nearest sofa. They came at you from all angles with trays of champagne, hors d'oeuvres, ices. The princess attempted a grand entrance from the other side of the ballroom, but there was such a press of footmen that it was difficult to see her, apart from her elaborate pink ostrich-feather headdress bobbing over them.

After we had exchanged princessly greetings and she had gone to speak to humbler guests, I deposited Lidia with a group of young wives who went into ecstasies over the fashionable shade of her latest fichu and wanted ones just the same.

Then I lay in wait for the general, and as soon as he arrived, I suggested a nice game of cards and propelled him into the card room.

The countess's cadaverous husband was already sitting at one of the tables. "Ah, General," he drawled. "What is it to be? Boston or piquet?"

"Wouldn't you like to learn a new game?" I asked. "How about I teach you animal snap?"

The count looked down his patrician nose at me as though I had suggested passing the port to the right rather than the left. "Surely you are not joining us, Princess Tamsonova?"

"Sure am!" I said with my best smile, sitting down beside him. And then to my dismay, I saw that Sasha had come into the card room as well, when he was supposed to be dancing with Lidia.

"Count!" he said. "I have the honour of bringing you a message from your wife."

That woman had a genius for getting in the way.

The count grunted.

"She wishes you to know that she will wait in the ballroom until you are ready to go."

The count grunted again. What sort of a message was that for the countess to send, anyway? Utterly pointless. I picked up the fresh pack of cards on the table and began shuffling them energetically, to allow Sasha to go back to the ballroom.

But instead he said, "May I make up a foursome?"

He was acting with his usual courtesy. A lot of games require four players and he thought we wouldn't be able to start without him. He wasn't to know that you can play animal snap with any number from two upwards. He had already sat down, and it would have sounded rude for me to send him away. I also couldn't tell him to go and dance with Lidia in front of the general. All I could do was to try to get the game finished as quickly as possible.

"Right," I said, "same rules as snap except different. When you see a card of the same number, you don't shout 'snap', you shout the animal noise of whoever played the two cards. To save time, I'll give you your animals. General, you're a lion, so you go *roar*. Count, you're a sheep so you go *baa*. Sasha, you're a wolf, so you go *aaawoo*, and I'm a frog, so I go *ribbit*."

"Why am I a sheep?" demanded the count.

"Surely it is much more appropriate that I am the sheep," said Sasha deferentially. "I beg you to be the wolf."

The count gave a curt nod.

"So are we clear about the rules?" I said. "If I put down a seven and the general puts down a seven, what do we say?"

"*Aaawoo*," said the count.

"No, we say the animal noises of the people who put down the cards. It's me and the general, so it's—?"

"*Roar ribbit*!" cried the general.

"Very good. Right noises, but not quite in the right order. I played the first card and the general played the second card, so—?"

"*Ribbit roar*?" said Sasha.

"Excellent!" I said, briskly dealing the cards.

"What are the stakes?" asked the general.

"Ten thousand roubles," said the count.

I had to intervene, or Sasha would be dragged into financial disaster. "This is just a friendly, since it's a new game for you all.

The winner gets a free glass of champagne from the next passing footman. And so do the losers. Except me, of course. I'll just have a glass of tea."

We started playing. After a few rounds, the general played an ace and the count played an ace. I paused to let them shout out. Nothing happened. "*Roar aaawoo*," I prompted.

"Ah!" said the count. "So when a card is repeated, we make the noise of the people who played the cards."

The count definitely hadn't had the finest education in the world. "Yes, that's it," I said wearily.

The game resumed.

"Shona Fergusovna," whispered Sasha. "I think I saw you drop a card."

I bent down and looked. "I can't see anything."

"Count, General, perhaps it landed on your side of the table?"

They bent down as well, but even though the general was nearer the floor than the rest of us, no card could be found.

"Forgive me, it must have been a trick of the light," said Sasha.

He had just played a ten and the count put down another ten. I couldn't believe it. The card the count played was quite clearly from another pack of cards entirely. "*Baa aoooo!*" he said in triumph.

I wasn't having that.

"Count!" I remonstrated. "You great big cheat!"

It was as though I'd said something dreadful. The horror in the room was practically palpable. All of the players at the other tables dropped their cards, wide-eyed and open-mouthed.

The count jumped to his feet, overturning his chair. "What did you say?" he hissed, his thin lips white.

He needn't think he could intimidate me. When you've survived a bollocking from a Marcia Blaine maths teacher, you can survive anything.

"I said you're a great big cheat." I picked up the offending card and flapped it in his face. "Look, it's not even from the same deck."

"I played," the count snarled, "from the cards you dealt me."

The players at the other tables got up and began edging out of the room.

"Clearly not," I said. "And this is not at all sportsmanlike. But if you apologise and promise not to do it again, I'm prepared to let you back in the game."

The count's pale face flushed. "If you were not a woman, I would horsewhip you."

I was about to invite him to come and have a go if he thought he was hard enough when the general intervened.

"How dare you insult a lady!" He stretched up and swatted at the count with a glove, managing to hit his upper arm.

"Forgive me, Count. If you would oblige me?" he murmured.

"Of course, General."

The count bent down and the general whacked him across the face with the glove.

"Thank you, Count."

"Not at all, General."

"And who is your second?"

The count looked round without any great interest, and fixed on Sasha. "This young man will do as well as anybody. And you, General?"

I felt I owed the general a debt. "I'll be his second," I volunteered.

"You?" Contempt dripped from the count's tongue.

"Yes, me. Got a problem with that? Is it the woman thing again? We're not in the dark ages any more. This is 18—" I looked round hopefully to see if someone would complete the date for me, but nobody did. "Anyway, these are modern times. I presume, General, that you've got no objection?"

The general hesitated. "It's not usual." Then he beamed. "But no, I have no objection."

"Then the two seconds will sort out the arrangements for the field of honour tomorrow morning," snapped the count.

My extensive reading hadn't covered this. "I don't know what to do," I said. "Sasha, how about you?"

Sasha gave a gracefully apologetic bow. "I'm afraid I have never been involved in a duel."

"I've been involved in hundreds," snorted the count. "And I've always won."

"I've been involved in hundreds as well," said the general. "And I've always won."

"That's handy," I said. "So you'll be able to tell us what to do."

"The most important thing is secrecy," said the general. "At all costs, we must avoid discovery by the authorities."

It was just as well that all the other card players had disappeared.

"I favour the secluded glade in the forest on the edge of town," said the general.

"That is one of my favourite duelling locations," agreed the count. "Would eight in the morning be convenient?"

"It's already quite late, and we must get some sleep, so perhaps ten past?"

"Of course. I am entirely at your disposal."

They were so matey that they seemed to have forgotten that some of us still weren't up to speed.

"General, I've no idea where you're going—can I come with you?" I asked. "And do I have to bring anything?"

He shook his head. "I shall bring a brace of pistols and I assume the count will do the same."

The count inclined his head.

"All that the seconds need do is check the weapons and attempt to effect a reconciliation," the general added.

"An attempt that will be doomed," said the count. "I shall now go home to write my will, although, I assure you, I have no intention of dying."

He stalked out of the card room.

"I shall do the same and my intention is similar," said the general and followed him.

I turned to Sasha. "I feel a bit bad about this," I confessed. "I sort of wish I hadn't accused the count of cheating."

It was the weirdest thing—I had another optical illusion. It was as though Sasha's eyes were glowing red. I looked round to see where the red light source was coming from but I couldn't find anything. When I turned back, Sasha's eyes were as blue and limpid as ever.

"You had no choice," he said gently. "Your integrity allowed you no other course. The fault is entirely the count's, for trying to deceive us all in such a blatant manner and then for denying it."

It had to be said that he talked very good sense. And he was unbelievably good-looking. It would be impossible to find a more perfect husband for Lidia. And if the count happened to kill the general, there wouldn't be a single obstacle in Sasha's way.

I had to get home if I too was going to get a few hours' sleep before the duel. Lidia, who was wilting under the barrage of young wives' fashion questions, was happy to leave. Once we'd dropped her at her mansion, I asked Old Vatrushkin to make sure I got to the general's in time to be at the secluded glade in the forest on the edge of town by ten past eight.

"Of course, your excellency."

It crossed my mind that he might think I was involved in some sort of dodgy assignation, so I thought I'd better explain. Given that I was on a mission, it was important I was seen to be working.

"I'm going to be a second in a duel," I said. "Between the count and the general. I felt I had to be involved, since I sort of started it when I got cross with the count for cheating at cards."

The carriage lurched wildly and I had to cling to the side to avoid falling out.

"Your excellency!" Old Vatrushkin gasped. "It's a wonder the count didn't horsewhip you."

"He did threaten to, but the general stood up for me. Of course, it took a while for everyone to notice he was standing up."

Old Vatrushkin didn't even smile at my joke.

"Who heard what you said?" His voice was tight with anxiety.

"Only the people in the card room," I said.

He let out a groan. "So they will have told everybody else at the party, and now the whole town will know. Oh, your excellency, the count will never forgive you."

OLGA WOJTAS

I gently pointed out that I didn't require forgiveness since I wasn't the person at fault. Old Vatrushkin groaned again, and pulled the drozhky into the side of the road. He peered all round in the darkness.

"What are you doing?" I asked.

"Ensuring that nobody can overhear us," he whispered. "The matter we are forbidden to speak of—I am about to speak of it."

I leaned forward, intrigued. "Speak away."

"It was the night before the count's wedding. He and his imperial majesty the tsar and some other gentlemen had gone to some drinking dens to celebrate the count's last night of freedom. It is one of our traditional marriage customs."

"We have something similar," I said. "It rarely ends well."

Old Vatrushkin lowered his voice still further. "As was the case here. They were playing a game of piquet and the tsar accused the count of cheating. The count said that if the tsar were not the tsar, he would horsewhip him. And the tsar said he *was* the tsar and exiled him. The wedding was hastily rearranged from the town to the church in the village of N—, but it was only after the ceremony that the count told the countess about being exiled."

"I imagine the countess wasn't best pleased," I said.

"It is rumoured that they have not exchanged a civil word since then."

In the distance came the clop of horses' hooves and the clatter of carriage wheels. Old Vatrushkin grabbed up the reins and set off at high speed.

"I was afraid it might be the count," he panted as we reached home. "But I think we are safe for the moment. Oh, your excellency, I beg you to be careful—he is a very dangerous enemy."

"So you reckon he'll win the duel tomorrow?"

"Impossible to say, your excellency. They are both superb shots. And they both have physical advantages. The count is so thin and the general is so small that they leave little for their adversary to aim at."

I pondered this as I got ready for bed. It would solve all Lidia's problems if the general got shot. The atmosphere at social gatherings would be much improved if the count got shot. The ideal, surely, would be if they shot each other simultaneously. And yet the only reason the duel was taking place was that the general had defended me. I couldn't wish him ill after that. And even though the count was totally obnoxious, I could scarcely stand by and watch him get killed. I had to find a solution.

I know very little about firearms, beyond knowing that they're dangerous and should be banned. I have a cursory working knowledge of duelling pistols, just basic stuff, like the difference between flintlock firing mechanisms and percussion lock mechanisms, and how the priming gunpowder leads to the main charge. And as I considered the mechanics, I realised what the solution was. If only I had...

I raced over to my underwear drawer and wrenched it open. There, just beside a multiway bra, was a paper bag. A small bag, but it was full.

"Thank you, Miss Blaine," I said into the ether.

The paper bag was safely in my reticule when Old Vatrushkin drove me to the general's. The wee guy was already waiting for me outside, a plain white shirt under his black jacket, which was covered in military medals. He was holding a large wooden box.

"My lucky pistols," he explained. Then he gave a piercing whistle, and a large black horse appeared from round the corner and trotted up to us. "My lucky horse," he explained. I was surprised that the servants hadn't already harnessed it to the carriage.

"After you," the general said, indicating the horse, which I now saw had a saddle on it. The general detected my look of slight surprise.

"I'm a simple old soldier," he said. "I don't believe in modern fripperies like carriages."

There was no way I could sit astride without exposing a scandalous amount of leg.

"We could go in my carriage," I offered.

The general shook his head. "Secrecy is of the utmost importance."

Old Vatrushkin stepped forward. "If his excellency the general would take his place, I shall assist you to mount."

The general walked away from the horse, then turned and started running. At the optimum point, he jumped, got a foot in a stirrup, and swung himself into the saddle. I was still gazing at him with new respect when Old Vatrushkin grabbed me and lifted me up bodily to sit in front of the general, side saddle without a saddle. The general reached round me to take hold of the reins, his arms stopping me from falling off. The only problem was that I completely blocked his view of the road.

It was just like the advanced motoring test, giving a running commentary on everything I could see. "Avenue with lime trees," I announced. "Small dusty road to the right. Small dusty road to the left. Woman in headscarf with basket full of hens about to cross. Slow down. Woman in headscarf has dropped basket full of hens. Hens on road. Veer left."

We proceeded very effectively. I have excellent eyesight and the general had excellent reflexes. There was very little else on the road ("Haycart ahead. Haycart wobbling. Haycart tipping over. STOP!") and then I spotted a carriage in front of us, containing a lean cadaverous figure and another that, even from the back, looked stunning.

"Count's carriage directly ahead, travelling approximately twenty versts per hour. We can just keep behind it and follow it to the locus," I said.

"Twenty versts per hour?" said the general. "And you want us to follow them? I wouldn't dream of going so slowly, even if my horse was lame in all four legs." The next thing I knew we were accelerating.

"Pull into the outside lane!" I yelled just before we careered into the back of the carriage, and we overtook with only dyuims to spare.

"Are you crazy?" the count shouted after us. "You could have killed me!"

"Give me time," murmured the general, and we hurtled on, cackling like loons. I was warming to the wee guy.

"This is fun!" I shouted.

"It's even more fun when you're under enemy fire," said the general, breaking into a battle song in a fine baritone. There was more to him than met the eye, which was just as well, there being so little of him. Considering things rationally, the only way I consider them, all I had against him was that he wanted to marry Lidia. And if he had been younger and taller, I would have had no objection to that. Was I guilty of being ageist and heightist? No: the general might be a perfectly decent bloke, but Lidia deserved better than that. She deserved a soulmate, someone as good and as beautiful as herself, and that was Sasha. As soon as the duel was over, I was going to the station to get rail tickets to the village of N— to complete the background checks.

We were crashing through the forest now en route for the rendezvous, the horse's hooves and general's voice scattering small creatures and the occasional elk.

"Wooded glade!" I announced, and the general pulled on the reins, bringing the horse to an emergency stop.

"I always like to arrive first," he said. "It creates a psychological advantage." He scrambled off the horse, and was stretching up to assist me when I told him I could manage. I sprang down, landing proficiently on my DMs.

"You would have made a fine aide de camp," said the general.

I shook my head. "I'm not keen on wars. I believe we place too little reliance on diplomacy."

"Then you would make a fine Metternich," he said.

Another clue. It must be before 1859, when the Austrian empire's celebrated diplomat died. I was narrowing down the timescale.

The general handed me the large wooden box with his lucky pistols. "We will allow the count to choose which weapons he prefers," he said.

The count's carriage was too bulky to come into the forest, and eventually Sasha and the count appeared, scrambling through the trees. I appreciated the general's tactics. Here he was, composed, prepared, unruffled, while the count was dishevelled, tired and fractious, which didn't bode well for a steady aim.

"I've never seen such hazardous riding!" he greeted the general.

"I'm sure you haven't, since you have never thought it your duty to join the army," the general responded.

Duellist trash talk.

Sasha was smiling at me, an open, sincere smile that spoke not only of pleasure at seeing me but also recognised the absurdity of the situation we were in.

"The pistols," demanded the count.

Sasha and I opened the boxes. The general's pistols were practical. The count's were blingtastic. They must have been a present from the countess.

"You have the choice of weapon," said the general politely.

"I should normally choose yours, as being the ones you are most used to, but mine will allow you the opportunity to enjoy a much superior firearm," said the count.

They each lifted a pistol out of the box.

"Aren't we forgetting something?" I said. "The seconds have to check that everything's in order. I mean, they might not be primed correctly, or they might have the wrong type of lead shot."

I handed them to Sasha, who glanced at them and pronounced them acceptable.

"You don't mind if I have a proper look, Count?" I asked. "I've never seen such beautiful pistols. Wogdon & Barton, are they?"

"Joseph Manton," he grunted.

"The acme of weaponry!" I breathed. "I should have known that's what you would have. They're amazing. Eleven-millimetre calibre, I suppose?"

He grunted again.

"Nice platinum touch holes. And that's an impressive frizzen."

I had covertly taken the paper bag from my reticule before retrieving the pistols from Sasha, and as I ran my fingers along them in apparent admiration, I shook the aniseed balls out of the bag and swapped them for the ammunition. There was now a faint scent of liquorice in the air, but I hoped everyone would just think I was wearing a new perfume.

I gave a pistol to both the general and the count.

"Right, then. May the best man win."

"Now you are forgetting something," rasped the count. "There must be a final attempt at an apology."

"Thank you," I said. "It's a bit late, but I'm happy to accept it."

"No, you brainless idiot!" he snarled. "I am the wronged party! It is up to you to make the apology!"

I felt the wronged party was the one being called a brainless idiot, but under the circumstances, I was prepared to let it go.

"Count, I'm very sorry I said you had cheated at cards."

"So you admit making an unjustified slur?" he grated.

"You're not listening," I pointed out. "I said I was very sorry I said you had cheated. It's not an unjustified slur, because you did cheat. But I'm prepared to allow that it may have been a bit rude of me to point it out, even if it was unfair on the rest of us for you to attempt to win through deception. But I'm prepared to overlook your fundamental dishonesty in the interests of avoiding bloodshed. There, apology accepted?"

The count's nostrils flared. "General, let us begin."

It seemed he was determined to fight. The two combatants, pistol in hand, measured forty paces between them, turned and began walking slowly towards one another. I knew they would aim and fire when there were only ten paces between them. As I concentrated, I unconsciously inched forward in time with their pacing. Just as they both lifted their pistols and fired, I tripped over a stray branch and stumbled forward.

There was noise and smoke and a smell of burning aniseed balls. But as I fell, I felt an odd tug at my pelisse, and I could have sworn I heard three shots rather than two. I examined my pelisse and found a hole in it, the edges still smouldering. I made a quick geometrical calculation and realised that if I had been standing upright, the lead shot would have gone straight into my heart.

CHAPTER 8

"Count, you're still alive," shouted the general. "But I aimed directly at you and I never miss."

"And I aimed directly at you and I never miss," the count shouted back.

"And somebody aimed directly at me and definitely didn't miss," I said, getting to my feet, and displaying the hole in my pelisse.

Sasha rushed over to me, concern on his handsome face. "How terrible, Shona Fergusovna. One of the pistols must have misfired."

I shook my head. "From the angle, whoever shot at me must have been behind you. Did you notice anybody?"

"Forgive me, I was watching the duel. I saw nothing else. But who in the world would want to shoot at you?"

It was a no-brainer. The location of the duel had been decided with the greatest secrecy, so it couldn't be a stranger.

"Count, did you tell your wife you were going out duelling?" I asked.

He stared down his aquiline nose at me. "Of course. She had a right to know she might soon be a widow."

The countess had clearly bribed or bullied the count's coachman into an assassination bid. He had crept through the forest after the count and Sasha, secreting himself behind a nearby tree, and then shot at me under cover of the opponents' fire.

But it would be imprudent of me to complain to the count about his wife in case it provoked another duel.

"We've had an early start, so I'm sure we could all do with some breakfast," I said.

I asked the general to drop me off at the station and told him I would make my own way home. He was really upset about not killing the count, saying he had never lost a duel in his life and he must be losing his grip.

It was tempting to tell him that he was as good a shot as ever, but that aniseed balls do very little damage. Instead, I bought him breakfast. We sat companionably on a station bench eating kasha and pelmeni.

"This getting married thing," I said. "Are you sure it's for you? Isn't it nicer to be your own boss and do exactly what you want?"

"But that's what I did when I was married," he said.

I gave him a significant look, which he interpreted correctly.

"The marriage was arranged by our families. My wife and I disliked each other from the start," he said. "I only went into the army to get away from home. Now, in the twilight of my life, I yearn for the happiness that I see other people have. And this time, I shall choose my own bride. When I first saw Lidia Ivanovna, I thought she was the most beautiful creature I had ever seen. And my regard for her only increased when I discovered her woodwork skills."

"I can see the benefit to you," I said. "But what's the benefit to her?"

He thought for a while. "I'm quite old, and will leave her a wealthy widow."

"She's wealthy already," I said. "Anything else?"

He thought some more. "No," he said, in a voice almost as small as himself.

"Oh, come on!" I said. "You're a great singer, a superb horseman and an expert marksman. I'm sure today was just a blip."

"You think so?" he said earnestly. "Oh, Shona Fergusovna, we made a good team. Are you sure you—"

"Absolutely sure," I said. "I told you already, I've got no wedding plans."

"A pity." He sighed. "We could have gone on gallops together around my estate."

"But by all accounts, that's just flat and muddy. It wouldn't be any challenge."

"Would you prefer us to live in town?"

I was about to explain, kindly but unmistakeably, that there was no us and never would be. And then I realised that I could keep him away from Lidia while I was carrying out my investigations in the village of N—.

"That would certainly be preferable," I said. "I'm not fond of the country. Or mud."

"Matrimony is a matter of compromise," he said. "I would consider living in town."

"And I'll consider your kind offer," I said. "In the meantime, don't go proposing to anyone else."

Once I'd bought the train tickets, I headed home. I was passing a drinking den of the most disreputable kind just as half a dozen unkempt individuals were being ejected. There was something familiar about them.

"Mikhail!" I exclaimed as a figure was strong-armed into the street and collapsed at my feet. I recognised all the members of the band from Lidia's party who had gone off to enlist in search of certain death. "You're not in the army?"

"We were on our way," he groaned. "But we got sidetracked."

"Of course," I said. "You're musicians. It's a pub. It's only natural. But are you sure I can't deflect you from the certain death thing?"

"It's all that is left to us," said the leader. "After two days' drinking, we had to sell our instruments in order to continue."

"That would include the accordion that was going to get hurled to the ground and have the kazachok danced on it so that nobody could profane it after I'd played it?" I said, with just the faintest tinge of sarcasm.

He spread his hands. "What choice did I have? I had run out of money. And now all of us have run out of money and have been thrown out of the inn, which leaves us no choice except to die."

I had already saved two people from certain death that day; I felt I was on a roll. And just as I was formulating my plan, I was hailed by Old Vatrushkin from the drozhky.

"Aren't you supposed to be painting?" I demanded.

He hung his head. "I have been looking for you, your excellency. I thought that if the general was killed, you would have no means of returning."

"Surely the count would have brought me back in his carriage," I said.

Old Vatrushkin looked astonished. "Of course not, your excellency," he said. "He will never forgive you."

I suddenly wondered whether it was the count who had organised the attempt on my life. But there was no point in dwelling on that, since there were more pressing matters. I had a few hours before the train left to get the band sorted out. And I knew just the person who could help.

"Old Vatrushkin, is Ludwig van Beethoven still in town?" I asked.

"Indeed he is, your excellency," said Old Vatrushkin. "He has been hired to conduct concerts every evening this week, although he has never yet appeared in the concert hall."

"They really need to get a better system than knocking on his door," I said. "Do you know where he's staying?"

"Of course, your excellency. He's staying at the home of the concert manager."

That was peculiar. You would have thought the concert manager would have worked out an adequate means of communication.

"Right," I said, "can you take us all there?"

"You and these seven—" Old Vatrushkin paused as he searched for an appropriate word.

"Musicians," I said, and he gave a nod of understanding. "Yes, just the eight of us—they've sold their instruments."

"But the drozhky is built for only two passengers," Old Vatrushkin protested.

"We'll just pile them all in on top of one another," I said. "They're totally rat-arsed."

"Rat-arsed, your excellency?" enquired Old Vatrushkin. "I don't know this word."

I tried some more direct translations into Russian. "Hammered, steaming—oh, just take a look at them and you'll work it out. Now help me get them in."

We heaved them up into the drozhky, taking care to place them in the recovery position.

"But there is no room for you, your excellency."

"I'll be fine hanging on at the back. Just don't take the bends too fast."

As we set off down the road, an ornate carriage approached from the opposite direction. When we drew level, the window opened and a familiar head appeared.

"Princess Tamsonova! What are you doing standing on the footplate?" asked the princess.

"I've got an orchestra inside," I explained as we cantered on.

"What a marvellous idea!" the princess called back and I heard her instructing her coachman to find the nearest orchestra, and her footman to get off the back of the carriage so that she could stand in his place.

Old Vatrushkin pulled up gently outside the concert manager's house. I had been going to take the band with me, but they were all snoring contentedly and it seemed a shame to wake them.

It was clearly no use knocking on Beethoven's door if he couldn't hear, so I decided on the strategy I had thought of during the concert—climbing in a window. The windows at the front were all closed, but one at the back was ajar, and I easily gained access. That room was empty, but when I walked into the next one, I found myself in the presence of the great man himself. When I saw that bulky figure, that brooding expression, that leonine hair, I couldn't help it: I turned into a total fangirl again.

"Oh my God!" I gasped in German. "I can't believe I'm in the same room as Ludwig van Beethoven! This is amazing. I just love all your music, though at the start of the Fifth Symphony, I've always wondered why you decided to write the clarinets in unison and not in octaves?"

His expression changed from brooding to utter terror. He had mistaken me for a mad stalker. I wanted to reassure him, and tell him he was entitled to do what he liked with the clarinets, but I was so star-struck that all I managed was to say "Ludwig van Beethoven!" again.

"*Ja*," he said.

That was odd. It wasn't odd that he had replied, since he should surely be able to lip-read his name at the very least. But I had expected a Bonn accent with Viennese overtones, and he sounded Bavarian. Thanks to Marcia Blaine's language teachers, I have a very well-developed ear. Two, in fact.

"If I talk slowly, can you follow what I'm saying?" I asked.

"*Ja*," he repeated. I was pretty sure he was Bavarian.

"Nice to see you in Russia," I said. "I suppose you're taking the opportunity to visit Count Razumovsky, who commissioned you to write the Razumovsky string quartets?"

"*Ja*."

Bavarian, absolutely no doubt about it.

"You're not Beethoven," I said.

"Yes I am."

"No you're not," I said. "There's no way you were born in the Electorate of Cologne. And you can't visit Count Razumovsky because, as you would know if you were Beethoven, he's the Russian ambassador in Vienna, where he's been living in seclusion since 1814 and I know it's at least 1825."

He tugged at his cravat as though it was choking him. "Pavel Pavlovich!" he shouted.

Immediately, another man entered the room and I dropped into an appropriate martial arts stance for fighting two attackers at once. But the fake Beethoven was backing away and the newcomer was a weaselly bloke who posed no threat whatsoever.

"Pavel Pavlovich, she knows I'm not Beethoven!" he wailed, still in Bavarian German.

"You fool, what have you been saying?" hissed the weaselly bloke whose execrable German accent immediately gave him away as Russian.

I intervened. "He's said 'yes' three times, and 'Pavel Pavlovich', which has been quite enough for me to work out your whole nefarious plan," I said in Russian and then quickly translated into German for the fake Beethoven's benefit.

Pavel Pavlovich was about to speak but I held up my hand. "You've been stupid going along with all of this," I said in German to the fake Beethoven. "But you," I said in Russian to Pavel Pavlovich, "are the concert manager, and you're the one I blame. You're an unscrupulous shyster. You've put on a programme of Beethoven, which you know audiences will be suspicious of because it's modern and difficult. You decide to entice them in by claiming that the composer himself will be conducting. But Beethoven's hearing has been deteriorating since the turn of the century and he's had to stop conducting. So you hire this Bavarian doppelganger—" (the fake Beethoven, who clearly didn't speak Russian, had been looking perplexed but perked up at hearing this reference to himself) "—who looks like the maestro but knows nothing about music, so can't be allowed near an orchestra. But he can be seen about town so that everyone knows he's here, and then you come up with excuses for why he hasn't turned up to conduct. You get massive ticket sales and you don't have to shell out an enormous fee for the real Beethoven. I'm guessing you're paying the doppelganger—" (the fake Beethoven looked pleased to get another mention) "—peanuts."

"That's not true. I'm paying him real money, fifty kopecks," said Pavel Pavlovich and then clapped his hand over his mouth. He turned on the fake Beethoven, addressing him in excruciatingly badly pronounced German. "You must have told her! How else would she know every single detail of our plan?"

"I didn't tell her anything!" the fake Beethoven wailed.

"Someone as crooked as you wouldn't recognise the truth if it bit you on the ankle," I said to Pavel Pavlovich, in German, so that the fake Beethoven wouldn't feel excluded. "But the truth is exactly what he's telling you."

"Then you must be a witch!"

I shook my head. "I'm not a witch. I'm not an angel. I simply had the finest education in the world, which enables me to assess the evidence in front of me and make logical deductions."

I could see grudging admiration in Pavel Pavlovich's eyes, alongside a strong desire to hack me into tiny pieces. "I suppose you want a proportion of the takings," he said.

"Don't insult me," I said quietly.

He paled. "You want all of the takings?"

"I don't want any money," I said. "At least, not directly. I've got an orchestra outside. Violin, double bass, bassoon, clarinet, trumpet, percussion and an accordion. You're going to make them famous and very rich. They're extremely versatile—I suggest in particular that you get the accordionist playing a transcription of Bach's Goldberg Variations. Or Clementi, if you want something a bit more contemporary. But their speciality is Scottish country dance music, which, as you know, is extremely fashionable these days."

A greedy expression came over the manager's face. "I heard there was an astounding orchestra playing Scottish country dance music at a grand party a few days ago. With a truly exceptional female accordionist."

Modesty forbade me. "She's off doing other things," I said. "But otherwise it's the same line-up."

"So I'll be very rich as well," he said thoughtfully.

"All in good time," I said. "First, they'll need a new set of instruments."

He sighed. "They've sold them for drink?"

I nodded. "And I'm afraid they're still a bit drunk. They're just outside, piled up in my drozhky. You'd better come and have a look at them."

We went outside, the fake Beethoven following us. Pavel Pavlovich surveyed the dishevelled snoring heap. "Yes, I can see they're professionals all right. I agree to the deal."

I raised an eyebrow. "I'm not just going to accept the word of a crook. Do you think I came up the Dvina on a banana boat?"

"No, of course not," he said. "No one has ever come up the Dvina on a banana boat."

"I'm glad we understand each other. Just a minute." I signalled to Old Vatrushkin, who jumped down from the drozhky, and took him aside to avoid being overheard.

"I'm leaving for the village of N— later today, but I don't want anybody to know. First, I've got to stop the band from enlisting and facing certain death. The princess said Kirill Kirillovich was the best lawyer in town. Do you know where his office is?"

Old Vatrushkin pointed. "Just across the road, your excellency."

"Perfect. I'll sort things out with the concert manager while you go home and get the maid to pack for a couple of days away. I'll meet you both at the station."

I avoided telling Old Vatrushkin about the attempt on my life in the forest, since I knew he would fret.

"And it might be cold in the country, so make sure she brings my fur coat," I added. Again, there was no need for him to know I was aiming for protection from more than the weather.

With some difficulty, Old Vatrushkin, Pavel Pavlovich, the fake Beethoven and I managed to drag the seven musicians out of the drozhky, and then Old Vatrushkin drove away.

"I believe the best lawyer in town is just over there," I said, changing to German in order to include the fake Beethoven.

Pavel Pavlovich nodded.

"Then that's where we're all going."

"I don't think they're going anywhere," said Pavel Pavlovich, indicating the inert figures on the ground. "Not until they sober up, which will take hours."

In 1817, Beethoven himself referred to Dietrich Nikolaus Winkel's new invention, subsequently patented by Johann Maelzel.

"Do you have," I asked Pavel Pavlovich, "such a thing as a metronome?"

He looked very smug, like one of those geeks with the latest must-have from the Apple Store. "Of course."

"Of course!" repeated the fake Beethoven in sudden understanding, scampering off to get it.

It was a Maelzel original, a beautiful thing, rosewood and brass. I set it to fifty-six beats per minute and waited. The musicians' eyes flickered open and they began nodding their heads in time to the ticking. I held the metronome up in front of them, and they staggered to their feet, their bodies swaying to the rhythm. As I set off with the metronome, they clumped along in unison behind me, speeding up as I changed the tempo from lento to adagio.

I announced myself and my business at the lawyer's, and a troupe of scriveners rushed to get enough seats for us all in Kirill Kirillovich's office, the musicians collapsing into them when the metronome stopped.

I succinctly outlined the contract to be drawn up between Pavel Pavlovich and the band, ensuring that the band's rights were absolutely watertight. There was a slight hiccup when Pavel Pavlovich tried to insist on a larger percentage but he saw sense when I pointed out that I could completely destroy his career.

"One last thing," I said. "There's going to be an extra concert at the end of this Beethoven series." The fake Beethoven hadn't been following the conversation, since we were speaking Russian, but on hearing his name, he smiled and nodded.

"I thought he was deaf," the lawyer whispered.

"He is," I said, "but he can pick up vibrations. That's how he still manages to conduct."

Pavel Pavlovich was squirming in his chair as though someone was prodding him with the business end of a piccolo.

"You will of course know," I said, "that Maestro van Beethoven's Opus 108 is a set of arrangements of Scottish songs?"

The lawyer nodded vigorously. People are terrified to admit that they haven't a clue about contemporary composers.

"He initially wrote it," I went on, "for voices, violin, cello and piano, but he has been so impressed by these musicians that he has reconfigured it for violin, double bass and accordion, with the non-playing band members doing the singing."

Pavel Pavlovich now looked as though someone had whacked him over the head with the double bass.

"So we need a codicil covering that specific performance, which will be conducted by Maestro van Beethoven himself."

Pavel Pavlovich sagged, his hands over his face, as I dictated the codicil giving all proceeds to the band.

Kirill Kirillovich finished writing, laid down his pen and scrutinised me over his glasses. "You are obviously an eminent legal expert," he said. "How is this possible when your gender cannot attend university?"

Another tribute to the finest education in the world. "I don't have any formal qualifications. Jurisprudence is just a bit of a hobby of mine," I said. "If you could make the necessary copies of the contract, we'll get these gentlemen to sign it."

When the lawyer went out to round up some scriveners, Pavel Pavlovich clutched my arm. "Why are you determined to ruin me?" he moaned.

"Ruin you?" I said, reverting to German so that the fake Beethoven would know what was going on. "I'm making your fortune. Nobody will realise he isn't the real thing. All he has to do is stand on the podium, look moody and wave his arms about."

"I can do that," the fake Beethoven said, waving his arms about.

"But that's not conducting," Pavel objected.

"He doesn't need to conduct," I said. "He just needs to look as though he's conducting. These boys are self-starters. They'll sort themselves out, the transcription, the singing, everything. They'll be great. I've played alongside them, and I know."

Too late, I realised I had given myself away.

"So it was you!" said Pavel Pavlovich. "You are the virtuoso accordionist who captivated everyone at the grand party."

"It was just a wee jam session," I said.

"If you will do a concert tour for me, I will give you all the jam you want," he said.

I briefly considered it. Playing in front of an audience for a maximum of half an hour, ten minutes' practice just to make sure I remained at my peak, and the rest of the day to myself. It was appealing. And I like jam. But I was now on the fifth day of my mission and running out of time.

"Just be happy with the deal you've got," I said as the lawyer returned with the documentation. I started up the metronome again and the band members revived enough to make their marks alongside the others' signatures, with me and a scrivener as witnesses.

"You have the most incisive legal mind I have encountered," said the lawyer. "Would you consider coming into partnership with me?"

"You're very kind," I said. "But I'm afraid I've got a train to catch."

In a couple of hours, I had saved nine lives, ten if I included my own when I fell over the branch. I reckoned that ought to please Miss Blaine, and stand me in good stead for the speedy completion of my mission.

I headed for the station. With any luck, a newspaper proprietor had begun publishing again and I would find out what the date was. But before I could look for a vendor, I heard a scream.

I ran to the source and found the maid collapsed against the drozhky, Old Vatrushkin tentatively patting her shoulder.

"She thinks she saw someone," he said in explanation.

"I don't *think*!" she snarled at him and I gave Old Vatrushkin a warning look. "I know what I saw!" Now that her audience had doubled, she started wringing her hands theatrically. "The man! The big man! The big sinister man!"

I tentatively patted her other shoulder, and asked Old Vatrushkin if he had seen this alarming character.

"No, your excellency. If she could read, I would say she had been reading too many Gothic novels."

I had a brief hope that this would let me pinpoint the date until I remembered that the first Russian Gothic novel was Nikolai Mikhailovich Karamzin's *Island of Bornholm* in 1793.

"You think you're so clever just because you can read and write!" the maid snapped at Old Vatrushkin.

"I can do a lot more than read and write," he retorted. "I can carry out the packing duties of a lady's maid."

"And why weren't you doing the packing?" I asked her.

"I was out," she muttered. "It was awful. The big sinister man followed me all day. I had to keep moving."

"Followed you where?" I enquired and she looked sulky.

"Just visiting some maidservant friends," she said, and I knew she'd been swanking around in my clothes again, upsetting people. It was what she did best. "He's been everywhere I've gone and now he's here at the station. I'm sure he wants to sell me down the Bosphorus as an odalisque."

"Don't start that again," I said. "You're in absolutely no danger. Old Vatrushkin got you here safely, and I'll be with you on the train." I normally dismissed most of what the maid said, but just in case she was right for once, I said, "It's a bit chilly. I'll wear my fur coat for the journey."

Old Vatrushkin raced to get it and helped me on with it. "I apologise for taking upon myself the delicate task of packing for your excellency," he said in an undertone, "but the maid was in too distraught a condition to perform it adequately. May I assure your excellency that I kept my eyes closed at all times. Particularly when packing your excellency's...accoutrements."

"Excellent," I said, feeling nostalgic for the simplicity of a serf-free life. But he was handy for carrying my luggage, and ushered us towards the nearest carriage.

"Here, your excellency. I shall install you in the first-class saloon, beside the conductor."

"There," I said to the maid. "Now do you believe you'll be perfectly safe?"

She looked sceptical, but as we approached, the conductor rushed up and led us into the plush compartment with its velvet-covered sofas.

"I shall be just next door, your excellency," he said. "If there is anything at all you need during the journey, simply send your maid to fetch me."

She gave a snort that told me I'd be quicker getting him myself. I waved goodbye to Old Vatrushkin, shouted at him to go and get on with his painting, and had just got myself settled when the whistle went, and the wheels squeaked and clanked against the rails as we set off.

"This is nice," I said to the maid. "You must be looking forward to seeing your old colleagues."

"No," she said. "I hate all of them."

"Not all of them, surely."

There was a pause, as she pondered. "Yes, all of them," she concluded. "I can't wait to see their faces when I turn up dressed in all my finery."

"Dressed in all *my* finery," I pointed out, at which she turned her back and stared grouchily out of the window at the passing countryside.

I relaxed into the comfortable sofa and listened to the soothing rumble of the wheels. But over the noise of the train, I could hear other sounds in the conductor's room next door. Raised voices, an indistinct exclamation, a shout that ended in a hoarse gurgle and a heavy thud, as though a body had fallen to the floor.

There was clearly a need for my first-aid skills. I was moving towards the connecting door when it opened to reveal a menacing figure brandishing a bloodstained knife.

The maid screamed. "That's him! That's the man!"

Steel flashed through the air and there was another scream. This time it wasn't the maid.

CHAPTER

9

I surveyed the intruder, now pinned to the carriage wall by half a dozen razor-sharp knives that a moment earlier had been secreted up the sleeves of my fur coat.

With my usual precision, I had been careful not to draw blood, while ensuring that he was immobilised. Two knives secured him by the shoulders of his greatcoat, two by his sleeves, and two at his waist.

The maid had been right: he was big and sinister. But his head, hands and feet looked disproportionately small, almost as though he was wearing a ridiculous number of layers of clothing, including two coats. His cap was pulled down over his brow: the rest of his face was concealed by a beard and moustache so shaggy that they made Old Vatrushkin's spectacular foliage look like designer stubble.

"Stop wriggling," I advised. "I've got a few more of these little beauties up my sleeve—you have no idea how many—and the way this train is lurching, I can't guarantee I'll miss your more delicate areas."

This was doubly untruthful. I had used up all the knives, and I had no doubts as to the accuracy of my aim. But I believe there are some rare instances, notably when dealing with villains, when one can be economical with the actualité. To add credence to my threat, I used the voice that had so chilled the audience when I played Mr Hyde in our fourth-year dramatisation of Robert Louis Stevenson's novella.

The intruder stopped wriggling.

"Now," I said, "you're going to tell us who you are and what you're doing here."

The would-be assassin spat at me.

"Missed," I said. "Your aim's terrible, by the way. I know all about you stalking my maid but that knife went nowhere near her—it came straight at me."

The maid was cowering behind the sofa, yowling.

"Okay," I said in my most silkily scary voice. "Since you don't seem to want to tell me anything, let me tell you something. You see this coat? Pure haggis fur. Haggis are very, very wee and very, very quick, but they're not as quick as me. It took hundreds of them to make this coat and I trapped and skinned every one of them myself. In fact, I've developed a bit of a taste for skinning things. If you don't talk, and talk fast, I'm going to make a start on you."

The intruder slumped in defeat, and I congratulated myself on my fine theatrical skills. I waited for him to make a full confession, but with sudden energy, he burst out of his great-coat, revealing another greatcoat underneath, wrenched open the compartment door and plunged out into the darkness.

I did a quick calculation. Given the velocity of the train and the angle of his trajectory, the most he would suffer would be a few bruises. He had been more cunning than I thought, and my mission had extended yet again—now I had to keep the maid safe from her would-be assassin.

For once, she was too traumatised even to scream. She was staring at my coat, her eyes wide in terror.

"You didn't believe any of that, did you?" I said. "This is fake fur. I'd never dream of hurting a wee haggis."

My levity went unappreciated. The maid's gaze had swivelled from my coat to the connecting door, which had swung open with the rattling of the train. The conductor was lying in a pool of blood. I went to check his pulse, but there was little point since his throat had been comprehensively cut. The maid's would-be assassin was already a ruthless killer.

Taking paper and pencil out of my reticule, I quickly wrote a full account of the incident, including not only a clear description of the killer but also a rather good sketch, and the coordinates of where he had leaped from the train. I then enclosed a significant sum for the conductor's dependents.

The maid had now turned miserable and grumpy, which I realised could be a coping mechanism following trauma, trying to make everything as normal as possible. But I needed the answer to a question. It could provide a clue as to who was trying to kill her.

"Tell me," I said, "did you tell anybody we were going to the village of N—?"

She hesitated, her eyes flickering. "No," she said.

"Unless you want to be re-emancipated, you tell me the truth, and you tell me right now," I grated.

She folded her arms across her chest, glowering. "Didn't tell anyone," she retorted.

I had one more sanction. "If you don't tell me the truth, you won't get the other three roubles."

She crumbled. "I might have told Sasha," she muttered. "It was when you sent me to see if he was all right. So it's your fault."

I remembered: it was after Old Vatrushkin had mistakenly thought Sasha was attacking me, when he was merely trying to check my pulse. Telling her to enquire about Sasha's health wasn't the same as giving her carte blanche to reveal my travel plans. But I could scarcely blame her for talking to him, since he was the last person anyone could suspect of anything underhand. And yet, I could see how things might have gone wrong.

"Tell me," I said, "was this at the countess's?"

She looked shifty.

"Three roubles," I reminded her.

"Yes," she admitted. "I know how to get in the back door."

So now all was clear. The maid had told Sasha. The countess could have overheard. Or perhaps Sasha had mentioned it to her without understanding the implications. He didn't know how dangerous she was, how ruthless and proprietary. She was still smarting over the maid's infatuation with the count. I was in no doubt: the countess was the only person who could possibly have hired a hit man. Or one of the two only people, since the count himself might have wanted to get rid of his unwise dalliance.

Knowing that we were travelling to N— gave the countess (or possibly the count) her (or possibly his) opportunity. Murdering the maid in town was too risky because of potential witnesses. A journey was ideal, but the hired assassin wouldn't have known how or when we were going to N—. So he had kept the maid under surveillance and followed us on to the train.

That was an advantage. His own train journey would have been unexpected, and it would take time for him to return to town and report back to whichever one of the couple had hired him. That still left me an opportunity to complete my investigations in N— before I sent the maid away for her own safety to somewhere distant, such as Irkutsk. Or Omsk. Or Tomsk.

In the note for the authorities, I contemplated naming the countess (or possibly the count) as having hired the conductor's murderer. But I decided not to, out of politeness. There's nothing authorities loathe more than amateur detectives, and it implied that I didn't trust them to reach the right conclusion on their own. In any case, I had my own mission, and it was important to fight the temptation to interfere in other matters.

When we arrived at the village of N—, I made my way up to the driver's cab and explained that the train crew was now minus one member. I handed over the note containing the report of the murder · and the financial support for the conductor's family, and the driver assured me the matter would be dealt with as soon as he stopped somewhere that had a policeman.

The maid was still in the compartment, as useless as ever, sitting in a morose heap and glowering. I summoned a porter, who summoned a carriage, and before long we were trundling down a lime tree avenue to the countess's country mansion.

The carriage was visible from a long way off and by the time we arrived, the staff were lined up to greet us, led by a motherly housekeeper. As I was working out what to say, the maid emerged from the carriage, to be met by a collective groan.

"Nice to see you too," she jeered, strolling up and down the line like a sergeant-major, adjusting an apron here and a collar there. "As you can see from my clothes, I'm now one of the most important members of the household, the countess's personal assistant, which means you all have to do as I say."

This provoked a number of incredulous outbursts, which were quickly shushed by the more nervous members of the household.

"The countess sent me, her personal assistant, to personally accompany a real live princess who wants to visit the area," she went on. There were gasps of surprise and anticipation.

"Princess Tamsonova!" she announced and I stepped out of the carriage, reprising my fifth-year Shakespearean role as Cleopatra. There was a lot of bowing and curtseying but I distinctly heard someone say, "Her frock's not a patch on the maid's," which I suppose was only to be expected since the maid had purloined all the best ones.

She was barking out orders, getting the luggage unloaded, the coachman paid, tea and delicacies prepared, beds made up. The housekeeper, whose authority she was completely usurping, stood in disbelief until she remembered herself and brought me into the parlour. She was getting me settled with quiet efficiency when the maid bustled in.

"Get back to peeling potatoes," she snapped at the house-keeper. "You don't know how to look after a grand lady."

"She's looking after me perfectly well," I said, and the maid turned to me with a simper that made me feel quite nauseous.

"Oh, Highness, you are too good, too accepting of inferior service! I cannot let this lowly creature pollute your parlour any longer."

Before I could say anything, she had shooed the housekeeper out of the room and flopped down on an easy chair.

"I could do with some tea," I said.

The maid shrugged. "I'm a lady's maid, not a footman. Samovar's over there."

I had created a monster.

"Just remember, you don't get the other three roubles until my business here is satisfactorily concluded," I reminded her and she grudgingly poured me a glass of tea, as well as one for herself.

"I'm going to have a look round tomorrow," I said. "But I think you should stay in your room."

She began to protest.

"It's for your own safety," I wheedled. "What if that maniac has followed us and is planning another attempt on your life?" He would be making his way back to town and wouldn't be anywhere near the village of N——, but if the maid was confined to her room, it would greatly improve the quality of life for everyone else.

I could see warring emotions re-enact the battle of Waterloo on her face. Then Wellington triumphed and she decided that it would give her extra kudos if she was known to be at risk of assassination.

She went off to disseminate the information throughout the household. "Someone tried to kill me today!" I heard her announce in the corridor.

"Just one?" said the housekeeper in an undertone, coming back into the parlour to check that I had everything I needed.

"Pour yourself some tea and sit down," I said and she looked startled. This obviously didn't happen when the count and countess were in residence. She perched on the edge of a chair, holding the glass in front of her as though she was a toddler in an egg-and-spoon race.

"Have you worked long for the count and countess?" I asked.

"I worked for the count before he was married, which was very pleasant since he was never here," she said, and then realised this was a bit of a gaffe. "I don't mean any disrespect, madam, what with you being a friend of theirs."

"Not a friend," I said firmly. "An acquaintance."

She nodded, and settled into a more comfortable position in the chair. We understood each other.

"And then?" I prompted.

"And then came the incident of which we are forbidden to speak."

"Yes, I know all about it," I assured her.

"That meant the count and his new wife were obliged to live here. It has been a great relief to have them move back to town."

We contemplated this for a while, sighing companionably.

"Something else I wanted to ask you about," I said. "I want to find out about a young man, blond, blue-eyed, really gorgeous, the countess's protégé."

The housekeeper didn't snigger, presumably because she didn't know French. "A terrible business," she said. "I have never known such depravity."

I didn't need to ask her what she meant. I'd had glimmers of suspicion, but always steered away from them. Now I knew for sure. A guileless serf, too handsome for his own good, preyed on by the dissolute lady of the manor. I must save him, and get him safely married to Lidia.

"Am I right in thinking," I said delicately, "that all has not been well between the count and countess?"

"We are obviously forbidden to speak of it," said the housekeeper.

"Obviously," I nodded.

"But from the very beginning, nothing has been well between the count and countess because of the incident of which we are forbidden to speak."

I could see that the new bride, desperate to become a socialite in town, would be pretty miffed to discover she had to stay in the back of beyond. But that was no excuse for seducing serfs.

"If I wanted to find out more about the depravity, where should I start?" I asked.

The housekeeper put down her tea glass and stood up.

"I'm afraid, madam, that's not a matter with which I can help you."

"You misunderstand me," I said. "I'm not seeking any personal involvement in the depravity. I'm as shocked as you are by what's been going on, and I want to put a stop to it."

She dropped back into the chair. "You're a member of the Skoptsy, madam?"

I searched my memory: the Skoptsy were a weird extreme sect who went around campaigning against lust. But before I could assure her I wasn't an extremist about anything except feminism, she said, "I thought it was a myth that the female Skoptsy went to great lengths to avoid arousing passion in men, but looking at you, I see it is true. You should talk to the schoolmaster of N——, the most important man in the village. Apart from the priest, he is the only person who can read and write."

"He doesn't sound a very good schoolmaster if his pupils can't read and write," I said.

"Oh, save us, madam, he doesn't have any pupils—he's much too grand for that," said the housekeeper.

So I set off for the village, having warned the maid to stay indoors. She seemed happy enough, now wearing my second-best dress. The housekeeper was horrified that I was going to walk and wanted to call a carriage, but I had on my DMs and it was a sunny day. I definitely didn't need the fur coat and just put on a light pelisse that I found in my luggage. It struck me that Old Vatrushkin packed better with his eyes closed than the maid would have done with her eyes open.

It was a pleasant walk, along an isolated woodland path leading past a picturesque pond. When I reached the village, I made for the biggest house and knocked on the door. A flustered middle-aged woman appeared, clutching a feather duster.

"Hello," I said, "I'm looking for the schoolmaster."

"Dmitri Dmitrievich?"

"If that's the name of the schoolmaster, then that's the very chap," I said.

"Do you want him to read something for you, or to write something for you?" she asked.

It would be showing off to tell her about my literacy skills. "No, I just wanted a chat," I said. "I'm from town."

Her eyes grew large and she dropped the feather duster. "From town! I used to live in town. Is it still as beautiful?"

"It's very nice," I said. "Any chance of a word with Dmitri Dmitrievich?"

"Of course, of course! A chat, you say? So you're a visitor? In that case, let me show you to the drawing room. His study is for clients, not for visitors. Dmitri Dmitrievich! We have a visitor! Who wants a chat!"

An elderly man with spectacles and a long flowing beard emerged from what was presumably his study.

"A visitor, you say, wife? Who wants a chat?"

"Yes, this young lady!" The wife flung her arms wide as though she were a magician presenting a very large rabbit. Had she known the word, she would undoubtedly have said "ta-da!"

"How very remarkable," said the schoolmaster.

"Yes, isn't it? I said you would chat to her in the drawing room. I'll make tea." She turned to me, bursting with pride. "We have sugar."

The drawing room was small but very well dusted. The wife flung open her arms beside an armchair in another "ta-da!" moment, and I realised this was where I should sit.

"Very comfy," I said. Too overcome with delight to speak, she rushed off to make the tea.

The schoolmaster had chosen a plain wooden seat, more in keeping with his ascetic demeanour. "Now, young lady, what do you want to chat about?" he asked. "I can chat about astronomy, history, geology, moral philosophy and metaphysics—"

"Yes, I can chat about all these things too," I said, to reassure him that I wasn't a time waster. "But I want to ask you about a local serf."

"Ah yes," he said. "I know all of the local serfs. They come to me if there is something they need to have read or written. In other villages, they would go to the priest, but the priest here is a very inflexible man who does not believe in helping sinners."

How very unlike the Reverend John Thomson of Duddingston Kirk.

"It's one of the countess's serfs, a young man called Sasha."

The schoolmaster frowned behind his glasses. "I don't know any such young man."

"You must do. Sasha. Twenty years old."

The schoolmaster stroked his beard. "No. I do not know him."

"Twenty years old, unbelievably good-looking," I prompted.

He shook his head just as his wife reappeared with the tea and sugar. And there was simultaneously a rap at the front door. The wife took a step forward, then a step back, then another step forward. She'd have been a natural for the Gay Gordons.

"I'll see to it," said the schoolmaster testily. "You stay here with the visitor." He left to answer the door.

The wife beamed at me. "Clients are seen in the study. Visitors take tea in the drawing room."

Perhaps I would have better luck with her. "I'm enquiring about one of the countess's serfs, Sasha, twenty years old, unbelievably good-looking?"

She screwed up her face in concentration. "No," she said finally. "I don't know him."

I thought. There must be an explanation. There always was. Sasha could read and write, and must have been taught by the schoolmaster, since the priest didn't sound likely to have helped.

It must be another of these things that people were forbidden to speak of. The countess wouldn't want people knowing that she was having Sasha educated as part of her dastardly plan to take him into society with her. The wife was patently telling the truth —I wouldn't put it past the countess to have insisted that the literacy lessons were completely secret, to be concealed even from the schoolmaster's wife.

"I know you came to chat to my husband," she said, "but would it be all right for us to chat as well? I would so like to hear about town."

"What would you like to know?"

"Is it still big? With boulevards? Lots of people, lots of carriages?"

I nodded. She clasped her hands to her bosom. "Ah, that is exactly as I remember it."

"Where did you stay?" I asked.

"With a grand family," she said. "My husband was a tutor. But now he is a schoolmaster." A schoolmaster seemed to outrank a tutor in her hierarchy, so I said I was very happy for him.

"How did he come to change career?" I asked but she appeared to be distracted. I could very faintly hear the voices of the schoolmaster and his client, a man with a gruff bass voice, although I couldn't make out any words.

"That voice...I thought..." said the wife dreamily and then shook herself. "My son is in town," she said with sudden excitement. "Perhaps you have met him? His name is Aleksandr Dmitrievich. He is twenty years old and he is the most handsome man in the world."

Bless, I thought, mums and their sons, they always think they're perfect.

"Sorry," I said. "I haven't met him. But as I say, it's a big place."

"Perhaps you will meet him at some point. Perhaps you could give him a message from me? Tell him—tell him..." She burst into tears.

She was obviously distressed by the topic of her son. The best way to distract her was by changing the subject. I went back to the question she had never answered: "How did your husband come to change career?"

She burst into tears again. I leaned forward and patted her on the shoulder. "There, there. Have some more tea. With sugar."

She cheered up at the mention of sugar, the symbol of a prosperous household. "Ah, we had sugar all the time in town when my husband was tutor to the grand family! I remember it as though it were yesterday, even though it was twenty years ago. When we came here, I said, the first thing we do with these monthly payments is buy sugar."

"Monthly payments?" I said.

She dropped her gaze. "I've said too much."

Or, from my point of view, not enough.

"So what's your son doing in town?" I asked.

She burst into tears again.

"He left us!" she wept. "He overheard us talking, and he was so angry that he walked out. With that dreadful woman."

That's the other thing about mums with sons. They just can't stand the girlfriends. Nobody's ever going to be good enough for their wee boy. The lad had heard his mum being rude about the woman he loved so he'd made his choice and left home. I couldn't blame him.

The schoolmaster came back into the room. "A simple note. As always. There is never anything to test my scholarship." He noticed his weeping wife. "I told you," he hissed, "we can keep hens."

"But there won't be enough money for sugar!" she wailed.

"Sugar's actually quite bad for you," I said. "Most experts now agree that it's worse than fats, even saturated ones."

The schoolmaster sat down on the hard chair again. "Shall we resume our chat?"

I had all the information I needed. Sasha had been groomed by the countess and taught in secret by the schoolmaster. But out of politeness, I stayed for another fifteen minutes and chatted about astronomy. There was a difficult moment when I mentioned the moon landings and the schoolmaster flatly refused to believe it, but you get that all the time with people who think the Apollo programme was filmed in a studio by Stanley Kubrick.

"Well, this has been lovely," I said. "But I must get back. I'm staying at the countess's."

The wife burst into tears again and ran out of the room.

"We do not mention that woman's name in this house," said the schoolmaster severely. It must be some weird village protocol not to speak of the lady of the manor, like not looking film stars in the eye on set.

"Sorry. It's been very nice chatting with you. Please thank your wife for the tea and sugar. If you're going into livestock farming, you should consider pigs as well as hens, and that will bring in enough to buy as much sugar as she needs."

He stroked his beard thoughtfully. "A good suggestion. That will make her happy, or at least as happy as a mother can be who has lost her adopted son."

"I hadn't realised he was adopted," I said. "He's very lucky to have been brought up by such a nice couple and given a good start in life. Well done."

On the way back to the countess's, I gave myself a stern talking-to. What had I done, despite warning myself not to? I had assumed. I had assumed the schoolmaster's son had walked out over his mother's disapproval of his girlfriend. Did I have any evidence for that? No. Instead, he must have walked out because he had found his natural mother. That was the dreadful woman the schoolmaster's wife had been referring to.

I was still berating myself as I approached the countess's mansion. The housekeeper emerged and ran towards me, her face haggard.

"Dreadful, dreadful news, madam!" she gasped.

"Good heavens. What?"

"Your beautiful coat!" she gabbled. "It is ruined, completely ruined."

"What happened to it?"

"It got utterly soaked."

"That's a pity," I said. "I suppose that's fake fur for you. It was probably dry clean only."

"It's all the fault of that wretched maid!" said the housekeeper.

This surprised me. I would have thought the maid's strict views on demarcation would have prevented her from doing any laundry.

"Still," I said, "it was nice of her to try to clean it."

"She was doing nothing of the kind!" said the housekeeper. "She was wearing it when she drowned herself. We did everything we could when we dragged her out of the pond, but it was no good—the coat will never be the same."

CHAPTER 10

"Did you say 'drowned herself'?" I asked cautiously.

"Yes, but please don't upset yourself, madam—I shall take over her duties while you remain with us."

"Why would she drown herself?" I went on. I was going to say, "She always seemed so cheerful", but it would have been less than accurate.

The housekeeper snorted. "Why indeed? That girl was a law unto herself." She rummaged in her apron. "But perhaps this will help, madam. She left a suicide note, kindly written for her by the schoolmaster, but of course none of us can read. Perhaps you can help us?"

I unfolded the crumpled piece of paper and found a note written in a clear, bold hand. I read it aloud: *My many sins are too much to bear. Goodbye, cruel world.*

The housekeeper sniffed. "An appropriate note, at least."

"What were her many sins?" I asked, intrigued.

"You met her, madam," said the housekeeper. "Cheeky, lazy, greedy, sulky, snobbish, churlish."

One more, and she could have been a septet of dwarves.

"And she was guilty of the sin of pride," the housekeeper went on. "She put on your beautiful fur coat, despite my remonstrances, and said she was going to the village to show everyone how important she now was. I've never known a more sinful creature."

I pointed out that she actively seemed to revel in her behaviour. I hadn't got the impression that her sins had weighed heavily on her, certainly not enough to drive her to suicide.

"Perhaps she had a visitation from an angel," the housekeeper suggested.

"Perhaps," I said. People round here seemed tremendously keen on angels. "So have you informed her family?"

The housekeeper seemed surprised. "But we all know."

"Yes, you all know, but don't you think you should inform her family?"

"I'm sorry, madam, I don't quite understand. We all know—me, her father and her sisters. Ah, of course, madam, you're not aware of our various duties. My husband is a gardener and my other daughters work in the laundry. Nobody is far away in the fields, so the news got round us quickly."

It takes a lot to surprise me. This was a lot. "You're her mum?"

"Please don't think badly of me, madam," said the housekeeper. "I don't know where she got it from."

I began to offer her my condolences, but she brushed them aside.

"Thank you, madam, but that's not necessary. None of us could stand her. When she was a baby, I left her on the steps of the convent. But after a week, the nuns brought her back. They said if I tried it again, they'd get the priest to excommunicate me."

"Well, at least let me help pay for the funeral," I said.

"Oh, madam, there will be no funeral. The priest would never allow such a thing for a suicide. No, madam, she will be deposited in an unmarked grave in unhallowed ground."

That didn't sound at all fair. I decided to go back to the village and have a word with this priest of theirs.

I walked along the woodland path until I reached the pond. It seemed quite shallow. But if the maid had been absolutely determined, I knew it was possible to drown in 30 millimetres of water. I went over to the edge to check how deep it was.

And then something cannoned into me, and I fell in. The pond was definitely deeper than 30 millimetres. And what had cannoned into me was a person, a person who was forcing my head underwater and was determined to keep it there. If I had realised in advance, I would have taken a gulp of air before I went under, and then I would have been fine—I have excellent lung capacity. But I had had my mouth open in surprise, and had already ingested enough water to finish off most people. As the grip on my head and neck tightened, I knew I was drowning. My life flashed in front of me, much of it consisting of walking across the platform at prize-givings.

But I couldn't die. I was on a mission. I had to get back to town and ensure that Lidia married Sasha. One thought reverberated in my increasingly waterlogged brain: *Save me, Miss Blaine!* And the answer came ringing back: *Save yourself.*

I kicked downwards and my feet touched the bottom, the DMs giving me valuable purchase. I thrust an elbow into my assailant's solar plexus, and with a grunt, he relaxed his hold for a fraction of a second. It was long enough. I manage to twist round, clawing at his face, aiming for his eyes. Instead, my fingers closed on the tangle of a beard. I grasped and tugged.

And then I was rolling over and over, my assailant having shoved me aside as he escaped into the woods. I was still holding the beard.

It would have been a vital clue in an era of DNA testing, but all I could do was leave it for a bird to make a nest out of it. I felt quite shocked. Someone had just tried to murder me. But why? Nobody had any reason to take such exception to me.

My dress was soaking and I was covered in mud. I could go back to the house to change, but I was already halfway to the village. A brisk walk would dry things out a bit—it's an old wives' tale that going out in damp clothes with wet hair gives you a cold, since a cold is an airborne virus. I covered up the worst of the damage with my pelisse, which had fallen off when I was propelled into the water. Had I been at home, I would certainly have reported the matter and would probably have booked a therapeutic massage, but I was on a mission with a deadline, and had no time to waste feeling sorry for myself just because someone had tried to murder me.

When I eventually reached the church, it looked in much more need of repair than I did, which gave me an idea. The priest might be theologically hard-line but hopefully he was fiscally flexible.

He certainly didn't look friendly when he answered the door, noting my crumpled muddy clothes with distaste. "You have disturbed my meditation," he snapped.

I was going to say that meditation was supposed to calm you down, so he must be doing it wrong, but that wouldn't be the best start.

"Sorry, Padre," I said. "I'm not one of your parishioners, but there's something I'd like to ask you."

With obvious reluctance, the priest beckoned me into a gloomy parlour. There were two armchairs, but with a disapproving snort, he pulled out a rickety wooden stool for me to sit on.

"Actually," I went on, "I'm not even of your faith, but I have the greatest respect for spiritual leaders. Not of mad cults, obviously, but you're not anything unorthodox. Obviously."

He gave an impatient riffle of his breviary. "What do you want?"

"Nothing much. I'd just like to book you for a funeral."

"But why have you come to me? Nobody in the parish has died or is on their deathbed." He frowned. "Apart from...not five minutes ago, I had word of a shocking act of self-destruction."

Apparently news got round a small village almost as fast as it did in Morningside.

"Yes," I said. "The maid. I'd like her to get a decent send-off. I wouldn't dream of insulting you by offering you a fee, but I'd be happy to make a very generous donation to your onion dome fund."

"Apostate! Do you think you can bribe me into heresy?"

"Perish the thought. But your church looks as though it could do with a wee bit of refurbishment, and how about a nice Bokhara rug for in here? It would cheer the place up."

The priest rose to his feet. "Avaunt!" he bellowed, pointing to the door.

I didn't move. "Sit down, Reverend, and let's finish our conversation. On the great day of judgment, you wouldn't want to be found to have made a mistake, would you?"

The priest's brow furrowed. "What do you mean?"

"You're refusing the maid a Christian burial because you assume she killed herself. But you don't know that she killed herself."

A look of cunning came over his face. "I don't know that she didn't," he said.

"Precisely. This is one of these cases where we have to go on the balance of probabilities. So let's go over what might have happened."

My mind raced. Somehow, I had to take the facts, and mould them into a plausible case for the maid not having killed herself.

"When she joined me at the station to come here, she was terrified. She said a man had been following her, a big, sinister man. And this man subsequently burst into our compartment with a knife and tried to stab her to death. It could have been this very same man who drowned her in the lake."

"What nonsense is this? Who was this man? Why would he want to murder someone as unimportant as a maid?"

I knew this one. "He was working for the countess," I said. "Or possibly the count. The countess was jealous of the maid, because the maid was in love with the count."

The priest raised his eyes to heaven. "Now I know you are mad. Nobody is in love with the count, not even the countess. Especially not the countess. She would not have been jealous of her maid."

"Well, maybe not jealous," I conceded. "Maybe just cross. She'd already emancipated her."

"Then she had already got rid of her. Why would she want to murder her?"

This line of argument wasn't going down at all well. I had to think even faster and mould the facts into a different shape. "She didn't!" I said in triumph. "She wanted to murder me!"

"Why would she want to murder you?"

I thought faster and faster. "I'm foreign?" I suggested. "Oh, and I've inadvertently humiliated her publicly several times, in front of the princess."

The priest stroked his beard thoughtfully. "Go on, my child."

Faster than a missile from a Trident submarine. "There's no doubt that the countess, or possibly the count, sent him after me."

"Why would the count want you dead?"

"He got a bit annoyed with me when I caught him cheating at cards."

The priest crossed himself and broke into prayer.

"Anyway," I continued, "let's say the countess hired the big sinister man. When he was following the maid, she was wearing my dress and bonnet. He thought she was me. Yesterday, she went out wearing my coat. He thought she was me and drowned her."

I was quite pleased. This sounded even more convincing than my first narrative.

"But she left a suicide note," said the priest.

"A note that wasn't signed. It could have been supposed to come from me just as easily as from her."

"True. It referred to many sins," said the priest with malice. "You look to me like a hardened sinner."

I considered reminding him that casting stones was on the banned list, but didn't want to antagonise him further.

"Another thing about the note," I remembered. "It couldn't have been written by her because she couldn't write."

"Of course she couldn't write. Nobody here can write except the schoolmaster and myself. She went to the schoolmaster to get him to write it for her."

"That's just ridiculous," I said. "If she had dictated a suicide note to him, he would have intervened, warned the rest of you, got her some counselling."

The priest looked scandalised. "The schoolmaster is a man of utter rectitude! He might act as amanuensis but he would never dream of reading a private note."

"Well, I can assure you she didn't go to the schoolmaster," I said confidently. "She was with me from the time we arrived in the village until I went to see the schoolmaster, and she was dead by the time I got back. She couldn't have…" Then I paused, uncertain, remembering the visitor.

The priest noticed my hesitation and was on it like a ferret up a kilt. "What have you failed to tell me?"

"The schoolmaster did have a visitor, somebody who wanted something written. But it was a man."

The priest gave a nasty smile. "Someone sinful enough to take her own life would not hesitate to disguise herself."

"Really, I'm sure it wasn't her." But my certainty was wavering. I clutched at another argument.

"I've just remembered something else. I was walking past the pond just now, and somebody tried to drown me. That's why I'm looking a bit bedraggled. He had a beard and I grabbed it and it came away in my hand. The big sinister man had a beard. It could have been fake. So that proves it was me he was trying to murder in the first place."

Even to me, it sounded far-fetched.

The priest shook his head. "What a remarkable capacity for delusion you have. I advise you to go home and repent."

"I know you're not totally convinced, but could you not make an exception just this once? Go on. Nobody need know."

The priest raised an accusatory arm. "Now I know you for what you are! You are the Evil One, sent to tempt me!"

"Now who's got a remarkable capacity for delusion?" I demanded. "I haven't exactly got a forked tail and cloven hooves."

The priest shook his head. "The Evil One can take many forms to deceive us. I know of a priest in town who was summoned by one of the finest families to discuss the sacrament of baptism. As soon as he saw the infant, he knew. 'You have been deceived into thinking that this is an innocent new-born babe,' he said, 'but it is the Evil One himself. I have never been in the presence of such evil. You must destroy it immediately.'"

I was indignant. "Destroy a wee baby? I've never heard anything so outrageous!"

"It was the embodiment of every diabolic wickedness. As soon as it heard the priest's words, its eyes glowed red and it vomited green bile."

I was going to tell him that his colleague had been conflating *The Omen* and *The Exorcist* when I remembered that cinematography didn't emerge until the 1890s. A book might make its way through the ether, but it was unlikely that an entire home cinema system would.

"So what happened?" I asked.

"This was a righteous, God-fearing family, so of course they destroyed the child. Had they kept it, it would have cunningly learned to control its outward appearance so that nobody knew of its inner iniquity. Much the same as you have done."

The whole thing sounded to me like a priestly urban myth. But this man was so rigid in his views that nothing would ever persuade him he was mistaken. Despite my best efforts, I had been unable to come up with a convincing story. For once, I was going to have to admit defeat. I stood up to leave.

"Yes, go. Who do you think you are, to come and disturb me?" snapped the priest.

"Just someone trying to do a little good as I pass through, Padre," I said. "Long story short, not only am I not of your faith, I'm not of your country. I'm from Scotland."

"Scotland?" The priest looked alarmed and crossed himself. "The land of John Knox?"

"That's the bunny. Sorry, that's just an expression. Not appropriate in this case, since he wasn't exactly cuddly and fluffy. More like a raging lion, seeking whom he could devour."

"That is from the scriptures! You know the scriptures?"

"I know more or less everything," I said. And then I felt I had to elaborate, remembering the litany of the maid's alleged sins. "That's not the sin of pride, by the way, it's a simple statement of fact. I had a very good education. Oh, listen, you'll like this one—a minister is preaching to his flock, and he says, 'Miserable sinners that you are, you'll all be burning in the fires of hell and suffering agonising torments, and you'll look up at the Almighty in heaven, and you'll say "Lord, Lord, we didn't know!" And the Lord will look down upon you and in his infinite mercy and compassion, he'll say, "Yes, well, you know now."'"

I waited for the priest to laugh, but he was just staring at me, his eyes bulging.

"Just a wee Presbyterian joke there," I explained. "It's actually a lot funnier when you hear it in Scots but I didn't know how to translate it."

He crossed himself. "John Knox! Presbyterianism! How can I save my flock?" he moaned.

"Sorry?" I said.

"What can I do to persuade you?" he gabbled. "I will do anything, anything at all, if you leave my humble, insignificant parish in peace, and proselytise elsewhere. There is a much more wicked parish in the village of Y—, not fifty versts from here."

I leaned back in my chair and stared thoughtfully into the middle distance. "Oh, I don't know about that," I said. "I'm on a mission to convert the whole country. I wouldn't be doing my job properly if I left this bit unpurified."

"Please, I beg you, there must be some way I can persuade you to pass us by?"

I pondered. "No, don't think so. Right then, I'm off to call a meeting in the village hall, and judging by my past results, they'll all be good Calvinists by the end of the day. Bye, Reverend. Nice meeting you."

I hadn't got halfway to the door before the priest cried, "Wait! I implore you—what if I hold a funeral for the maid?"

I wrinkled my nose. "The maid? I'm not really bothered about her any more. I'll just get on with my converting."

"I will give her the finest funeral anybody has ever seen," coaxed the priest. "Everyone will attend."

"Absolutely everyone?" I said.

"I swear it on the holy icon of Saint Basil the Blessed, Fool for Christ."

"Including her mum and dad and sisters and the schoolmaster and his wife?"

"All of them!"

"Even if they don't want to come?"

"I will threaten them with excommunication if they are not present."

"I really shouldn't...but all right," I said.

I had promised the maid another three roubles when she had successfully convinced the countess's household that I was a princess. She had fulfilled her part of the bargain. I handed a banknote to the priest.

"Here's three roubles. Organise her a nice catafalque and keep the change."

The priest crossed himself and clasped his hands in prayer. "And you promise that if I do all this, you will leave us in peace and unconverted?"

"I'll be off on the first train tomorrow morning, your Autocephalousness," I said. "Pleasure doing business with you."

When I got back to the house, I found everyone was dressed in mourning, which I thought was really nice, considering they all claimed they didn't like the maid.

"That was quick," I said. "How did the message reach you so fast?"

"The message came by the speediest horse available." It must have come along the main road while I went back through the woodland path. "But how did you find out, madam?"

"I got it straight from the horse's mouth," I said. I thought it was a pretty good joke, but the housekeeper looked baffled. The idiom must be different in Russian.

"It's just an expression," I said. "Anyway, I'm glad you all know. It sounds as though it will be a spectacular funeral, with everybody there. More of a celebration really."

The housekeeper stifled a gasp, and I reflected that the concept of a funeral celebrating a life well lived or, in the maid's case, a life tetchily lived, was probably not yet generally accepted.

"Sorry, I shouldn't have said that."

"I'm honoured that you feel able to speak so freely in front of me, madam," said the housekeeper.

"And I'm happy you're honoured. Anyway, I'm leaving first thing tomorrow, so I'll just go and pack."

"But you have no maid, thanks to my wretched daughter's thoughtlessness. Let me come and help you."

The housekeeper proved quick and efficient, cast in the same mould as Old Vatrushkin.

"Such a tragedy, such a tragedy," she muttered. "Your poor fur coat."

"You know what would be nice?" I said. "I think the maid should be buried in it."

"That beautiful coat in an unmarked grave? Excuse me, madam, but how could you suggest such a thing?"

I stopped in the middle of folding up an afternoon dress. "But it's not an unmarked grave. She's having the finest funeral anybody has ever seen, remember?"

The housekeeper dropped a spare pelisse. "The priest has agreed?"

"Of course," I said. "That was what I was talking about when I came in. What were you talking about? Why are you all in mourning?"

"Why, madam, because the count is dead."

CHAPTER

11

"Dead?" I repeated. "Another duel?"

The housekeeper shook her head. "The countess's bust."

"Ah well," I said, remembering how the general had got wedged in her cleavage, "I suppose he died happy."

"His skull was split open like a watermelon," said the housekeeper. "They think he dropped his pen on the study floor and when he went to pick it up, he accidentally nudged the table and dislodged the bust."

The marble bust. I had been in the count's study. I had seen that bust. I had tried to move it and I knew it couldn't be dislodged accidentally. The count must already have been lying helpless on the floor when someone dragged the bust to the edge of the desk and let it fall on him. This had been deliberate. But who would want the count dead?

"Tell you what," I said. "You've been working so hard at sorting out my packing. Why don't you sit in that easy chair and we'll have a nice glass of tea together."

I summoned the serving maid, who poured the tea and gave us each a dessert bowl filled with *kutia*, a delicious cracked wheat and poppy seed pudding that always goes down well at Russian funerals.

I took a spoonful. "I'm sorry I can't stay for your daughter's send-off," I said.

The housekeeper snorted. "You're lucky. We've had a message from the priest telling us we've all got to be there. Still, at least there's more pudding to look forward to."

The serving maid had now left and I felt able to speak confidentially. "I sort of gave you a bit of a wrong impression when I arrived. The countess doesn't actually know I'm here."

"I don't understand, madam. Then how could the countess have given you her maid to accompany you?"

"Because the maid wasn't her maid any more—the countess emancipated her."

The housekeeper's hand flew to her mouth. "No!"

"Yes, and then I gave her a job."

"She became your serf? And you allow her to be buried in your beautiful coat? You are truly the kindest owner anyone could wish for! On behalf of my wretch of a daughter, I thank you."

"Speaking of owners, how do you find the countess?"

The housekeeper's lips tightened. "She is a monster. She cares for nothing and nobody. She came from a country family and married the count only in order to win status and position and live in town. She blamed her husband for the unfortunate incident we are forbidden to speak of that obliged them to live in the country. She never forgave him, and she made all our lives a misery. It was a blessing for us when he was finally pardoned and could go back to town."

"Still, that's pretty rough, having to wait twenty years for a pardon."

"He would never have bothered asking if it hadn't been for her," said the housekeeper. "Nag, nag, nag, say you're sorry to his imperial majesty, and after twenty years of her going on and on about it every day, he finally cracked and apologised. The tsar sent him the most generous reply imaginable: he said he'd realised just afterwards that he'd mistaken a nine for a seven and that the count hadn't cheated at all. And now that the count had apologised for his outrageous insolence, he could come back to town any time he liked."

I stopped eating the *kutia*. "So you're telling me he needn't have been in exile here for twenty years? If he'd apologised at the time, he could have stayed in town? More to the point, the countess could have been living in town twenty years ago?"

"Exactly."

"She must have been livid."

The housekeeper shuddered. "It was horrible."

"Do you think she was angry enough...to murder him?" I waited to let my words sink in.

The housekeeper paled. "She was certainly remarkably cross."

I leaned forward confidentially. "She couldn't get rid of him before now. She needed him to be unexiled so that she could install herself in their palace in town. You should see it, by the way."

"I can imagine," said the housekeeper. "That woman wouldn't know good taste if it was floating in her borshch."

"Then," I went on, "once they were in town and she was launched into polite society, she didn't need him any more."

The housekeeper nodded. "Murdering her husband sounds exactly the sort of thing she would do. She's a most unpleasant woman."

"And then of course there's Sasha."

The housekeeper stifled a guffaw.

I hadn't even said protégé. "I don't think that's a very appropriate response," I said tartly. "Manipulating someone for your own ends, it's not decent."

"Maybe not, but it was still very funny watching him get the countess to take him to town. He played her like an accordion."

"Pardon?" I said.

"Yes, it was the pardon. The instant Sasha discovered the count had been pardoned, that was it. The maid didn't stand a chance."

"Sorry?" I said.

"The maid. My wretched daughter. The one nobody liked. The one he seduced."

"No!" I said. This was impossible.

"Yes. He used her to get to the countess. Being the maid's lover gave him an excuse to hang around here and he was always putting himself in the countess's line of sight. Lumbered with a misery guts like the count, of course she was going to fall for a handsome young lad like him."

"But that's not how it was," I protested. "The countess groomed him. He was her passport into society."

"And she was his passport into society."

This was making no sense at all. "So did he work far away in the fields?" I asked.

"Why would he work in the fields?"

"Bringing in the harvest?" I suggested. "Planting maize? Sorry, I haven't really paid attention to what kind of fields you have round here." Whatever type of serf he had been, he couldn't have worked in the house or he wouldn't have needed the maid to get himself noticed by the countess. And how on earth had he learned to read and write so quickly?

"Bless you, madam, the schoolmaster's son doesn't work in the fields," the housekeeper said.

It must be some sort of couthy aphorism, denoting acceptance of the status quo and condoning class privilege. "We're all the children of Jock Tamson," I rejoined.

We stared at each other for a while. Then, slowly, so that she would understand, I said, "I was just wondering what kind of serf Sasha is."

And equally slowly, she responded, "Sasha is not a serf, he is the son of Dmitri Dmitrievich, the schoolmaster."

"I'm talking about Sasha," I said. "Blond hair, blue eyes, chiselled cheekbones, totally stunning."

She nodded.

The schoolmaster's wife had talked about her son, Aleksandr Dmitrievich. The pet name for Aleksandr was Sasha. It seemed we were indeed talking about the same person. This was good news. Lidia had said she would be prepared to marry a serf for love, but a schoolmaster's son must be a few rungs up the social ladder.

The housekeeper had, however, got one thing terribly wrong. It was quite impossible that someone so guileless and transparent as Sasha could have considered seducing the maid and the countess. He was the victim here. I wouldn't put it past the countess to have set up the maid as a honey-trap, although that just proved what a poor judge of character she was.

"Right," I said, finishing off the last spoonful of pudding, "let's get on with the packing."

"May I ask one last thing, madam?" asked the housekeeper. "Why did the countess emancipate my wretch of a daughter?"

I hesitated. It was wrong to speak ill of the dead—but it was also important to tell the truth.

"I'm afraid your daughter was chasing after the count."

The housekeeper shook her head. "Never. She was cheeky, lazy, greedy, sulky, snobbish and churlish. But she wasn't dopey."

The housekeeper certainly was, with these crazy theories about Sasha. Thank goodness I was there to separate fact from fantasy.

But I still felt I hadn't quite worked out everything. On the train back to town the next morning, I sat back on the sofa, listening to the soothing rumbling of the journey, and letting my subconscious take over from my rational mind. You can get so far with rationality, but the subconscious is not to be sneezed at. I half-dozed, half-meditated as the versts went by, five, ten, fifteen, twenty. Twenty.

I sat bolt upright. Of course. All had become obvious, just as Miss Blaine had said it would. Sasha was twenty. The countess had got married twenty years ago. The countess was Sasha's mother. I was slightly hazy on the precise details, but since Sasha didn't live with the countess, he must have been the result of an indiscretion before the countess married the count. She had placed her baby with parents who lived nearby so that she could watch him grow up, paying them monthly to ensure he was well looked after. He had heard his adoptive parents discussing these payments, and had sought out his birth mother, who realised it was time he took his rightful place in society. Now that he had moved out, the countess had cancelled the payments, and then gone on to murder the count to avoid embarrassing explanations.

I'd thought the countess was an obnoxious, pretentious egomaniac. But now I understood that she had simply been fraught at social events, worried about the impression her wee boy was making. The next time I saw her, I would apologise for thinking badly of her. All I had to do was reconcile her to the idea of Lidia as a daughter-in-law, which should be no problem given Lidia's fabulous wealth and the fact that she was now a favourite of the princess.

Getting Lidia onside would be no problem. All she had to do was be in love with Sasha, and who could fail to be in love with Sasha? Nanny would be sniffy about the illegitimacy element, but with the count out of the way, Sasha could be presented as the long-lost legitimate heir.

I had worked it all out in the nick of time and would complete my mission today with a day to spare. Miss Blaine would be proud of me.

The train pulled up and I remembered I was going to see if newspapers were being published again, so that I could find out the date. I clambered down from the carriage with my luggage— no need to look for a porter, I can bench press 80 kilos—and was just looking round for a newspaper vendor when a bearded figure hurtled down the platform towards me.

Instinctively, I went into a forward combat roll and felled my assailant with a hammerfist strike.

"Welcome home, your excellency," choked Old Vatrushkin. "Seeing your excellency is the boys."

I knelt down beside him. "Old Vatrushkin! I could have really hurt you."

Old Vatrushkin tried to gulp in some air and winced. "Let me reassure your excellency that you have indeed really hurt me."

I helped him to his feet and let him hang on to me until he caught his breath. I seemed to be suffering from PTSD, going into automatic defence mode at the sight of big beardie blokes.

"Why on earth did you run at me like that?" I demanded.

"I could not let you carry your own portmanteaux," he said. But he had to, since every time he tried to hoist them onto his shoulders, he buckled at the knees. I regretted having hit him quite so hard. I got him on the driving seat of the drozhky and warned him that if he didn't stop apologising, I might consider smacking him again.

"So you were just passing?" I asked as we set off.

"Yes," he said, "a very happy coincidence."

"Anything been happening while I was away?" I said casually.

"I don't know, your excellency," he replied and then realised he had fallen into my trap.

My voice was as silky as a very silky silkworm. "But coachmen know everything. Surely something must have happened? Could it be—and please correct me if I'm wrong—that you've been waiting outside the station since I left? Despite the fact that you were supposed to be painting?"

"Please don't be angry with me, your excellency!" he begged. "My job is to be your coachman. Painting is merely my hobby."

"You're never going to get anywhere with that attitude," I said. "If you organise things so that your hobby's your job, you need never work another day in your life. Anyway, let's see what wages I owe you. That's at least twelve hours at twenty kopecks an hour—let's just call it three roubles and have done with it."

"No, your excellency," he protested. "You have already given me far too many coins for what your excellency describes as working antisocial hours."

"No more coins, I promise," I said, shoving the three-rouble note in his coat pocket.

An ornate carriage approached in the other direction. "My dear Princess Tamsonova!" came a patrician voice. "I have the most extraordinary news! But perhaps you have already heard it from your coachman."

"No, Princess," I said. "My coachman seems to be surprisingly short of news right now."

A sob broke from Old Vatrushkin's lips.

"I'm just heading home after a trip to the country," I said. "Do you want to come in for a cup of tea?"

"That would be delightful. I have so much to tell you. A cup of tea would be—what do you say in your charming language?— the very dab. Coachman! Follow that drozhky."

The princess's coachman performed a reckless three-point turn, scattering pedestrians and street traders, and dislodging the footmen standing on the carriage's footboard.

When we arrived home, Old Vatrushkin leaped off the box so that he could meet the princess at the door as the major-domo, then sprinted past her up the marble stairs in order to be ready with tea and pastries by the time we reached the salon.

"I suppose this is the gardener?" she asked, not having any idea that she had seen him before.

"I work in the orangery, highness," he said.

"What a splendid idea! As soon as I get home, everyone working in my orangeries shall be a footman."

"And it's time for you to get back to the orangery," I said meaningfully. "And stay there. I'll pour the tea—I know how the princess likes it."

The princess took a mouthful of milky tea and smacked her lips. "Delicious. And such a welcome change from champagne. I drank so much champagne last night, I feel like..." She cast around for a suitable simile.

"A Nebuchadnezzar bottle from Veuve Clicquot?" I suggested, and she delved for paper and pencil and wrote it down.

"Darling Princess Tamsonova! You make me laugh more than..." She looked at me challengingly. A metaphor this time.

Had we been back home, I would immediately have said, "Someone at a laughing gas party," since nitrous oxide was used as a recreational drug among the smart set from 1799. But that was only in Britain. If a Russian princess knew about nitrous oxide at all, it would merely be as an analgesic during surgery and not a source of amusement.

"...a hyena being tickled by a centipede," I concluded.

It took her a while to write this down since I had to explain and spell both hyena and centipede. She might know her Scottish literature, but her knowledge of zoology was sadly lacking.

"So where was all this champagne drinking?" I asked.

"It was the most marvellous concert—the premiere of a sensational new orchestra. I had no intention of attending, but it turned out to be so popular that not a single ticket was to be had. So of course I insisted that they accommodate me. Let me see, there were four singers, a man with a violin, a man with a very big violin, and a man with a small piano attached to his chest," she said. "Oh, Princess Tamsonova, you would have loved it. They sang the most charming Scottish songs. And the conductor—a foreigner, but such an energetic young man, constantly waving his arms about. I'm sure I would have enjoyed it very much had I not had to concentrate on the champagne."

It was good to know that Pavel Pavlovich had carried out his side of the bargain, and got the band their gig with the fake Beethoven. I imagined they would be off on a European tour shortly, although probably not to Teutonic areas where people might pick up on the Bavarian accent.

"Ah, yes!" the princess went on. "I have not yet told you the extraordinary news!"

"Don't tell me," I said.

"But that is why I am here, to tell you."

"It's just an expression," I explained. "What I mean is that I've already guessed what you're going to tell me. Another lady has fallen downstairs."

"Yes, she fell, but not downstairs," said the princess. "These days, it is commonplace to fall downstairs. I told you this was extraordinary."

"You haven't told me who it was yet."

"Why, the countess."

"Is she all right?" I asked.

"Oh no," said the princess equably. "She is completely dead."

CHAPTER 12

The princess took some more tea. "It was so very dramatic," she said. "It quite put the concert in the shade. We were all obliged to have more champagne in order to recover from the shock."

"She was at the opera?" I said. "Just after her husband had died?"

"But of course," said the princess. "Black is particularly flattering to someone of her girth. And since she had inherited her husband's entire fortune, she had treated herself to a diamond tiara, which she was most anxious to show off."

"So what exactly happened?" I asked. "Cardiac arrest? Apoplexy? Cholera?"

"She toppled out of her box. Her embonpoint." The princess gestured. "Top-heavy. She must have seen an acquaintance in the stalls and leaned over to greet them."

"So the countess's bust killed both husband and wife," I said thoughtfully.

The princess shrieked with laugher. "Oh, Princess Tamsonova, I wish I'd said that!"

I watched her write it down. "You will, Princess, you will."

"It caused quite a stir—the concert had to be delayed by a quarter of an hour. When she landed, she crushed three members of the audience to death, but thankfully they were from the provinces, so no harm was done."

"That's a relief," I said. My egalitarianism was roused yet again, but the princess failed to pick up the ironic tone.

"The delay in beginning the concert was longer than it should have been, because a German doctor sitting nearby insisted on examining the body and claimed—imagine!—that she had not broken her neck in the fall but had previously been strangled with the cord from the curtains in her box. But nobody paid any attention to him. You know how hysterical Germans are as a race, and how prone to exaggerate every little thing."

I scarcely heard her. I was thinking of poor Sasha, so recently reunited with his birth mother and now bereaved.

"Princess, I'm going to be terribly rude, but there's something I have to do. Would you mind awfully if I asked you to leave?"

"Please, no apology is necessary," said the princess. "I must start immediately on my round of visits to regale everyone with my epigram on the countess's bust." She sighed. "So the count's fortune went to the countess and now there is nobody to pass it on to. My ghastly cousin the tsar will add another palace and more estates to his collection."

At least, I thought, that wasn't going to happen.

A letter of condolence is never easy to write, and it's particularly difficult when you aren't supposed to know about the relationship between the deceased and the bereaved. I would have to make it clear that nobody had told me anything they shouldn't, and that what I knew was the result of my own detective work. It was going to require very careful wording.

"*Dear Sasha,*" I wrote. "*This is a very sad day for you. I spoke to your adopted parents, who didn't deliberately betray any confidences, but I managed to work everything out. Everybody else will find out because of your sudden wealth and at last you can be seen for who you really are.*"

It could be embarrassing for him to explain his parentage so I thought I should offer to take that burden on myself. "*I'm prepared to tell everyone all about you,*" I wrote.

It might not be the most elegant of letters, but I was sure he would appreciate the obviously warm and sympathetic sentiments. And *de mortuis nihil nisi bonum.* I picked up the pen again and wrote: "*Your late mother was a lovely woman. Shona.*"

I blotted the ink, and was about to call Old Vatrushkin. Then, just in time, I realised my mistake. I couldn't possibly ask him to deliver the letter, given his irrational belief that Sasha was a homicidal maniac. I nipped out into the street and found a loitering urchin.

"How would you like to earn a couple of kopecks?" I asked.

The urchin leaned back against the wall and surveyed me from under hooded lids. "Whatcha looking for? Vodka? Opium?"

"I am looking," I said with great deliberation, "for someone to deliver a letter."

"Paying off your gambling debts, is it?" he said.

I reflected that it wasn't his fault that he had such a jaundiced view of humanity. He hadn't had the advantages of being brought up in Morningside and having had the finest education in the world.

"The letter," I said with even greater deliberation, "is a message of condolence to a young man who has just lost someone very close to him."

The urchin jerked upright, his eyes snapping open. "You mean Sasha? You don't waste no time, lady, do you?"

"You know Sasha?"

"Everyone knows Sasha! The countess's 'protégé.'" He sniggered loudly and I wondered yet again what it was about a perfectly innocent French word that provoked such a peculiar reaction. Perhaps to an uneducated child, anything in a foreign language would sound intrinsically humorous.

"Sasha's our hero," the urchin went on. "We all wanna be just like him when we grow up."

It was really heartening that a small urchin, whom I might have associated with larceny, criminality and possibly even psychopathic violence, aspired to be charming and well-mannered. And I should do what I could to facilitate that.

"First," I said, "we now refer to the late countess. Second, of course I haven't wasted any time in sending a message of condolence. It's important to console the bereaved as quickly as possible."

"Oh, no offence, lady. Good on you. You get in there while the other old dears are still looking for their specs, let alone their writing paper." He shot me a quick conspiratorial grin. "All I can say is you better be loaded. These 'protégés' don't come cheap." Sniggering loudly, he snatched the letter and a five-kopeck piece from my hand, and scampered off.

It was a pity I wasn't going to be around for longer, to teach him to speak properly. But my mission had only one more day to run. Now I had established that Sasha was of noble birth, and wealthy in his own right, all I had to do was get him engaged to Lidia.

I could scarcely invite him to tea today, just after the letter of condolence, but I could get them both round tomorrow and throw an engagement party.

Old Vatrushkin was just finishing washing up, and I ordered him to get on with his painting and not to come back under any circumstances. Then I went upstairs for some pianoforte practice.

In honour of the band, which had played Beethoven's *25 Schottische Lieder* to such great effect after the countess's demise, I adapted the score for piano and alto. I was just getting to *Old Scotia, wake thy mountain strain* when my superbly acute hearing caught the sound of quiet, almost stealthy footsteps coming up the stairs. I went out of the salon into the anteroom, preparing to yell at Old Vatrushkin for not painting.

"Sasha!" I said. "What a lovely surprise! Sorry you had to let yourself in. I've given Old Vatrushkin the rest of the day off, and I see he's been sensible enough to leave the front door open."

Sasha's usual attractive smile was missing, and I realised I had been far too jaunty in the way I had greeted someone who had just lost a parent. Adopting a more serious tone and expression, I said, "So you got my letter? Come and have some tea—tea's always good for shock." I ushered him into the salon.

There was the sound of more footsteps on the staircase, footsteps that were all too familiar.

"Excuse me a minute," I said, yet again leaving the salon for the anteroom. Old Vatrushkin stood there, his lamb's wool cap clutched in one hand and a letter clutched in the other.

This was seriously awkward. I couldn't possibly let him know that Sasha was in the salon. He would start going on about how my life was at risk, and create an appalling scene. I had to get rid of him as quickly as possible.

"Forgive me, your excellency!" he burst out. "I was just strolling nearby when a courier arrived with this letter and I felt it was my duty to bring it to you."

"Just strolling nearby?" I mimicked sarcastically.

"I thought…" he mumbled, handing me the letter, "I thought your excellency might need me."

I deliberately hardened my tone. It was the only language Old Vatrushkin understood. Apart from French and Latin.

"Do you remember what I said to you? That you were absolutely without question to take the rest of the day off to paint? You claimed you understood, but apparently you didn't. Is there any way I can make it clearer?"

Old Vatrushkin kept his eyes firmly on the ground, the lamb's wool cap turning round and round in his nervous fingers.

"Haven't you wondered," I asked, "where the maid is?"

Old Vatrushkin stopped kneading his lamb's wool cap and stood very still. "Emancipated?" he whispered.

"Let's just say my patience is not inexhaustible." I grabbed him by the elbow and propelled him down the stairs. Then I pushed him outside, saying, "Orangery," and locked the door behind him.

As I went back upstairs, I opened the letter and began reading. It was written in a clear, bold hand that I immediately recognised as the same as the maid's putative suicide note. So it *was* written by Dmitri Dmitrievich, the schoolmaster.

"*Dear Madam,*" it began, "*We hope you are well. We are all well and enjoyed the funeral for my wretch of a daughter, especially the pudding. Thank you for the catafalque. We have spoken to the schoolmaster (who with his wife sends you their very good wishes but of course is only writing this and not reading it) who confirms that it was a big, sinister, bearded man who came to ask him to write a note (which of course he did not read), not my wretch of a daughter. It is a great comfort to know that she was murdered and did not take her own life because we all loathed her and could cheerfully have murdered her. We would love to have you visit again but the priest says you must remember your promise never to return.*

Anisya Federovna, Housekeeper."

I remember thinking what a nice letter it was. I remember thinking that it was very rude of me to leave Sasha by himself in the salon. I remember a damp pungent cloth being clamped over my nose and mouth. My second-last thought, before I lost consciousness, was that this was another useful clue: chloroform, invented 1831. And my last thought was that if I hadn't been so star-struck over Beethoven, I would have remembered that he had died in 1827…

CHAPTER
13

It was the most wonderful dream. I was in the arms of one of Scotland's best known and accomplished actors who was covering my face in tender yet passionate kisses.

"No," I protested weakly, "I'm on a mission. We mustn't—"

Fortunately, he ignored me. But I gradually became aware of an unpleasant odour. The actor's talent and attractiveness couldn't mask intense halitosis. I tried to extricate myself but the kissing continued.

"Mission!" I protested. "Stop!"

My eyelids fluttered open and I found myself staring at the animated floormop, who was enthusiastically licking my face. When he saw me wake up, he stopped and panted, open-mouthed, releasing another miasma of bacteria.

I tried to shift to dislodge the malodorous creature. But I discovered that my arms and legs were firmly pinioned. There was no point in struggling; I would only exhaust myself. But what had happened to me? My mouth was dry and I felt nauseous. I was lying in the anteroom. That's where I had been, reading a letter. There had been something in it...yes, the maid hadn't drowned herself, a big, sinister beardie bloke had dictated the purported suicide note to the schoolmaster.

I had glimpsed something out of the corner of my eye... something odd, something I couldn't quite remember. I rolled over to look round the room but could see nothing that jogged my memory.

Tresorka jumped on top of me, wanting to play. And then I noticed another smell. Two other smells. Singed fur and smoke. The animated floormop appeared to be scorched round the edges.

"Tresorka, what happened to you?" I whispered. "Are you all right?" The floormop panted fetidly some more, his other end quivering to indicate tail-wagging. After the Countess's demise, nobody would take responsibility for the poor creature, and he had sought me out as his best source of help. Except I wasn't currently in a position to be that helpful.

The smell of smoke was becoming more intense. I rolled round to see that at the bottom of the marble staircase, flames were beginning to emerge from my wood-panelled bedroom and were illuminating the hallway.

"You ran through the fire to get to me?" I asked. "What a good dog!"

Tresorka was quivering so much that he was in danger of causing a draught, which would spread the blaze faster. But who had set the fire and tied me up? The prime suspects would have been the count and countess, but they were both deceased. And I had been alone in the house with Sasha after sending Old Vatrushkin off to the orangery.

It was then that the truth hit me. They say your blood runs cold, and despite the increasing heat as the fire crept up the staircase towards us, I shivered. I had been betrayed, betrayed even more badly than the school had been by Muriel Spark.

Old Vatrushkin, whom I had thought so devoted, whom I had thought was my friend, was nothing but a callous, calculating killer. And the reason was obvious. If I died, there was no will, and Old Vatrushkin would win the ultimate honour for a serf, being owned by the tsar.

I had told him where the duel was taking place: he was the one who had shot at me. He had been in hiding then, but he had been hiding in plain sight when I fell downstairs. He tried to convince me that Sasha was strangling me, but it had been him all the time. The hands round my throat had been his, and he had attacked Sasha for trying to protect me.

Then there was the maid. She had never been the assassination target—I was. Old Vatrushkin had got on the train with us, wearing that ludicrous fake beard to conceal his own hirsuteness. Then, after mistakenly drowning the maid, he attempted to drown me. That was why he didn't know what had been happening in town—he hadn't been in town. And that was why I had gone into defensive mode when I saw him at the station. At a subliminal level, I knew Old Vatrushkin was a very bad man.

Now, with diabolical cunning, he had left me trussed up like a wild boar to be roasted alive. My bonds would be burned as well as me, and in an era before proper forensic investigation, people would just assume the fire was caused by a faulty domestic appliance such as a samovar or, worse, that I'd been smoking in bed.

If Tresorka hadn't managed to rouse me from my chloroformed daze, it might have been too late. In fact, it might still be too late. I would be incinerated if I stayed here at the top of the stairs. My only hope was to reach the salon and try to close the double doors behind me. The salon. Sasha had been in the salon. What had Old Vatrushkin done to him?

I couldn't waste more time trying to loosen my bonds. With a vigorous eel-like motion, I juddered my way along the floor of the anteroom into the salon, Tresorka frolicking around me and over me. I got through the doors and slammed them with an effortful kick.

"Sasha!" I called. There was no reply. I rolled this way and that, scanning every part of the room, but there was no sign of him. I forced myself not to imagine what terrible fate might have befallen him. He was brave, he was strong, he was resourceful. He would have escaped Old Vatrushkin's murderous attack and was probably even now alerting whatever rudimentary emergency services there were.

But as the fire continued to take hold, I couldn't wait. The windows. I had to break the windows. And first I had to free myself. I could easily smash the glass with my DMs, but the individual panes were too small for me to get through. I needed my hands to open an entire sash. And then I was faced with the conundrum of how to get from the first-floor window ledge to the ground without going splat. There was another imperative as well, arguably more important than saving my own life—saving Tresorka.

Smoke was beginning to creep into the room. I knew it was important to keep as close to the floor as possible to avoid smoke inhalation, so it was quite useful not to be able to get to my feet. I struggled as forcefully as I could against the ropes binding me, but there was no give whatsoever. Tresorka, who was obviously much smarter than the average lapdog, got behind me and started trying to nibble through them, but it was immediately apparent that his minuscule teeth would have no effect.

I was lying there beginning to feel quite sorry for myself when my gaze fell on the golden samovar. The golden samovar adorned with an eagle with a razor-sharp beak. I congratulated myself on my foresight in forbidding Old Vatrushkin to file it down.

I zig-zagged over to it and managed to haul myself into a kneeling position, my arms still tightly tied behind me. My knowledge of first aid had made me very aware that severing an artery was a serious matter, so I raised my wrists up extremely carefully to the eagle's beak and started rubbing the rope against it. The smoke was thickening, my lungs protesting, but I forced myself to go slowly. Haste could result in the loss of one or more fingers. And if I escaped with my life, I still wanted to be able to play the piano.

I shot a brief, regretful look at the pianoforte, which was about to be immolated. I thought back to how I had played it that first evening in my new home, and, scarcely realising what I was doing, I began to hum the school song. The majestic, inspiring tune gave me the perfect rhythm to rub the ropes against the cuspidate beak. And at the third repetition of Marcia Blaine's name, the bonds round my wrists gave way, and I was able to unfasten the ropes round my ankles. I ripped up the nearest cushion cover, soaking it in water from the samovar and holding it over my nose to help my breathing. Tresorka, who was as close to the ground as possible without being an actual rug, was doing much better.

I staggered to the window, wrestled with the catch, opened it and looked out. The classical dimensions of the house meant it was a very long way to the ground.

Someone was looking back up at me. "Your house is on fire," said Nanny.

"Yes, thank you, Nanny, I'm aware," I said. "There's a dog here that needs rescuing. Could you hold out your apron, and I'll throw him down."

Nanny clutched the corners of her apron as tightly as possible. I kissed Tresorka on the nose, told him everything was going to be all right, and then flung him out of the window with the élan of my winning ace during the school tennis championships. Tresorka landed in the apron, bounced slightly, landed back in the apron again, licked Nanny's hand, and then scrambled out onto the ground, looking up expectantly at me.

I could scarcely try the same tactic myself or I would squash Nanny as comprehensively as the countess had squashed the visitors from the provinces.

And then inspiration struck. "Nanny," I said, "have you got your knitting?"

Nanny flourished her needles, from which hung a very small amount of work. "I'm knitting another fichu," she announced.

"Could you knit it a bit longer?"

Nanny considered this. "If it's a bit longer, it won't be a fichu."

"Then could you knit a long sock?"

She shook her head. "I can't do socks. It's the heels, I don't have the right needles."

Flames were beginning to appear under the doors from the anteroom.

I tried to keep my voice steady. "Could you just do some long knitting?"

"I've only got green wool."

"Green is fine," I said. "And could you do it fairly fast? I need to climb down it before I burn to death."

"You want to climb down it? Bless you, my knitting will never take your weight. It's not as though you're slim like my little chicken. I'll have to find something else."

She disappeared round the side of the house, Tresorka trotting after her, as smoke swirled round me and the blistered door began to creak and curve inwards. I had two choices: I could stay, and perish in the blaze, or jump, and be smashed to pieces. As I stood there, contemplating my imminent demise, it struck me that this was the price of failure. Time had all but run out for the completion of my mission, and I had achieved nothing.

I bowed my head. "I'm sorry, Miss Blaine," I murmured. "I've let you down. I've let the school down. Worst of all, I've let myself down."

The double doors fell inwards with a crash and flames soared in, darting up the curtains, engulfing the cushioned armchairs, overwhelming the pianoforte. The words continued to echo in my head: "Let myself down let myself down let myself down..."

In a futile attempt to escape my fate, I tore off a length of smouldering curtain and fastened it to the samovar, which I wedged beside the window. I grabbed the charred material, stepped on to the window ledge, and let myself down.

This is never going to work, I thought. I was right. The curtain shredded between my fingers and I plummeted to earth.

Earth that was softer and more yielding than I had anticipated. The Founder had given me another chance.

"There," said Nanny. "That was more sensible than ruining my knitting. You can apologise to your coachman for ruining his horse's hay."

"Nanny," I said, "you're a lifesaver." For once, I didn't mean it metaphorically. "I know things have been a bit difficult between us recently, but I want to say—"

"No, don't say anything!" she interrupted. "I cannot talk to you about—about the things I cannot talk to you about."

The power of Miss Blaine must still have been lingering. A series of images crowded into my mind, images I hadn't quite been able to remember. When Nanny had turned so peculiar, summoning me to her room and then refusing to talk to me, I had felt there was something different about her room, but I couldn't work out what. I knew now. Her icon of the crinose Saint Volosiya was missing.

I had thought I saw Sasha in the driveway long after he was supposed to have left. And he had been carrying something, something the size and shape of an icon.

And then I remembered something else. What I had glimpsed just before I was chloroformed. A reflection in the burnished gold samovar of Sasha's head spinning round and round.

There was one final image. Me shoving Old Vatrushkin out of the door and locking it firmly behind him. He couldn't have got back in, even if he had a spare key, because I'd left mine in the lock. The only person who could have attacked me was Sasha.

Perhaps the fall from the first floor had left me light-headed, but I suddenly felt I had to sit down. It seemed I had been wrong. I had been wrong about Old Vatrushkin being bad, and I had been wrong about Sasha being good. I felt queasy, nonplussed, perplexed. Was this how other people felt when they were wrong? It was a new experience for me, and I didn't like it.

But how I felt was irrelevant. I wasn't here to feel, but to act. Miss Blaine had entrusted me with a mission, and I was virtually out of time.

I turned to Nanny. "Sasha's kidnapped Saint Volosiya, hasn't he?"

The old woman's face went rigid with terror. "Don't!" she whispered. "You don't know what he's capable of!"

I looked up at the flames licking the windows. "Actually, I think I do," I said. "And he's forbidden you to say anything."

Nanny's mouth clamped shut.

"Don't worry," I said. "I'll ask you questions and all you have to do is nod or shake your head."

A ray of hope came into her eyes and she gave a tentative nod.

"You know something you can't tell anybody?"

She nodded more vigorously.

"And he threatened to hurt Saint Volosiya if you talked?"

She raised her hand and made a stabbing motion.

"He had a knife?"

A nod.

"Do you know where he took her?"

A shake of the head.

"Did you ever hold her?"

A nod.

"In your lap?"

Another nod.

I signalled to the animated floormop, who bounded over to me. "Tresorka, we're going to help the nice lady who saved you." I gathered Tresorka up in Nanny's capacious apron again. "That's right. Have a good sniff. Get the scent that isn't you and isn't Nanny and isn't knitting. Now seek."

Tresorka, released back to the ground, scampered off and we followed.

"What were you doing here anyway?" I asked.

"I was out for a walk when I noticed the smoke and flames," said Nanny.

"Out for a walk without Lidia? Is she disrupting everything with her woodwork again?"

"She gave me the afternoon off," said Nanny. "I've never had an afternoon off."

"You've never had an afternoon off?" I repeated, outraged by this exploitation of a worker in the caring industry, but she mistook my reaction.

"Yes, it is odd, isn't it?" she said. "She gave all the staff the afternoon off."

A bell went off in my head, very like the school bell that rang at 3.30 pm every day, except alarming rather than liberating.

"I'm sure everything's fine," I said with a reassurance I didn't feel. "You'll get home and find she's put up a lovely set of bookshelves, or maybe she's building a conservatory."

Tresorka was scampering faster now, wheezing with excitement. He came to a halt outside a three-storey building guarded by a uniformed doorman.

"These are the luxury apartments where the general stays," said Nanny. "The countess must have installed…the person you mentioned…here."

"Well done, Tresorka," I said, scratching him behind his little ears.

"We can't go in," said Nanny. "We will have to tell the doorman who we are and who we're going to see. If the doorman tells—the person—" She broke down in tears. "I can't risk her coming to harm."

"We can still check. Sasha might not be in," I said.

"And in that case, the doorman will not let us in."

She looked utterly woebegone. We needed a plan. I pondered.

"Got it," I said. "Wrap Tresorka in your apron and carry him as though he's on a tray."

We approached the doorman, who gave us a supercilious stare.

"Now then, my good man," I said. "I am the Princess Tamsonova." I hated myself for pulling rank when I believed so passionately in equality, but it was in pursuit of a greater good. "I am here representing the imperial repository for the relief of comparatively indigent gentlemen."

I indicated Nanny, who was tottering behind me with every indication of carrying a laden tray under her apron. "Caviar to the general," I announced.

The doorman bowed low. "Princess. The general is in apartment three."

I was about to tell him that it was just an expression from the playwright William Shakespeare when I realised we had achieved our aim and got access to the building.

"The general!" said Nanny excitedly as we went into the vestibule. "We should take him with us! He would be useful to have around if it comes to a fight."

I felt two women were more than adequate if it came to a fight, particularly if one of them was me. But Nanny insisted on knocking at the door.

A cleaning serf passed us. "He's gone out," he said.

"We're actually looking for Sasha," I said.

"Flat five. But he's gone out as well."

We waited until the cleaning serf was out of sight. "We need to break in," I said. "But I don't have a hairpin."

"Neither do I," she said. "Nasty scratchy things. But I could give you a knitting needle."

It was perfect. A quick jiggle and a sudden twist and the door opened. Nanny let Tresorka out of her apron and he shot down the hallway to scrabble at a door. This too was locked, but the knitting needle performed its magic again. There were sheaves of paper everywhere, piles of bank notes, stashes of jewels. I stood looking round in astonishment, but Nanny was scuttling after Tresorka, who was scraping at a bureau and whining. Another lock, another flourish of the knitting needle, and it was open.

Nanny gave a cry. "My beloved! Are you all right?" She examined the icon from every angle, ascertained that it was unscathed, and planted a reverential kiss on Saint Volosiya's homely face.

"Right, Nanny," I said. "She's out of danger. You're free to talk."

"When Lidia was five," she said, "her saintly mother was to be blessed with another child. I say 'was to be blessed' but it was not a blessing—" She paused, reluctant to continue.

"Don't worry, I know all about it," I said. "The baby wasn't her husband's."

The look Nanny gave me could have fried a Mars bar at a hundred versts. "How dare you say such an outrageous thing, Shona Fergusovna!"

"Everybody knows," I said. "I believe it was ginger?"

"A complete lie!" she burst out. "He was the most beautiful baby in the world, after my little chicken!"

I could understand people getting aerated about the ginger thing, however true it was. "All right," I said. "Let's say auburn or Titian. Anyway, the point is that he was the result of an extra-marital affair."

The next thing I knew, she'd used her outstanding pitching skills to lob another ball of wool in my mouth.

"Do not dare to speak of Lidia's saintly mother in that way!" she shouted.

I spat the wool out. "Nanny," I said, "have you forgotten you told me yourself that she was no better than she should be?"

"Exactly. We should all be as good as we possibly can. How could she have been any better? It is impossible to be any better than your best."

It was another of these occasions when a foreigner misunderstood something that was clear.

"So if he was a perfectly legitimate baby who wasn't ginger, what on earth was the problem?" I asked.

"Pure evil!" said Nanny, shuddering. "We discovered when the priest came to discuss the christening."

"Do you know, I heard a very similar story the other day," I said. "It's one of these priestly urban myths."

"It was no myth," said Nanny. "I witnessed it all. The infant's eyes glowed red, its head spun round and round and it vomited green bile. And the language it used! Fortunately, Lidia's saintly mother had never heard such words before and thought it was speaking ancient Aramaic. The priest demanded that we destroy the child immediately, but Lidia's saintly mother and revered father could not bring themselves to do such a thing."

"Quite right," I said. "Infanticide is a crime. So I presume they put him in a basket and left him in the bulrushes?"

Nanny shook her head. "They knew of a tutor employed nearby who had not been blessed with issue. They gave the baby to him and his wife on condition that they went to live in the country, and every month, Lidia's revered father sent them money for the child's upkeep."

"That's an amazing coincidence," I said. "Sasha's adoptive parents were involved in quite a similar arrangement."

Nanny stared at me. "I am speaking of Sasha."

"No," I corrected her gently. "I am speaking of Sasha. You are speaking of Lidia's wee brother."

She spoke very slowly and distinctly, as though to a complete moron. "Sasha is Lidia's brother. I recognised him immediately when I saw him with my little chicken."

Again, that unaccustomed feeling of being wrong, except it was slightly less unaccustomed this time. The villain who had kidnapped Saint Volosiya and tried to incinerate me, Lidia's brother? I was pondering how different siblings can be when Tresorka trotted up to me with some documents in his teeth.

"Clever doggy," I said absently, scratching him behind his ears, taking the papers from him and laying them on the table. He trotted off and returned seconds later with more papers.

"Well done," I said, patting his head, and he rushed away and came back with even more.

"That's enough now," I said. "Go and lie down."

Nanny squinted at the papers. "These are all wills," she said.

I looked more closely at the papers I still had in my hand. It was the will of Madame Potapova, leaving everything she had to Sasha. It was entirely in order: she had signed it and had it witnessed. Nanny was leafing through the wills of the field-marshal's widow and the admiral's widow, Pillar Box Lady and Eye Patch Lady, which also left everything they had to Sasha.

Tresorka bounded up and dropped two bits of paper in my lap. The top one was the countess's will, leaving everything she had to Sasha.

"The demon!" cried Nanny.

"Now then, Nanny," I said. "She was a difficult woman, but *de mortuis nihil nisi bonum,* remember."

"I'm not speaking ill of the dead. Don't you see? That demon Sasha murdered the count, who left everything to the countess. Then he murdered the countess and forged her will."

"Forged?" I said. "If all these other ladies left Sasha their fortunes, why shouldn't the countess do the same? She seemed quite fond of him."

"All the wills are forged," said Nanny. "These ladies would never have dreamed of leaving him their fortunes. He must somehow have got their signatures and copied them."

"Nanny, we know he's done some wrong things, stealing your icon, and leaving me to burn to death, but you can't just accuse him of anything you like," I said. "This is a case of give a dog a bad name and hang it."

Tresorka whined.

"You're not a bad dog," I said. "You're a very good dog. What's this you're bringing me now? A book?"

Tresorka, the front cover between his teeth, pawed at my knee.

"You want me to throw it for you? We don't throw books. And we don't chew them. We treat them with respect. Apart from That Book."

I retrieved it from Tresorka to check. It was the copy of *The Bride of Lammermoor* I had given Sasha. I opened it. The title page, on which I had inscribed my good wishes, was missing.

Nanny pointed to the remaining document on my lap. It was a will, leaving everything to Sasha, and signed by Shona Fergusovna McMonagle, duly witnessed and bearing the date of the girls' afternoon tea.

"The scheming wee toe-rag!" I said. "That's just an expression, Nanny, it means—"

"I understand your meaning perfectly," she said. "I think we'd better see what else he's got in here." She started searching inside the bureau and gave a horrified gasp. "Oh, Chicken!"

I looked over her shoulder to find her holding a letter.

"Dear Aleksandr Dmitrievich," it began. Aleksandr Dmitrievich—that was what the schoolmaster's wife had called Sasha. *"Thank you for your message. Not a day goes by without my thinking of my poor deceased brother. It is something of which we never speak, so it is a great joy to hear that you have knowledge of him that you wish to share with me. I quite understand that it would entirely ruin my reputation if you, a young unmarried man, were to be seen to visit me, a young unmarried woman. So I shall do as you suggest for the sake of discretion. I shall give everyone, including Nanny, the afternoon off tomorrow, and leave the back door open so that we can have complete privacy. Your proposed arrival time of 3 pm is completely acceptable.*
Yours sincerely,
Lidia Ivanovna Chrezvychainodlinnoslovskaya."

"Oh, Nanny," I said. There was growing evidence that Sasha hadn't just made a couple of errors of judgment.

Nanny, with trembling fingers, picked up a piece of paper that had been lying underneath the letter. It was the draft of another letter, which had a few false starts until the writer got used to copying Lidia's handwriting.

"My darling General," it read. *"I am so very fed up that we never get to spend any time alone together. That interfering old nanny of mine and that awful Scotchwoman are always getting in the way. So why don't you come round tomorrow at 4pm? I'll make sure we have the place*

to ourselves and we can find something interesting to do together. Come in the back door. (And don't you dare get the wrong idea—I'm literally talking about a door!) Lots of love, Little Lidia."

"My chicken would never write a letter like that!" raged Nanny.

"Of course she wouldn't," I said. "It's appallingly badly written. She would never be insensitive enough to call herself little when she's so much bigger than him. And Scotchwoman isn't even a proper word."

I looked again at the top of the letter. "It's dated yesterday. So he's expected today at 4pm. And the real letter she sent Sasha is also dated yesterday. So he's expected today at 3pm."

We both glanced at the clock. Quarter to four.

"Whatever Sasha has in mind, we have to stop it. Come on," I said, but Nanny and Tresorka were already racing out the door.

Nanny might be tiny but she was nippy, and it took me all my time to keep up with her. As we ran, I tried to work out how I had managed to get it wrong. I approached it like a maths problem, going right back to the beginning to check the working-out. And that was it, right back at the beginning, the way my heart had thudded and my pulse quickened at the first sight of him. He had a bewitching smile and he had bewitched me. But I had to accept my share of the blame.

"I should have paid more attention to Tolstoy," I said. "I thought Sasha was lovely because he looks so gorgeous. Tolstoy warned about that. He said, 'It is amazing how complete is the delusion that beauty is goodness.'"

"Tolstoy?" said Nanny without slowing up. "That doesn't sound the sort of thing that Nikolai Ilyich would say."

"No, I mean his son, Lev Nikolayevich," I said, and then realised the great writer hadn't actually been born yet.

Fortunately Nanny didn't notice my slip. She was pointing at a horseman ahead of us. "Look! The general! Hurry up!"

She put on a burst of speed, Tresorka bounding behind her, and I suspected she might even be capable of breaking my record for the 1500 metres.

"He'll have to get round to the back of the house," she panted. "We'll get ahead of him—I've got the front-door key."

We sprinted the rest of the way, but we were too late. As we started climbing the stairs to the salon, we could hear Sasha's light, attractive voice, tinged with a mixture of shock and embarrassment.

"My dear Lidushka! You didn't warn me that you were expecting another gentleman caller this afternoon!"

"Lidia Ivanovna!" came the general's voice. "I am surprised!"

"No, general," said Sasha. "We are surprised. You are astonished."

I was going to tell Nanny that this was a very old joke supposedly made by the lexicographer Samuel Johnson, and Sasha was guilty of plagiarism as well as everything else, but she was wailing, "My little chicken is ruined!"

Then we heard a sound I had never heard before. It was Lidia giggling. And there was a distinctiveness to the giggling. I was about to tell Nanny that Lidia was totally rat-arsed, when I remembered Old Vatrushkin's unfamiliarity with the word.

"She's bladdered," I said.

"She sounds drunk to me," said Nanny.

Lidia was speaking now, slurring her words and only just comprehensible. "Silly general! He's my brother!"

"Merciful heaven!" cried the general. "What depravity is this?"

"We have to stop this," said Nanny.

"I have to stop this," I corrected. I was on a mission, and at last I knew what it was. My mission was to keep Sasha away from Lidia at all costs.

It would have been helpful if I'd had written instructions at the start. I must mention it to Miss Blaine. Assuming I succeeded. The clock was ticking and my time was running out. She had warned me that if I failed to complete my mission in the allotted time, there would be repercussions. She hadn't specified, but I didn't think they would be pleasant.

I burst into the salon to find Sasha and Lidia clasped in an embrace. This was not good. The general knew that. He had collapsed in a chair in horror and was staring glassy-eyed at the couple.

"You! Sasha, or Aleksandr Dmitrievich, or whatever your name is," I said in my prefect voice. "Get away from her."

"His name's Aleksandr Ivanovich Chrezvychainodlinnoslovsky," slurred Lidia. "Please don't tell him to get away from me. I'm feeling quite wobbly and I'll fall if he lets go."

"No, don't tell me to get away from her," said Sasha, his customary charm oozing from every syllable. "The only person telling people what to do now is me."

With a sudden graceful move, he produced a knife, which he held against Lidia's throat. I might disapprove of the action, but I had to admire the technique.

"You. Shona Fergusovna, or Princess Tamsonova, or whatever your name is, sit on the chair next to the general's."

Lidia had stopped giggling and her eyes widened in terror as she felt the knife edge press against her skin. She held herself very still, scarcely breathing, in an effort not to get cut. I had to save her, but I had to bide my time until there was a better opportunity. Pretending compliance, I sat on the chair next to the general.

"You. Old woman. Get out your knitting."

Nanny glowered at him. "I've got no wool left."

I was impressed. This was an outright lie. But she knew Sasha had a plan and she was undermining it. That would make him nervous and more prone to making mistakes, and that would give me my opportunity.

Sasha pressed the blade more firmly against Lidia's neck. She gasped. "Nanny, I'm afraid."

Nanny delved into her apron and produced wool and knitting needles.

"Wise decision, old woman," sneered Sasha. "Now knit two lengths of binding and then you will tie the general and this interfering Scottish fool to their chairs."

"Excuse me," I said, "we'd all get along better without the racial abuse."

He ignored me. "Quicker than that, or your little chicken will have her gizzard slit."

Nanny completed her knitting in record time.

"And tie them up properly. The instant I see one or other of them begin to free themselves, the chicken gets it." The threatening timbre of his voice was really very sexy.

Seconds later, Nanny was tying my wrists behind me and securing the ends of the wool rope to the arms of the chair. I had thought that despite Sasha's warning, she would have the nous to leave the rope loose enough so that I could free myself and take action at an opportune moment. But the daft woman tied me up properly. I couldn't even hope that Tresorka would surreptitiously nibble through the wool since he had crawled under a sofa and was lying there trembling.

"Now, sit down beside them so that I can see all three of you," Sasha ordered.

Nanny flopped into a chair. "Oh, Chicken!" she wailed. "What have you been doing?"

Lidia turned pleading eyes on Sasha. He gave her an attractively boyish grin. "Go on," he said. "Tell them."

Fighting back sobs, Lidia said, "I invited Sasha here to tell me about my brother. We had tea, and he said he was my brother, Aleksandr Ivanovich Chrezvychainodlinnoslovsky, and we had some more tea, and he said it wasn't fair that I had everything and he had nothing, and I said it wasn't fair at all, and we had some more tea, and he had a document saying that everything I had was his, and I said then I would have nothing, and he said I would marry the general and still be very rich, so I signed it."

"Evil, evil man!" wailed Nanny. "You have tricked my chicken out of her fortune, you have fooled the general into thinking she is a fallen woman so that he will not marry her, and now both her reputation and her finances are ruined!"

Sasha nodded. "Well done, old woman. Watching my beloved sister's miserable decline is much more satisfying than killing her, don't you think?"

The general cleared his throat. "I am afraid there can be no doubt that your little chicken—" (he nodded politely to Nanny in acknowledgement of the pet name) "—has been indulging in licentious behaviour. When I came in, she was in a passionate embrace with the young man, and I believe both you and Shona Fergusovna—" (he nodded politely to me) "—witnessed it as well."

"No," said Lidia, her voice shaky but determined. She was standing upright now, no longer leaning on Sasha, sobered up by terror. "No licentious behaviour. Only tea drinking. Then, when you arrived, Sasha ran over to me and gave me a great big cuddle."

"Nanny," I said, "I think he put something in the tea."

Nanny gave a sigh, which sounded quite theatrical. "Yes, Shona Fergusovna," she said. "probably something to do with the bottle of vodka sitting beside the samovar over there."

I had to admit there was nothing wrong with her eyesight.

"Anyway, your little plan hasn't worked," I said to Sasha. "Lidia has just assured us that she remains pure, so the general will still be happy to marry her. Not that I think that should have a bearing on the matter, and I think the double standards for male and female behaviour are absolutely disgraceful. But that's by the way. And no court in the land will uphold that document once we've explained how you conned Lidia into signing it. So you might as well crawl back to the primordial slime from which you emerged."

"Ah, Shonetchka, your grasp of the matter is, as ever, flawless. My plan has indeed failed," said Sasha, and I thought it was nice that he was able to be gracious in defeat. He turned to the others. "My intention was indeed merely to ruin my beloved sister. But now that this interfering Scottish fool has blundered in—" (he placed a distinct emphasis on "Scottish") "—I have been obliged to change my plan. Now you must all die."

Nanny and the general looked at me in an accusing sort of way.

"Wait," I said. I may not be a trained negotiator, but working in the library has given me good people skills. It was important to keep him talking while I devised a plan to free us all. "Lidia's lovely. Why are you being so horrible to her?"

"She has what is mine!" he snarled. I couldn't take my eyes off him. He looked even more delicious when he snarled. "She has a palace and hundreds of serfs—"

"Thousands," interrupted Nanny. "Four thousand, three hundred."

"I thought it was four thousand, two hundred and ninety-nine," I said. "Or were you just rounding up?"

"No, Yevdokia has just given birth to a son, God be praised," she said. She really was on top of serf management.

"God wasn't praised when I was born!" Sasha snarled gorgeously.

"He was to begin with," said Nanny. "Just not after the priest told us you were the Evil One."

The priest, I now realised, had been very perceptive.

There were flecks of green bile at the corners of Sasha's mouth and a red glow in his eyes. "My dear sister has a palace and estates and untold wealth while I was brought up in penury by a couple of yokels."

"Now, that's not true," I said. "I've been in your adoptive parents' house and it's very nice. They have sugar. And they're a very nice couple. I didn't have much of a chat with your dad, but your mum's very nice indeed and she's very proud of you. But I don't think she'd be very proud of you if she could see you now, do you?"

"That peasant is not fit to call herself my mother. They didn't even confess to me—they kept up the pretence that they were my parents, and it was only by chance that I overheard them complaining that the payment they received for my upkeep had stopped because my natural father had died."

"I got that wrong," I admitted. "I thought the countess was your mum."

"That gargoyle? She was nothing but my pawn. I seduced the maid to get to the countess and seduced the countess to get to town."

It had sounded so improbable when the housekeeper had said it, but now I saw Sasha in quite a different light.

"I appreciate you've had an emotional shock," I said. "But we've all had bad things happen to us when we were growing up. When I was ten, I lost a ball in the whin bushes up Blackford Hill, and I looked for it for ages but I never found it. We just need to get over it and get on with things. What doesn't destroy us makes us stronger."

"And now it is time for you to be destroyed," said Sasha briskly. "I shall take particular pleasure in seeing you dead at last, my dear Shonetchka. You have proved quite a challenge. I have tried without success to shoot you, strangle you, break your neck, stab you, drown you and incinerate you. This time I shall not fail."

It's amazing how things suddenly just fall into place, a strange mixture of intuition and deductive reasoning.

"It was you who shot at me at the duel?" I said. "You weren't just picking up the curtain cord at the concert? You left that cabbage pickle for me to slip on? You were the big, sinister beardie bloke on the train and at the pond?"

He gave me a roguish smile.

"You haven't only been forging wills," I said. "You've killed before, haven't you?"

He laughed, a gloriously melodic laugh. "Oh yes. Many times. So many times I have begun to get a taste for it."

"If you were the big, sinister beardie bloke on the train, it must have been you who killed the conductor," I said. "And drowned the maid." My thought processes were like quicksilver now. "Those old ladies you inherited from. I bet you pushed them downstairs."

He nodded. "Of course. I would have killed that ghastly old princess as well if she hadn't already written a will. And I found her staff too unpredictable to evade—one never knew whether they were doormen, footmen, coachmen, gardeners or major-domos."

I allowed myself a moment of princessly pride. Then I continued my indictment. "And Nanny was right. You murdered the count and the countess."

He frowned slightly. "I didn't expect to have to kill the count myself. I expected the general would do it for me. He and the count were both expert marksmen but the general presented a much smaller target."

The general leaned forward eagerly, as much as his bonds allowed. "Yes, that surprised me too," he said. "I aimed right at him, and I'm certain I didn't miss."

I allowed myself a small secret smile. It was tempting to tell them about my trick, replacing the ammunition with aniseed balls, but I didn't like to draw attention to my own acumen. And then I caught sight of Tresorka, who had emerged from underneath the sofa and was surreptitiously crawling along the edge of the room, circling his quarry. I had to distract Sasha.

"That was totally out of order, rigging the card game," I exclaimed. "You left that obviously bogus card for the count to play so that he'd be accused of cheating and there would be a duel."

Tresorka was closing in on Sasha.

"You are not a gentleman, sir," I went on. "No gentleman cheats at cards."

"I'm most certainly a gentleman and I have the fortune to prove it," he said.

Tresorka, teeth bared, prepared to attack Sasha's ankles. I held myself in readiness. The minute Tresorka's teeth met flesh and deflected Sasha from his murderous plan, I would shout instructions, ordering Lidia to run and Nanny to untie me. Then I would quickly get Sasha in an armlock and...

With a heart-rending yelp, Tresorka flew across the room. There was a sickening thunk as he hit the wall. Sasha, with some diabolical sixth sense, had kicked backwards with vicious accuracy.

Tresorka lay silent and motionless, one tiny leg jutting at an unnatural angle.

"You brute!" I shouted at Sasha, straining against the knitting. "You're pure evil!" As soon as I'd said it, I was relieved I had said it in Russian. I would have hated anybody to think I was talking Glaswegian.

"Killing people is wrong," I said, "but kicking dumb animals is—well, if it's not more wrong, it's at least equally wrong. Or if not quite equally wrong, then very nearly as wrong. In fact, why are we even discussing levels of wrongness? Wrong is wrong."

"Ah, killing people," drawled Sasha. "I knew there was something I meant to do. Thank you for reminding me. First, I shall cut the throat of my beloved sister."

I started thinking fast. I had to complete my mission. All these people were depending on me. I struggled to free my hands but they were tied fast. There was nothing the general could do because he was also tied to his chair. Lidia was rigid with fear. I would have to give instructions to Nanny. I knew she was very good at throwing things, but first I had to think of something for her to throw. I looked around.

While I was thinking fast, Nanny gave a sudden shout. "Chicken! Your owl!"

Lidia grabbed her awl from her pocket and jabbed it into Sasha's side. At that exact moment, Tresorka hurtled across the room on three legs and sank his teeth into Sasha's ankle. Sasha shrieked, dropping the knife as he tried to tend to his injuries. Lidia and Tresorka raced to safety as Nanny hurled an oil lamp at Sasha's head while the general threw the half-full bottle of vodka.

Bottle and lamp met in mid-air and the oil and alcohol exploded. An instant later, all that was left of Sasha was a small charred heap and a hideous stench of sulphur and burnt fat.

"Wow," I said in awe. "I think you've just invented the Molotov cocktail."

"No thanks to you," said Nanny testily. "Why are you just sitting there?"

The shock of the preceding events must have given her short-term memory loss.

"You tied me up," I reminded her. "With your knitting."

"And I deliberately dropped a stitch so that you could wiggle your fingers about and pull it all apart," she said. "The general's been free for ages, just waiting for my signal."

"Oh," I said, unaccountably unable to think of anything else to say.

"Well, I need to get this mess cleared up," said Nanny, going off to find a broom.

Lidia came over to untie me. "What a peculiar day," she said. "To find my deceased brother was no longer deceased and now to find him deceased again. It's probably for the best. I think our personalities were too different to allow us to be truly at ease together. But he made very good tea."

Once I was free, I rushed over to Tresorka. "Good boy," I said. "I thought you were unconscious but you were just lying doggo. How's the leg?"

Tresorka gave a weak wag of his tail. I investigated and found his leg was dislocated rather than broken.

"I can put this right, but he'll need something to bite on," I said.

"How about my hand?" asked the general, and I had to explain about tetanus and lockjaw. Nanny went off to the kitchen and found a ham bone, which Tresorka gnawed on while I manipulated the dislocated joint back into position. I made a splint from one of Nanny's crochet hooks, tied on with wool to keep the joint in place while it healed.

Meanwhile, Nanny was sweeping up Sasha's remnants.

"Oh, Nanny!" said Lidia, her eyes shining. "The parquet is completely ruined! It will take so much work to repair it—the whole floor will have to be replaced."

"I hope you are not forgetting my verandah," said the general quietly.

The way ahead was now clear. My mission was to help Lidia and I would complete it.

"It's at times like this that you realise what's important," I said. "We've done a lot today, and I think we just need to take it easy now. But I'd like to invite you all round to mine tomorrow afternoon for an engagement party."

I left Tresorka where he was, so that he could start recuperating, and showed Nanny how to carry out basic physiotherapy. She would bring him in her apron the next day.

It was only when I was halfway home that I remembered I had left the mansion ablaze. By now, it would be nothing but a pile of ashes. Like Sasha, only bigger and less pungent.

CHAPTER

14

There was no point in rushing home if there was no home to rush to. Since Sasha had set the fire in my wood-panelled bedroom, all of my clothes would have been destroyed. The gown I was currently wearing was too smoke-damaged to be suitable for a party, so I went to the nearest dressmaker and ordered a new one for the next day. Fortunately, I was wearing a multiway bra, which I could rinse out, and my DMs were tough enough to withstand any disaster.

I then paid a return visit to Kirill Kirillovich, the best lawyer in town. It all proved straightforward. He was slightly unsure on a couple of the more complex details, but I was able to direct him to the relevant legal authorities, and sign the necessary affidavits.

"One final matter," he said. "I would like to offer you a partnership. I shall have a scrivener write out the contract."

I shook my head. "That's very flattering, but I expect to be leaving shortly."

As I neared the mansion, I could hear a hubbub of voices, horses neighing, and the creaking of cart wheels. Then I saw the mansion itself, which looked the same as ever, only brighter and cleaner. Dozens of carts filled with workers and their paraphernalia were trundling away.

Old Vatrushkin was at the door. I felt a surge of affection. How could I ever have imagined he would try to hurt me? He wouldn't hurt an amoeba.

As I approached, I saw he was concluding some sort of business with a tanned, dark-haired man, and realised he had been supervising the repair work.

"Your excellency!" he cried when he saw me. "Please don't be concerned! There has been a small fire, but almost everything is as it was. I was in the orangery when I smelled smoke, and was able to summon help before the mansion was completely destroyed. Fortunately, so much of it is marble that it was able to withstand the blaze."

He paused and I saw his bottom lip tremble. "I was afraid that—that—I searched every room. I was…greatly relieved to find no human remains."

I noticed a bit of scorching to his hair and beard.

"In any event," he went on, "I am very glad that your excellency had gone out before the fire began. I rushed to get the repair work done before you returned."

There was no need to go into what had happened; he would only get upset.

"I can see you've done a grand job," I said, and nodded to the man he had been talking to. "Is this a serf friend of yours?" I asked Old Vatrushkin. "Should I give him three roubles?"

The dark-haired man spat out a short phrase, which I recognised first as Italian and secondly as extremely rude.

"Wretch!" roared Old Vatrushkin. "How dare you use language like that in front of her excellency!"

"I'll use whatever language I like. I'm a freeborn Milanese, a master craftsman, not a serf," said the man, still in Italian.

This could give me a clue as to the date.

"Tell me, have you had a Risorgimento yet?" I asked, also in Italian.

The Milanese ignored my question. "Lady, you aristocrats make me sick," he said.

"Hold on a minute," I said. "I'm no aristocrat. I'm a woman of the people."

An ornate carriage rolled past and a familiar head appeared. "My dear Princess Tamsonova!" called the princess. "Just heard about young Sasha, dreadful waste—still, plenty more fish in the sea. I'm hosting a small dinner party for a hundred on Thursday and of course you must be the guest of honour."

The master craftsman stared at me with loathing.

"It's really not how it sounds—funny story—you'll laugh," I began, but he interrupted, "You people should go down on your knees in front of your so-called serfs. Old Vatrushkin here has been racing round to hire the finest international craftsmen in town for you. We don't come cheap in the first place, and for a rush job like this, we charge well over the odds."

Old Vatrushkin shook his head. "I hired every local artisan in town as well, and they required very little beyond their usual rates."

"He's paid every one of us out of his own pocket, and now he doesn't have two kopecks to rub together," said the Milanese.

I turned to Old Vatrushkin. "Is this true?"

He shook his head vigorously. "An outrageous lie. I have nine kopecks left, more than enough for my needs."

"Where did you get the money?" I asked.

"Your excellency has been so generous to me, showering me in kopecks and roubles. I also had a small store of money from selling paintings in Paris."

The Milanese, who had boorishly kept his head covered while talking to me, pulled off his cap and bowed to Old Vatrushkin.

"Even with only nine kopecks, you're worth ten thousand of her," he said.

Old Vatrushkin's fist landed straight on the master craftsman's nose. "Ill-mannered cur! You've been paid—why are you still hanging around? Crawl back to your gutter."

Maybe it was just amoebas and me who were safe with him. Discreetly, I tore off a piece of my underskirt and handed it to the Milanese to staunch his nosebleed.

"You'd better go," I whispered. "There's no reasoning with him when he's in this sort of mood."

The master craftsman staggered off.

"So," I said conversationally to Old Vatrushkin, "you speak Italian? I'm impressed."

"No, no, no, it's no achievement on my part," Old Vatrushkin said. "Once I knew French and Latin, Italian was simplicity itself. *Il piacere più nobile è la gioia di comprendere.*"

Leonardo's apophthegm was extremely apt: the noblest pleasure is indeed the joy of understanding.

"Maybe it took me a wee while to understand why I was here, but everything's sorted now," I said.

"Not quite, your excellency," said Old Vatrushkin, tears welling up in his eyes. "Your bedroom is no longer completely wood-panelled. I was unable to locate a craftsman suitably skilled in woodwork to reconstruct it."

"Don't worry about that," I said. "I know just the person to sort it out."

"And...and..." With an obvious effort, he forced himself to continue. "The golden samovar—for reasons I cannot begin to explain, it was wedged beneath an open window. The eagle's beak was stuck fast in the wall, and when I attempted to detach it, it—it broke off."

"Don't worry about that either," I said. "The samovar and the beak served their purpose."

"But it is all my fault," he said. "After you instructed me to stay away, I obeyed for longer than I should have done. I shall never forgive myself. Your beautiful home."

"Never mind," I said. "I don't expect to be staying here much longer."

Old Vatrushkin was immediately alert. "Where are we going, your excellency?"

He looked so excited that I couldn't bring myself to tell him he wasn't going anywhere.

"First things first," I said. "I'm throwing a party tomorrow afternoon."

"I shall go and get the messages," he said. "Messages is the boys."

"I'm going to have an early night," I said. "Just bring them in at breakfast time."

I watched him leave and then went into the house, relieved that he wouldn't be with me when I saw the renovations. In those television makeover shows, you can always tell when somebody really hates what's happened to their house, however much they say it's lovely.

But despite having had the mansion renovated at breakneck speed, Old Vatrushkin had brought his painterly eye to bear on everything; each room was an oasis of peace and tranquillity. I particularly liked the hyacinthine colour he had chosen for the salon. I could just imagine it in my kitchen at home.

Unfortunately, all of the furniture had been destroyed. The salon and the anteroom seemed particularly austere. And then I realised that Old Vatrushkin's beautiful paintings had also been destroyed. The place cried out for art.

My gorgeous wood-panelled bedroom was now just an ordinary room. Without a bed. It definitely needed Lidia to restore its xyloid charm. But I can sleep anywhere, a skill I developed during geography lessons. I curled up in the corner and whispered into the ether, "It's okay, isn't it, what I've arranged with Kirill Kirillovich? After everything that Old Vatrushkin's done?" I felt a sensation of warmth and comfort and knew that it was indeed okay.

The next day began with Old Vatrushkin bringing in the messages and cooking utensils. I made him a breakfast fry-up, since it's only the sedentary twenty-first-century lifestyle that makes it dangerous. Old Vatrushkin burned up calories almost as fast as Sasha had disappeared.

And over the fried potatoes, I explained that I would sort out the party food, since I had a list of things for him to do in town. I handed him the paper on which I had carefully set out my instructions. He read through it, then rubbed his hand across his forehead.

"Oh, your excellency," he said brokenly. "What will I do?"

"You'll do what you're supposed to do," I snapped. "You'll obey me without question. Now get on with it while I wash up."

There was no cleaning to be done since the house was pristine. So I concentrated on making a batch of rye scones and a celebration cake with a cream cheese filling and "Congratulations on Your Engagement" in cream cheese on the top.

Mid-morning, my new dress was delivered, sprigged muslin with Brussels lace at the neck and wrists. It was good to change out of the soot-stained one, which still reeked of smoke. I nipped out to give it to the nearest female beggar I could find, but she was less than enthusiastic.

"I suppose I could turn it into dusters," she sniffed.

"Sorry, I thought you were totally destitute. I didn't realise you had anything to dust," I said.

She pointed at the ground where she was sitting and I saw it was indeed very dusty. I felt glad to have been of help.

Then, just as I got back to the house, a delivery cart arrived with two sofas. Once the delivery men had installed them in the salon, the foreman hesitantly produced a bill and seemed surprised that I was happy to pay it immediately.

"And of course it is minus nine kopecks, since your excellency's serf paid that as a deposit."

The first guests to arrive were Lidia, Nanny and Tresorka. I took them into the bedroom, where I explained about the log cabin look and the wooden bed like a sleigh. Lidia, eyes sparkling, wrote down notes and started measuring up.

There was a knock at the front door. Old Vatrushkin was still out, working through the list I had given him, so I let the general in, and took them all up to the salon for champagne and scones. I got the general to open the bottle, a Jeroboam of Veuve Clicquot.

"I'm not sure that my little chicken should have any, after all the strong drink she had yesterday," said Nanny.

"Darling Nanny!" said Lidia. "It was not strong at all—in fact, I could hardly taste the tea."

"I'm afraid I can't actually offer you any tea," I said. "There was a bit of a catastrophe with the samovar up here, and I need Old Vatrushkin to help me carry up the big one from the pantry. But I thought since this was a celebration, champagne would be more suitable. Nanny, I'm sure one wee drink won't hurt her."

Grumbling, Nanny poured Lidia a glass.

"I went to see Kirill Kirillovich, the best lawyer in town, yesterday," I said. "It turns out that Lidia, as Sasha's sole remaining blood relative, inherits his entire fortune. And it's a very considerable fortune, since it includes the fortunes of the count and countess, Madame Potapova, and the field-marshal and admiral's widows."

"Weren't those wills forgeries?" asked Nanny.

"Strictly speaking, yes. But the money would otherwise go to the tsar, and nobody wants that. Nanny, you're going to have several thousand more serfs to manage."

"Mercy on us!" said Nanny, looking delighted.

Lidia blinked. "But I am already one of the wealthiest heiresses in the land," she said.

"Well, now you're even wealthier," I said. "Obviously, it's entirely up to you what you do with the money, but if I could make a suggestion, you could maybe reinstate the monthly payments to Sasha's adoptive parents. It would be a nice way to commemorate him, and it would let them keep buying sugar."

"Of course!" said Lidia. "Where do they live?"

"In the village of N——, where you now have an estate. If you're ever there, you should call in on them. His mum likes having visitors. You can tell her that he died in a tragic accident, but it's probably best not to mention the pure evil bit. Look out for the priest, though. He's a bit of a radge."

Lidia nodded. "As always, I shall obey your wise words even when I do not entirely understand them."

My super-acute hearing caught the sound of the door opening.

"Back in a second," I said. "Help yourselves to scones."

I ran downstairs and thought for a second that a complete stranger was on the doorstep. Then I realised.

"Goodness," I said. "You scrub up well."

"Thank you, your excellency," said Old Vatrushkin. "I scrubbed the soot off the floors and walls as well as I possibly could. It's good of you to suggest that my efforts have been adequate."

"No, it's just an expression," I said. "I mean you look—different."

It was odd seeing Old Vatrushkin without his long hair, wild beard and moustache, his shabby coat and lamb's wool cap. But he suited the blue dress-coat and silk cravat, the high boots and the batiste shirt, the close-fitting trousers and the gold watch chain. He had a fine firm jaw and a handsome mouth.

"How does it feel to be emancipated?" I asked.

He gave a tentative smile. "Not as bad as I expected, your excellency."

I gave him a slap on the shoulder. "Stop that right now. You're a free man. You don't call anybody 'your excellency'. And if you try to call me 'your excellency' again, I'll set Tresorka on you."

I escorted him upstairs.

"Everybody," I said, "let me introduce my good friend Gregori Gregorievich Vatrushkin who's very kindly been letting me stay here. He's the actual owner of this house."

"Yes, I have the legal documents to prove it," Old Vatrushkin said nervously, pulling some papers out of his inside pocket.

"Gregori Gregorievich is known as a great wit," I explained and everybody laughed.

Lidia laughed so much that some champagne went down the wrong way and the general had to reach up and pat her on the back.

"That was very funny, Gregori Gregorievich," she said, "when you pretended to produce your title deeds."

"Thank you, your—" Old Vatrushkin began.

"You're very kind," I supplied smoothly, giving Old Vatrushkin a warning glare. "He'll be organising the woodwork side of the renovations, Lidia. I thought you could have a chat with him about that later. But first, let me welcome you all here for this engagement party. This is a happy day, after yesterday, which was a bit fraught. Old Va— old friend, could you see that all our glasses are filled?"

Old Vatrushkin went round everyone with the Jeroboam.

"Raise your glasses, please, and let's drink to the future happiness of the engaged couple. I give you the general and Nanny!"

"The general and Nanny!" repeated Old Vatrushkin.

"The general and Nanny!" repeated Lidia, sounding relieved.

"Me and Nanny?" said the general, sounding surprised.

"The general and me?" said Nanny, sounding thrilled.

"Obviously," I said, looking down at the two tiny figures. "You're made for one another."

It was so sweet the way they could look directly into one another's eyes without one of them having to crane backwards.

"Just one thing, Nanny," I said. "I know you're very devout. The general is a divorcé."

"My wife ran away with a miller," explained the general. "Well, she didn't so much run away as float away."

"She was a very silly woman then, leaving a lovely man like you," said Nanny. "Bless your heart, don't worry about having broken one of the most sacred sacraments. I'm sure we've all done worse."

"Word of warning," I said. "I wouldn't mention the divorce to the priest in the village of N—. But if you ever have any trouble with him, just mention my name."

But Nanny wasn't listening to me. She was gazing straight ahead at the tiny general.

"I can manage your serfs," she said. "And knit you curtains."

"And I," said the general, his voice husky, "can give you all the mud you want."

"And when you're in the village of K— you can manage Lidia's serfs just as easily from there as you can from here," I said.

"And the serfs near the village of N— as well," said Nanny. "Three lots of serfs, imagine! I can knit them all fichus."

"When you're not knitting me curtains," said the general affectionately. Then his face fell. "My verandah!"

"I'm sure Lidia will be happy to come for a holiday and sort out your verandah while she's there," I said. "Speaking of woodwork, Lidia, isn't it time you and Gregori Gregorievich had a chat?"

They withdrew to a corner of the room and were soon deep in conversation, Lidia's eyes shining as she gazed up at him, Old Vatrushkin's handsome mouth curved in a smile.

I sat down on a sofa and let the two couples get to know one another undisturbed. Tresorka hobbled over to me and sat at my feet, tongue hanging out, tail quivering.

"Oh, all right," I said. "Just this once." I picked him up and let him lie on the sofa. It was an atmosphere of bliss and harmony, and I allowed myself to feel a touch of pride that my mission was going so well.

Lidia and Old Vatrushkin drifted back to join us, and I cut a slice of the celebration cake for everyone. Nanny and the general sniffed at it suspiciously.

"Gregori Gregorievich and I have had such a lovely chat," said Lidia shyly. "We have an announcement to make."

She looked round at him, seeking reassurance, and he nodded. It was touching to see the deep understanding that had already developed between them.

"Gregori Gregorievich and I—" Her voice faltered.

Old Vatrushkin stepped forward and grasped her hand. "We are going into partnership together," he said.

He was a man, and men are rubbish at romance, but I was still a bit disappointed. "That sounds very business-like," I said.

"Oh, it is!" Lidia assured me. "We shall go to Kirill Kirillovich, the best lawyer in town, to ensure that everything is done properly."

"You're getting a pre-nup?" I asked. She was as unromantic as he was. Maybe that was how it worked when you were one of the wealthiest heiresses in the country.

"We do not have your vast legal expertise," said Old Vatrushkin, "and I do not know what a pre-nup is, but if we require one to go into business together, then we will most certainly get one. We are determined that our academy will succeed."

"Academy?" I said.

"Yes, we are setting up the world's first Academy of Fine Art and Woodwork," said Lidia. "We will charge rich students extortionate fees. And we will use those fees and my vast wealth to fund scholarships for serfs." She looked up with pride at Old Vatrushkin. "That was Gregori Gregorievich's idea."

"I thought you were getting married," I said. "I thought if you didn't get married, you weren't allowed out in society."

"I shall not be out in society, I shall be inside an academy, which I shall much prefer," said Lidia. "But we have discussed marriage also. If we find ourselves falling in love, we will certainly get married. Gregori Gregorievich has kindly agreed that in that case, he will take the name of Chrezvychainodlinnoslovsky and so my family line will continue."

I turned to Old Vatrushkin. "And you're happy to give up your name?"

He gazed doe-eyed at Lidia. "Whatever makes Lidia Ivanovna happy makes me happy," he said. "But I shall not be giving up my name. I believe I once told you, your—"

I glared at him and gave a warning nod towards Tresorka.

"You're forgetting my family tradition," he continued quickly. "If, God willing, I marry and have a son, he will be Old

Vatrushkin like me, my father and his father before him. Old Vatrushkin Chrezvychainodlinnoslovsky."

"And if it's a girl?"

"Old Vatrushkina Chrezvychainodlinnoslovskaya."

Boy or girl, the kid was going to have a rough time at school.

For a moment, I thought Old Vatrushkin had just outed himself as my ex-serf, until I realised that since he wasn't their serf, they had paid no attention to what his name was.

"What a charming family tradition," said Nanny. And then I felt a twinge in my abdomen, not excruciating, but noticeable. My mission was accomplished. I hoped Marcia Blaine was impressed, and that this would be the first of many.

"Are you all right, Shona Fergusovna?" asked Lidia anxiously.

"That's what comes of too much champagne," said Nanny.

"Perhaps it's the cake," said the general.

"There's nothing wrong with—" I began and then had to stop to catch my breath as the twinges came again, more strongly. "I'm going to have to leave you," I said.

"I told you the cream cheese was off," the general whispered to Nanny.

"I understand!" gasped Lidia, clasping her hands to her bosom. "I know you said I mustn't tell, but all of us here owe you such a debt of gratitude. Nanny, General, Gregori Gregorievich—Shona Fergusovna is an angel!"

They all nodded sagely.

"And the best mistress any man could hope to have," said Old Vatrushkin in a low voice.

"It's all right," I reassured Lidia. "His reference is to serfs."

Lidia reached for his hand and held it tight. "I have never known anyone with such a concern for serfs," she said. "It is an inspiration. I can't wait to teach them woodwork."

I was practically bent double now. "I really must go," I said.

In an undertone, the general exhorted Nanny not to eat any more cake but just to throw it in a plant pot.

Old Vatrushkin was looking at me with tear-filled eyes. "Are you really leaving us?" he whispered.

I realised I didn't want to. I wanted to see the academy being founded, I wanted to go to Nanny's wedding, I wanted to go to Lidia's wedding, I wanted to take Tresorka for walks in the park.

There was a yelp behind me. Tresorka had managed to collapse off the sofa and was limping towards me. How could I leave him? But how could I take him? It wouldn't be fair to leave him in the flat all day, and he wouldn't be allowed in the library.

I picked him up gently and kissed him on the nose. He licked my nose in return. Then I handed him to Nanny. "Look after him. Don't forget about the physiotherapy," I said, my voice cracking. Then I doubled over as another twinge caught me.

"You must return to your heavenly abode," said Lydia.

"It's not a bad wee flat," I agreed. "You know what would make it even more heavenly? Gregori Gregorievich, do you have any of that hyacinthine paint left?"

He swallowed. "Come with me to the orangery."

"There will be plant pots in the orangery," the general whispered to Nanny. "Bring your plate."

I had never been to the orangery before. It was south-facing, with long windows and a glass roof, and a large number of orange and lime trees. One corner had been cleared for Old Vatrushkin's art. I had assumed there would be dozens of canvases lying around, but I could see only one, an enormous thing propped on a huge easel and covered in a velvet cloth.

He fetched me a bucket of blue paint, which I could tell was going to transform my kitchen.

"And this," he said, his voice wavering. "This is for you."

He whipped the cloth off the canvas, and there it was. A full-length, larger than life-size portrait of me in what I had been wearing the night I arrived, the lilac evening gown and white kid gloves. Just peeping out from underneath the hem of the gown were the DMs.

"I couldn't," I demurred.

"Please."

"No, really I couldn't," I said. It was far too big for the flat. And while there are no written rules, I'm pretty sure that in Morningside you're not supposed to have larger than life-size portraits of yourself. It smacks of conceit.

Lidia put her arm round him. "Don't press her," she said. "She cannot take it. Angels have no possessions."

"She's taking a bucket of paint," he objected.

"We're allowed wee things," I said.

"Gregori Gregorievich," said Lidia softly. "The proper place for this portrait is your salon. Then every time we look at it, we will remember our beloved Shona Fergusovna and that will ease the bitter pain of parting."

"That's nice," I said. "You've definitely got the wall space."

But I sensed that Old Vatrushkin was still distressed. Just behind the easel, I caught sight of an A4 sheet of paper with a drawing on it. "I'd really like to have one of your pictures," I said. "What's that?"

He brought it over. It was a preparatory sketch for the portrait. It looked great.

"Would you be so good as to allow me to take this instead?" I asked.

He nodded, too emotional to speak.

I was determined to let him know how much it meant to me. "This painting," I said, "is the boys."

He leaned over and kissed my shoulder. "Your excellency," he said.

It was a beautiful moment.

Lidia collapsed with laughter. "He's pretending to be a serf! You're right, Shona Fergusovna! Gregori Gregorievich is so amusing!"

In the background, I could see Nanny scraping her bit of cake into a bucket of white emulsion.

"I'll just go then," I said. The scene around me began to shimmer and the temperature started to drop.

"Oh, one last thing—" I said, before I was forced to close my eyes. It was like being in the middle of a wind tunnel.

When I opened my eyes, I was in the kitchen of my flat, holding an A4 sketch and a bucket of blue paint that, now that I saw it against the kitchen units, was completely the wrong shade.

The remainder of my sentence echoed across the room, "—what year is it?"

ACKNOWLEDGEMENTS

My sincere gratitude to the following:

The Scottish Book Trust, in particular Lynsey Rogers, Caitrin Armstrong and Will Mackie, without whose New Writers Award this would not have been written;

Linda Cracknell, not only a generous and encouraging mentor, but also an ace companion when crossing the Moroccan desert by camel;

Sara Hunt and all at Saraband, especially *editrix mirabilis* Ali Moore;

matchmaker Al Guthrie;

Iain Matheson, Elaine Thomson, Margaret Ries and Michelle Wards who read drafts without complaint and with brilliant suggestions;

for their kindness, help and encouragement: Helen Boden (in whose Writing Room at the Southside Community Centre Shona was born); Simon Brett; Jenny Brown; Mike Cash; Bill Kirton; Helen Lamb; Theresa McInnes; Colin Mortimer; Marina Partolina; Lesley Rowe; Vicki White;

Dame Muriel Spark and Count Leo Tolstoy;

James Gillespie's High School where I was taught by the finest English teacher in the world, Iona M Cameron;

and above all, Alistair, who has the Latin.

AUTHOR'S NOTE

Clever readers may have noticed that if Shona had been a bit more on the ball she could have found an additional clue about the year during her interactions with the folk in Russia. Alas she wasn't and she didn't! Will she overlook any important details during her future missions?